Girl Fignts Back

An Emily Kane Adventure

Jacques Antoine

Other books by the author:

The Emily Kane Adventures

>*Girl Punches Out (Book #2)*

>*Girl Takes Up Her Sword (#3)*

>*Girl Spins A Blade (#4)*

>*Girl Takes The Oath (#5)*

>*Girl Rides The Wind (#6)*

>*Girl Goes To Beijing (#7)*

Taking Back Earth

>*Atavism (Book #1)*

>*Phosphorous (#2)*

>*Descendants (#3)*

Girl Fights Back, copyright © 2011 by Jacques Antoine

Cover Designed by Torrie Cooney (torriecooney.com)

ISBN: 149035929X
ISBN-13: 978-1490359298

CONTENTS

To Roxie and Miki,

For taking the initiative.

CHAPTER ONE
A RELUCTANT COMPETITOR

"Sensei, what's my sparring gear doing back there?" Emily Kane asked.

Seiji Oda winced to hear the question, having hoped she wouldn't notice, though it could hardly be concealed much longer. He pretended to concentrate on driving through downtown Roanoke.

"You promised me it would only be *kata* today," she continued.

He grunted, face like stone, stoic, impervious.

"You know I hate fighting."

"It's sparring, not fighting," he replied. "And it is what your father wishes."

"Fine," she harrumphed, the reminder of her uncle-father adding to her irritation. "Will he even be there?"

Sensei Oda eased the minivan along a crowded, tree-lined parking area on the edge of the Virginia Western campus, and picked his way over to a spot not too far from the large building, where a throng of people in various martial arts uniforms pressed through three sets of double doors. Emily groaned.

"Your father wishes it," he repeated. "And you may find in it a path to deeper things."

With the hatch open, he pulled out the equipment bag for her, and slung a camera bag over his shoulder.

"I hope you don't mean that for me," she said, tapping the camera bag with the ball of her left foot. "Because I can do without memorializing the event in a video."

"Don't worry, Emi-chan. This is only for the other kids."

Once inside the doors, she peered resolutely out the plate glass window by the entrance, while he arranged for her tournament registration with two women sitting at a plastic folding table nearby.

"How old is she?" asked one woman in a loose white *gi* with a black belt and a large USKA patch. She wrote Oda's response in a small rectangle on the form: seventeen.

"Style?"

Oda paused to think it over. *What exactly was her style?* The other students in his *dojo* studied *Shotokan*, but that wasn't exactly what he'd been teaching her.

"*Wu shu,*" he replied finally, borrowing a Chinese term.

"I've never heard of it," the other woman said.

"Doesn't that just mean fighting?" the first one asked.

"Then put down *kung fu,*" he said, retreating a bit.

"How many years?"

"Twelve," he replied, taking a moment to calculate.

"*Kyu?*"

"Black."

"*Dan?*"

"No *dan.*"

"I don't follow," the first woman said. "Is she first *dan?*"

"We do not use levels. She is equivalent to highest *dan,* any style."

"Don't you have several other students registered for today under *shotokan?*" the second woman asked. He nodded.

"Her training is different, not limited to one style."

The first woman glanced over at her, standing by the doors, wearing camo-cargo pants, a black t-shirt, and a navy blue hoodie—the typical high school invisibility outfit.

"She'll need a uniform. This is a formal competition."

"What she's wearing is her uniform."

The woman grunted disapprovingly. "You're signing her up for the advanced adult *kumite*?"

"Men's division," he said.

"I don't think so," the second woman said. "Liability issues. Besides, she wouldn't stand a chance with the men. Have you seen those people? I'm sure they're much too strong… and fast for her. She could get hurt."

"No liability," he said. "I have a waiver signed by her father." Oda produced a folded paper from inside his jacket. "He put a note at the bottom about the Men's division, all notarized, official."

"We've never done anything like that in all my years with this tournament. She'll have to compete in the women's division, just like the rest of us."

"What's the problem, Sensei?" Emily asked, walking over to the table.

"Honey, do you really want to spar with the men?" the first woman asked.

"What?"

"Your sensei wants us to put you in the men's division. Is that what you want?"

With a pale face and wide eyes, she turned to look at him.

"It's what your father wants," he muttered. "You can do it," he added when she didn't say anything.

The two women retreated a few feet away to confer with an older man who wore a black *gi* and a very worn black belt, with several red velvet stripes decorating one end.

"I don't understand, Sensei."

"You are not just learning to defend yourself against women, Emi-chan, and you have plenty of experience sparring against the boys in the *dojo*."

"None of them even has a black belt yet," she replied.

"It makes no difference."

"And what belt do I even have?" she asked. "You've

never given me one."

"You are the highest rank. You are ready."

"Thanks for letting me know," she huffed.

"Colored belts are a distraction, only useful for people whose concentration needs reassurance. You do not need a belt."

The women returned to the table, followed by the man in the black *gi*.

"I'm sorry," he said. "We can't let you compete in the men's division. It's too dangerous."

"Do you think the black belts here lack control?" Oda asked.

"Miss, do you really want to risk it?" the man asked Emily.

"The women's division will not provide a sufficient challenge for her," Oda said, cutting her off.

"It's what my father wishes," Emily said, eyes fixed on the stripes on the man's belt.

The man mulled over her response and looked to the two women for an indication. One of them shrugged her shoulders.

"Let us talk it over," he said, looking at the waiver letter in his hand. "In the meantime, why don't you compete with the women. Their *kumite* starts in a few minutes, and the men's isn't until this afternoon. Show us what you can do there, and then we'll decide."

~~~~~~~~

Colored duct tape marked off twenty or so rings on the main floor of the gymnasium. Red tape set out the limits for competitors—step over that line and you're disqualified—while a larger square of black tape indicated a safe distance for spectators. All ten of the basketball backboards had been raised to a horizontal position overhead by a pulley system. A few scattered benches and folding chairs with specially padded feet provided limited seating, though most people either stood or watched from the retractable bleachers that had been pulled out for the purpose.

On one end of the floor, little kids competed in *kata* and weapons demonstrations, while their parents squeezed around each other to train video cameras at them. Older kids, up to age sixteen, sparred in four nearby rings where the crowd had fewer parents, but more teenagers. At the opposite end, musical *kata* occupied two rings next to the ones devoted to *chambara*, which featured foam-covered PVC "swords."

The largest ring, on a raised platform specially constructed for the purpose, resounded with the stomping of feet as two women in the advanced adult division lunged and circled each other.

"It'll be hard to sneak up on anyone with all that noise," Emily said.

"*Shotokan* uses loud noises and stamping feet to disrupt the opponent's *chi*," Oda replied. "But you already know that."

Emily nodded. "Should I stamp my feet, too?"

"That's up to you. Breathing is what matters. It's more important to hear your own *chi* than to disrupt your opponent's."

"Do you think I've forgotten everything?" she asked, one eyebrow raised.

One of the women in the ring scored a point by showing a front kick and following through with a hammer fist to the top of her opponent's head. She responded in the next point with an outward crescent kick to block a punch, followed by a roundhouse kick to the side of the first woman's headgear. The match was decided by a blocked punch that created an opening for an inside reverse punch, delivered from a back-stance.

"What did you observe?"

"They're fond of high kicks, and they're limber," Emily

said.

"The last point was more efficient."

"Yeah, but it was just lucky. She took a chance before she really knew what to expect."

He grunted his approval.

By the time Emily's turn came, the man in the black *gi* and the two women from the registration table had found seats on one side of the ring and motioned to Oda to join them. Emily pulled on foot and shin guards, and threaded her long, black, braided ponytail through one of the holes in the back of her headgear. She bit down on her mouthpiece, pulled on padded grappling gloves with articulated fingers, and stepped into the ring.

Emily's opponent, a tall, lanky woman, stared down at her over well-worn gloves with tiny cracks in the vinyl. The referee dropped his hand between them to signal the start of the match. Three points would win, awarded for any blow judged sufficient to temporarily incapacitate the opponent had it been delivered with full force.

The lanky woman stepped forward with a front kick, followed by a pair of lunging punches, and Emily retreated to the safety of the edge of the ring, where she heard the man in the black *gi* say "Your girl looks a bit skittish. You sure she's even up to this?"

"She's just taking her measure," Oda replied.

"If you say so."

The lanky woman circled around to her left and launched a high roundhouse kick, forcing Emily to retreat once again. After a second high kick and retreat, she barked out "C'mon, girl, face me," and gestured at Emily with her gloves.

After a deep breath and a sigh, Emily stepped back to the middle of the ring and held out her hands in an unusual pose, one hand held open, as if in a greeting, the other held out low, as if to receive a gift. When her opponent tried to raise her leg for another high roundhouse kick, Emily kicked her shin guard to block it. When she lunged forward to punch, Emily blocked first one hand, then the other. But her block was strangely sticky. She curled her hands around her opponent's wrists, not grabbing on, but making it impossible for her to pull her hands back without leaving an opening for a strike. When the woman tried to strike from that position, Emily rotated her arms, maintaining contact while preventing any attack. Finally, when the woman pulled back in frustration, Emily slid one hand along her arm, until it became a ridge-hand strike to the side of her headgear, and in the ensuing confusion jabbed to the center of her chest.

"Score," the referee shouted, as two of the corner judges raised little red flags, Emily's color.

"She's studied *wing chun*, I see," the man in the black *gi* said. Oda grunted.

The lanky woman shook her head and stared into Emily's eyes. When the referee dropped his hand between them again, she lunged a quick left jab towards Emily's face and followed it with a right hook. Neither one made contact as Emily leaned out of the way each time. A second left jab followed by a front kick missed as well, but this time Emily kicked the shin again to block, then hooked her opponent's foot with hers and pulled her forward and off balance. As she fell to the side, Emily tapped the side of her headgear and then pivoted to place the heel of a side kick directly in front of the woman's nose.

"Score," the referee shouted again.

"She held my foot," the woman complained. "That's against the rules, isn't it?"

"Trapping with the hands is," he replied. "Not the feet."

Back in the center of the ring, the woman eyed her warily, and Emily did what Sensei was always telling her to do; she breathed in and out and listened as the noise of the tournament drifted away. She could feel the woman's frustration, even see it in her eyes, and in the clenching of her jaw, often a sign that a decision's been taken.

When the hand dropped, the woman launched a sudden roundhouse kick aimed at her head. Emily leaned out of the way and waited for the next one. The woman kicked with the same leg three more times. "It must be her favorite kick," Emily mused, and toyed with the idea of sweeping her other leg out from under her during the next kick. It would be against the rules, but also a good lesson. At the fourth kick, the woman's technique had deteriorated, and to maintain balance she let her hand guard fall to the side. Instead of leaning away, Emily stepped in with a sharp block to the shin guard—the woman yelped, more from surprise than pain—and then punched several times to the chest and face, all controlled strikes, none full force, and none could be defended against.

"Score," the referee shouted, and gesturing to Emily, he called out: "Winner."

Emily gave a shallow bow to the woman and the referee, fist pressed against palm, then removed her headgear as she stepped out of the ring and sat by Sensei Oda. He grunted his approval and she tried to suppress a smile.

"I can see you've got some skills," the man in the black *gi* leaned over to say. "Why were you so timid at the beginning?"

"I hate fighting," she mumbled in reply.

"Then why train?"

"Sensei says so I won't have to fight."

"Yeah, but what do you say?" he pressed.

"I train because my father wants me to."

"But you don't enjoy it?"

"Oh, no," she said, suddenly animated. "I love training. I just hate fighting, and *kata* is beautiful, like dancing sometimes."

"I see," he said. "Are you still determined to compete in the men's *kumite*?"

Emily shrugged. He turned to the two women who'd

8

been in charge of registration and whispered something, then turned back to Emily.

"I'd like to see you go up against Charlotte here. She's won the women's *kumite* for the last three years."

"My friends call me Charley," she said with a smile. "I won't go easy on you, okay, hon?"

Emily nodded and then fidgeted with her gear.

After the last of the first round matches, the man in the black *gi* waved the referee over. Charley and Emily stepped into the ring, the first match of the second round. The referee reminded them of the rules: three points, no grappling, no full-force contact to the head, and no direct contact to the face.

"Don't worry, sweetie," Charley said. "You won't get hurt here."

Emily wondered what sort of expression people were seeing on her face. "It's not me I'm worried about," she muttered. She took in a deep breath and let it out slowly as Charley circled to her right, gloves up and stepping lightly. As she exhaled, it occurred to her that this woman had a good deal more self-possession than the other competitors she'd seen. Her eyes shone blankly, bright but almost unfocused, no sign of fear or anxiety, not even of aggression. Slightly shorter than Emily, and perhaps fifteen years older, she exuded confidence and, above all, patience. After a few seconds, it was clear she wanted Emily to make the first move. But Emily preferred to respond to an attack, a fighting posture called *go no sen* in Japanese.

"I guess she's read me pretty well," Emily mused. "Here goes nothing."

She led with a very traditional technique, starting with a quick front kick to her opponent's knee. When she leaned in to block it, Emily shifted her hips and flicked the same foot up into a roundhouse kick to the side of Charley's headgear.

"Score," the referee called out.

Charley adjusted her gear and stepped back to the

center of the ring. "Nice form," she offered through her mouthguard.

On the offensive this time, Charley tried a similar technique, a low kick followed by a high one, though this time, after Emily blocked her high roundhouse kick, she switched feet and pivoted through a crescent kick followed by a ridge-hand strike to the side of Emily's head. An extremely quick combination, Emily only barely managed to lean out of the way of the ridge-hand, but not the sneaky reverse punch to her chest.

"Score," the referee called, and the side judges held up white flags. "One-one, tied."

Emily nodded her head in appreciation once they were back in the center of the ring. The referee dropped his hand between them and Charley once again circled to her right. Another deep breath and Emily shut out all the sounds of the room, all the noise of the other rings and the spectators, the cacophony of hopes and fears pounding in the hearts of all the competitors. All that remained was the sound of her own heart, and Charley's. She could practically hear the flow of energy inside her opponent, free and unconstrained, until suddenly it seemed to gel into the form of a decision. From one side, with a loud shout and a stomp, Charley surged forward with a front kick, followed by two lunging jabs. But Emily had anticipated everything, sidestepping the kick and the first jab, one arm up to deflect the second, and the other arm extended in a sharp reverse punch to the center of Charley's chest.

"Score."

This time, her opponent seemed bewildered, no longer in possession of the serene self-confidence Emily saw at the beginning of the match. Another deep breath and she could almost hear the confusion in Charley's heart and expected something dramatic. When the referee's hand dropped, she spun through a series of high kicks—reverse crescent, crescent, pivoting into a wheel kick, switching feet each time—that led into a spinning back-fist and finally a ridge-hand/reverse punch combination. An elegant sequence of moves, beautifully choreographed, and perhaps too elaborate for tournament sparring, where points are usually decided by a simple punch or kick delivered with good timing and intensity.

Emily leaned out of the way of the kicks, not stepping back, so that when the final hand strikes arrived, they found her standing closer than Charley expected, too close to strike her effectively. In the tiny moment it would have taken her opponent to realize her mistake and adjust, Emily landed three quick punches to the center of her chest. She could have landed more, but there was no point.

"Score, winner."

Emily bowed to the referee and to her opponent, though Charley was too dumbfounded to notice. Mouth agape, stunned at having been defeated by a newcomer, practically a kid, she stumbled back to the bench where the man in the black *gi* and Sensei Oda sat.

"Well," the man said expectantly. "What'd you think?"

After a long pause, Charley stammered out, "I... I have no idea... what just happened?" After another pause she turned to Emily, who was now sitting next to her. "How did you do that?"

"Are you okay?" Emily asked.

"I'm fine. It's just... you know, no one's ever done anything like that to me. How'd you do that?"

"*Sen,*" she replied. Oda grunted next to her. When the woman showed no sign of understanding her, she explained. "It means initiative. I just didn't allow you to take the initiative."

"Yes, but how...?"

"It's all in the breathing. I try to get so quiet inside that I can really feel what I need to do."

Charley shook her head slowly, incredulous, apparently comprehending this explanation even less than the match itself.

"I suspect you'll be able to hold your own with the men," the man in the black *gi* conceded, after a long moment. "At least in terms of your skills. It's just that they hit harder. Are you really ready for that?"

"Isn't it just light contact in *kumite*?" Emily asked. "I mean, isn't that what the rules say?"

"Yeah, but light contact in the men's side is a bit heavier, and sometimes they can get carried away."

Emily frowned and glanced at Oda, who grunted, but said nothing. The man stared at the two of them intently for a moment, and then shrugged.

"I tell you what, there's a free ring at the far end. Spar with me, show *me* what you can do, and then maybe we'll let you in the men's *kumite*. Does that sound fair? Charley and your sensei can be the judges."

Emily nodded. "What's your style, Sensei?" she asked.

"*Wado-ryu*. And you can call me Steve."

"I'm not familiar with that style," she said, feeling a bit perplexed.

"It's not so different from the *shotokan* you've obviously studied. Some of the *katas* are similar. But, you know, sparring is less about style than about centering yourself and keeping focused. You shouldn't have any problem with that. Right?"

"I guess."

Since the musical *kata* competition had ended a few minutes earlier, the far end of the gym was relatively quiet, at least at first. But it didn't take long before some of the black belts around the room began to notice that Sensei Steve was up to something down there.

"Don't be afraid to hit me a little harder," Steve said. Emily nodded and Sensei Oda dropped his hand to begin things.

Neither one moved for several seconds, each apparently waiting for the other to initiate the action. Emily peered over her gloves at him and let her breath go in and out, slowly. He was resolute, untroubled and unflappable, that much she could see, and nothing she heard in her heart told her anything different.

"I can do this all day," he said, with a smile distorted by his mouthguard.

"Fine," she muttered, and began with the same very traditional move, a light kick to the knee and a foot flicked up into a high roundhouse kick. He would block them both, she knew, so she was ready to block the sneaky little jab he stuck in her face.

"Good, you kept your guard up. Most folks drop it to maintain balance when they kick up there. Now show me what you got."

Since he was bound to block her first move, she jabbed with a lunging punch to the chest, and when he tried to sneak a reverse punch in behind his block, she was ready. A quick punch to the bicep knocked his arm to the side. This left her open to a hook from the other hand, which she leaned away from, staying just close enough to sneak a quick ridge-hand strike in under his chin. Startled by the blow, he glanced into her face, and she stepped in to deliver a sharp knuckle to the soft spot at the center of his chest, just below the ribs. He staggered back, struggling to catch his breath.

"Point," Charley called out, with a snort. "She's tougher than she looks, huh, Steve?"

"Are you okay?" Emily asked. "You said to hit a little harder."

Steve raised his hand, still bent over at the waist, hands on hips, and said, "I'm okay... just give me a second."

Once he'd recovered, the two of them stood at the center of the ring.

"That was a pretty good punch. Is that as hard as you can hit?"

"No, I guess not. I mean, I wasn't trying to hit you as hard as I could."

"Have you ever been hit before, you know, sparring at your *dojo*?"

"Yeah, sure. The boys there, they don't always have good control."

"Well, let's try one more time."

Oda dropped his hand, and Steve circled to his left. By this time, some fifteen or twenty people were standing around the ring, mainly men sporting black belts.

"Who is that?" one of them whispered.

"Is this a private lesson?" another asked.

"She's pretty good. Can I have a lesson too, Sensei?"

In a sudden surge, Steve stepped forward with a low front kick followed immediately by a high kick with the other foot. The energy of the movement lifted him off the ground. Emily took a step back to evade the second kick, and then stepped forward under his leg to push him away. Once he'd regained his footing, Steve lunged forward a second time with a long jab, to set up a hook-uppercut combination. Emily blocked or ducked all three punches, but in the midst of the onslaught, he managed to sneak an inverted crescent kick in, making contact with her cheek in a glancing blow, but hard enough to knock her back.

"Point," Charley called out.

Her face stung, even through the headgear. *How did he manage to get his foot up there at such an awkward angle?* She hadn't expected anything like that, and that stung more than the pain of getting hit by it. One thing she was sure of, she wasn't going to let any tears come to her eyes.

"Are you okay?" he asked.

"Uh huh," she grunted, and held her gloves up ready for the next point.

"Well, you're a gamer, I'll give you that… and you can take a solid hit."

"Sensei, can I have a turn?" asked a young man in a stiff white *gi*. "Looks like she's had enough."

"Do you still want to compete against guys like this?"

Steve asked.

Emily turned to Sensei Oda, who gave no indication of how she should answer, but certainly no suggestion that she might get out of it now she'd been hit in the face. She shrugged and nodded in Steve's general direction.

"You may get to see whether she's had enough, first hand... in the *kumite*," he said to the young man. "She's competing in the Men's division."

Emily had no time to savor the consternation this news brought to the faces now directed at her. A crowd was already forming around the center ring.

CHAPTER TWO
SPARRING WITH THE BOYS

In the first few rounds of the men's *kumite*, Emily blocked, leaned, ducked and otherwise evaded almost everything her opponents threw at her, and delivered just as many surprising kicks and hand strikes. She was struck twice in three matches, once to the face, in violation of the rules, and once to the chest, knocking her to the floor. Each time, she glanced over to Sensei, and each time he returned a stony nod.

"She has a very eclectic style," Steve observed to Sensei Oda as the two sat together on one side of the center ring. "What exactly have you been teaching her?"

"*Kung fu*," Oda replied. Steve stared at him quizzically.

"You mean her training isn't just in karate, right? Her footwork is direct, like *shotokan*, but she also uses the circular patterns some Chinese styles favor. And she moves her hands like *wing chun*."

"Yes," Oda grunted. "She learned *aikido* first, and mastered *shotokan* by the time she was twelve. Since then, softer styles have suited her better, so we focused on *wing chun*, but without the wooden dummy."

"I wouldn't mind seeing her grappling skills, if her hands are strong enough."

"She is stronger than she looks, very deceptive."

"But she seems so timid, as if she doesn't know how good she really is."

"Not timid, observant."

Oda glanced over at Emily, who knelt nearby on the edge of the ring watching the match underway—two young men circling each other warily. He could guess what she was thinking: sometimes waiting is best, but not always. Sometimes it's best to lunge in before an opponent can make a decision, depriving him of the time and space he needs to take the initiative.

Sen, the initiative, is the key to every contest, and controlling it is essentially a matter of finding one's own *chi*. Breathing is the key, the only way Oda knew to unlock the power of *chi*, and Emily was as in touch with her own vital spirit as anyone he'd ever known. The boys and men he'd taught over the past four decades always struggled to understand this lesson, if they ever grasped it at all. That's the way it was with boys—bigger and stronger, usually faster, but too fascinated by their strength to attend to the truly important lessons. They learned all the techniques designed to make them strong and fast, they broke boards, wore their knuckles raw punching the heavy bag, but learning to listen to their own breathing remained elusive. In the dojo, Oda would drone on interminably about becoming still inside, breathing in and out, feeling everything—not just the sweat on your opponent's brow and the little jitter in his chest— feel that, too, of course, but so much else in addition. Feel the stillness every blow interrupts, and the return of the stillness afterwards. A boy's heart had no room for this lesson. Not yet. Maybe later. But she'd absorbed it all.

A quick kick-punch combination caught one of the men in the ring off guard. He stumbled back and pivoted away from a second kick directed at his chest. Oda smiled to see the intensity with which Emily watched the match. The man regained his balance to pivot a second time into a spinning backfist that struck his opponent's headgear from behind. Match over. Emily stood and took a seat next to Oda.

"That was a lucky break," Steve said, and Oda frowned.

"Not so lucky, I think," Emily said. "He lost his footing, but his opponent was over-extended. It was only a matter of time."

Steve nodded. "You're up next, I think." He watched as she put gloves and headgear back on, then turned to Oda. "Is she your best student?" he asked, after she stepped into the ring.

"Third best," Oda grunted. "She needs... what's the word? Not confidence, more like drive."

"That's why you want her to compete against the men."

"Her father's idea. He was my best student."

"Now that's someone I'd like to meet," Steve mused.

At a nod from Steve, the referee motioned Emily and her next opponent to the center of the ring and reminded them of the rules. The quarterfinal round, the remaining eight competitors had yet to lose a match, and Emily's opponent towered over her, tall and lanky, a slight swagger in his step, the top of his *gi* gapping open nonchalantly. The referee dropped his hand between them to begin the match. A long leg swung out on her right and she ducked under. When he tried to put his foot back down to start the next attack, Emily kicked it out from under him, and then watched calmly as he lost his balance, striking him several times around the chest and throat as he fell.

"Score," the referee called out.

She won a second point in similar fashion: a long, slow roundhouse kick, this time she leaned out of range, then surged forward behind his extended thigh, pushing him over and striking the back of his headgear. Finally, recognizing that his high kicks were too slow, her opponent focused on jabbing with his long arms. At least he wouldn't lose his balance this way, he must have thought. A few left-handed jabs achieved little, since Emily held her ground and blocked or leaned one way or another to evade each one. A hook-uppercut-jab combination had some intensity behind it, but produced similar results. Emily dodged the first two punches, slapped the jab across his chest, effectively sealing off any further attacks, then hit him with a sharp hook just under the ribs before he could disentangle his arms. One last reverse punch slipped under his arm caught him in the center of the chest. He stumbled back from the force of the blow, a bewildered, half-embarrassed expression on his face, but at least still on his feet. He gathered himself to bow after the referee declared her the winner.

~~~~~~~~

In the final match, Emily found herself up against a much more focused opponent, a somewhat older man, perhaps in his early thirties—which seemed almost antique to her—with a shock of curly blond hair and a wispy beard. A fire burned in his eyes, and she felt the intensity of his desire to win, to defeat *her*. The referee dropped his hand between them, and Emily backpedalled a few steps to buy a moment to breathe while peering over her gloves at him. The air filled her lungs, and when she exhaled, it carried the noise of the room away with it, until only the sounds of her own body remained, the slow beating of her heart, the sloshing of the blood in her veins... and perhaps even the sounds of his body. His heart beat resolutely—if that's what she was really hearing—urgently. If only she could divine his intentions.

He flicked his eyes to the side, perhaps so she'd see his left foot twitch and move to block it, leaving him an opening for a left jab. It would be a good move, just grazing her chin and followed by a quick front kick to her left knee, and then as she was falling to the mat he might finish her with a right hook to the left side of her face and a ridge-hand to the throat. The feint with the left foot would be necessary to prevent one of those sneaky kicks to the side of his head—he'd had plenty of opportunities to see how limber she was—as he leaned in with that first jab.

Could she really *feel* what he meant to do? Not in so many words, of course, but with each breath her confidence grew that she would recognize exactly when he had decided to make his move, and what direction it would go to and where it would come from. Sensei pushed her to do just this all the time, and maybe she was getting good at it with the other kids at the dojo. But here, in a noisy competition with a blackbelt, someone a whole lot more skilled than her usual opponents, and much more determined... she had everyone in her own dojo cowed, but not this guy.

Emily exhaled and stepped back to the center of the ring. He flicked his eyes down, twitched his leg and waited for her to block. She obliged and he leaned in with the jab. Before he knew what had happened, she had stepped just inside his fist—it grazed her ear as she punched him hard to the center of the chest. He thought of kicking before she could hit him again, but her left knee struck his raised thigh as he fell backwards. She hit his chest, cheek and chin three more times before he hit the floor.

"Score," the referee called out.

As they returned to face each other at the center, she could almost hear Sensei's voice echoing in her head, telling her she'd hit him too hard. "It left you overcommitted," he would probably tell her—even had told her on several occasions. There was no flaw in her technique, but she had overcommitted emotionally. In the thrill of the moment of insight, she had allowed herself the satisfaction of hitting him as hard as he had meant to hit her, and it left her out of balance emotionally, no longer sensing the flow of *chi* in the room. She'd given herself over to the boyish thrill of hitting hard and fast, of triumphing. It took an extra instant to pull herself back, to collect herself emotionally, to open herself again to the energy of the room. She had not yet learned to control that reaction.

Her opponent lunged at her suddenly, relying on quickness to get past her defenses. She blocked a jab across his chest and moved to strike under his arm, but he pivoted into a spinning back-fist that caught her on the side of the head. He hit her much harder than she could have expected, driving her to the floor, where she lingered for a moment while the referee awarded the point to her opponent. When the referee didn't respond to her look of righteous indignation at the rules violation he'd allowed, she turned to Sensei and Steve imploringly. When no comfort appeared from that corner, she picked herself up and girded herself to face her opponent again.

They traded the next two points, decided in the first case by a high wheel kick she managed to slip under an errant jab, and bring around to strike the back of his head. On some level, she'd felt an urge to strike his head as hard as he'd hit her in the previous point, and yet she held back, somehow unable to let him experience the full force of her resentment. In the following point, she thought he cheated again, grabbing her block to create an opening for a reverse punch to her chest. At least this time she didn't bother to complain, even silently. It wouldn't accomplish anything, she supposed, and maybe Sensei had a point. In a real fight, there would be no rules to shield her from whatever might come.

The referee dropped his hand for the last time, and her opponent lunged forward with a low front kick and left jab. She kicked his shin before his kick could reach her, then hooked his foot in the crook of her ankle, pulling him forward and off balance. His technique was good enough to block her strikes as he fell to the floor. He rolled to one side to elude a kick and sprang to his feet, and then into a leaping back kick that caught her by surprise full in the chest. She staggered back, gasping for breath, and collapsed to the floor. Grumbling loudly, she shooed away the referee's attentions, bowed slightly to her opponent, and stepped out of the ring.

Emily glowered at Sensei and prepared a cutting remark for him, something to the effect that she hoped he was satisfied. But before she could spit out the words, something else caught her eye. Sitting some small distance from the other side of the ring, she spied him, her father. How long had he been there? She ran along the edge of the raised platform, and when he stood to meet her, she threw her arms around his neck. "Daddy," she cried. "You came."

"Of course, I did, Chi-chan," he whispered in her ear. Everyone else knew her as Emily, but he called her Michi or Chi-chan. "Did you really think I wouldn't?" She raised an eyebrow. "Well, I'm here now," he said.

"How much did you see?"

"I saw it all, sweetheart. You were wonderful."

"Even if I didn't win?"

"You know what Sensei would say, right?"

"Yeah, winning a tournament means nothing, only winning a fight."

"You did well to ignore the cheating," he said, and she rubbed her cheek resentfully.

"I hope you don't expect me to go to any more tournaments, Dad," she said to forestall further discussion of this one. "I hate sparring."

"I'm glad you did this one. It's important... and don't worry, I know, it sucks to get hit."

"Yeah, it does," she said. "But that's not really it."

"Oh... then what is the problem?"

"It's having to hit people, Dad. I mean, getting hit's no fun, but hitting someone, that totally sucks. It's like stealing a little bit of their *chi*, you know? It's kinda gross."

George tilted his head as he looked at his daughter, and smiled his puzzlement at her sentiment.

~~~~~~~

On the ride home, her resentments and frustrations about sparring faded, and Emily bubbled over, telling her father how it felt to avoid strikes without blocking, how she heard her opponents' *chi* through her breathing, and how she understood *sen*, which no one else seemed to... no one except Sensei, and him.

Trees shot by the passenger window, industrial buildings peeked through here and there, warehouses, a lonely farm house or two, eventually giving way to empty fields, some recently harvested, others fallow for more than one season. The drive back from Roanoke eventually pulled her attention away from the tournament and martial arts. The swaying of tall grasses and weedy-looking scrub-trees turned her mind to another preoccupation, the camping trips she shared with her father. In her memory, the previous summer consisted of a series of weekends spent in the woods. Mostly with him, though also occasional daytrips with Anthony, the boy she babysat; she longed for those days to return. During the school year, homework intervened all too often. US History or AP English commanded much of her free time, and those weekends when they left her some space to breathe, her father had to go on some mysterious errand for Mr. Cardano.

"Are you done with your homework?"

"Yeah, pretty much," she grunted through clenched teeth, which was the way she usually responded to this inquiry. Then she thought better of it. "I got that essay on the Cherokee Removal back. Mr. Jameson wants to post it as an example paper for the rest of the school."

"That's great news, Chi-chan," her father gushed, and she let the feeling of his approval wash over her. It's not like he hid his feelings from her, but to everyone else he could seem as impervious as stone, and she noticed the contrast. He shared with her what he would never let the rest of the world see… except maybe Yuki, the cook at Mr. Cardano's estate. Emily knew he opened up to her, even if he tried to hide it. An occasional touch, a quiet word whispered into her hair that brought a smile. Once she even spied them holding hands when they must have thought no one could see.

"He wants to advise me on colleges."

"Have you thought about what you might want to study?"

"I don't know… maybe." The conversation had grown oppressive, in ways she might have anticipated, and she felt the irony of her desire to talk about these things with her father, and her fear that if she let him in to her deliberations about college, careers, even life itself, she'd lose the freedom to make her own decisions.

Just before Covington, her father turned off the freeway for the two-lane road that threaded its way north, through the foothills of rural Virginia to their home outside of Warm Springs. In the twilight, the sun crested the treetops, and shadows grew deeper and stretched long fingers across the road.

"I thought we could spend the night in the woods," he said, and her heart leapt to hear it, even if she suspected it was just to make himself feel better about making her spar. "You have Monday off, right? So we could even spend two nights out there. You up for it?"

"Are you kidding?" she practically shrieked, though she caught herself before it could turn into outright giggling. "Can we bring the slings?"

"Sure, sweetheart. But I thought we might bring the guns."

"Not more field-stripping, Dad. That's getting old. I could probably do that in my sleep at this point."

He smiled and said, "Nah, I was thinking we could do some target practice." Her eyes lit up at these words.

"Can we bring the semi-autos?"

George nodded as he turned through a gap in a tall

hedgerow that had skirted the road for the past mile or so. A gate swung open to admit the car and the familiar lawns spread out on either side of the entrance. The house—a three-story brick colonial with curving wings and a white portico—the garages and other utility buildings off to one side of the paved apron at the top of the drive, the lawns that stretched for at least a hundred yards on every side, and the forest that loomed in the distance and compassed it all, belonged to the family for whom he worked as chauffeur.

"Why don't you see what Yuki has for your dinner while I put the car away."

Emily hovered in the mudroom just outside the kitchen, uncertain whether she wanted to be noticed. The clatter Yuki and her assistant, Josefina, made putting the kitchen back in order covered her crossing to the corridor leading to the dining room. It must have been an early dinner for the family, no guests, no soirée, no social niceties to be observed. Lurking in the shadows gave Emily a moment to compose herself, maybe take a deep breath and get ready to face the onslaught of Yuki's attentions once she noticed her, which should happen shortly.

Family photos decorated the wall—she'd contemplated them many times—mainly pictures of Anthony and his mother, Andie, and his father, Michael, who towered over her father. Emily could recall the occasions many of these pictures memorialized. She'd been present when Anthony came home for the first time, a little bundle in Andie's arms, another day a few years later spent at Virginia Beach dodging the waves, his first day of school holding Emily's hand to board the bus. She found her way into a few others, but only by accident, or so it seemed. The camera hadn't meant to catch her. When she looked at them, she felt like collateral photographic damage, so to speak. In one photo, showing Anthony running after her toward the tree-line for an afternoon of play in the woods, she had to be at least a part of the photographer's target.

Josefina steadied a large pot on one edge while Yuki ladled the contents into several containers, and Emily stepped quietly through the door to look at another picture, this one unframed, held by a magnet on the walk-in freezer door... her second favorite. Shot with a long lens—she had no idea who had taken it—it showed her walking in the garden, Yuki's hand on her shoulder, four-year-old fingers clutching a few wildflowers.

She knew all too well Yuki was not her mother. Her uncle-father had explained it to her years ago, though Emily still knew next to nothing about her real mother. He'd met Mei Li in Japan—an American sailor stationed at Yokosuka and the youngest daughter of a merchant family from Taipei, sent to study nursing at Showa University. They married and she returned with him to the states, over the objections of her family. A turbulent marriage, she left shortly after Emily was born, and they never heard from her or her family again. Her own name seemed to be a sort of anagram for her mother's name, and she clung to that. Otherwise Yuki was the closest thing to a mother Emily had ever known, and looking at the photo on the freezer door always soothed her. She felt a large hand chucking her head from behind.

"What word from Roanoke, young warrior?" Mr. Cardano asked, towering over her by almost a foot. The teasing tone annoyed, but she swallowed it, since she knew he meant her a kindness by it. *Adults could be so clueless* "Any glory to be had?"

"Second place in sparring."

"Second place," he roared, in mock amazement. "You mean the woman who could best you lives... and she's in Virginia?"

By some miracle of kitchen air currents, or perhaps the racket of the cooktop exhaust fan, Yuki seemed not to have noticed her yet. "*Con permiso, hita,*" Josefina purred as she squeezed by to put an armload of plastic containers in the freezer.

"Second place in the Men's *kumite*," she added.

"Whoa… you're kidding, right?" he said, examining her face. "You must have kicked some serious butt."

"The Men's," Yuki exclaimed from across the room. "Just wait 'til I get my hands on that man…"

"It's okay, Mom. I did fine. Nothing happened."

"I don't care," Yuki snarled, pulling off an apron and twisting it into a weapon of some sort. "What on earth was he thinking? And that fool of a *sensei* went along with it, I suppose."

"It's not *sensei's* fault," she tried to explain.

"You are not fine, Emi-chan. Your face is all bruised up."

"It's nothing, Mom," she said, as Michael bent over to examine a red mark along her jaw.

"Looks like someone tagged you there," he said. "And you have a little mouse under your eye."

"Josefina, bring me a bag of frozen peas," Yuki said. "Where else did you get hit?"

"Stop it, Yuki. I'm fine. It's nothing." Calling her anything other than 'Mom' was like opening an old wound, and Emily could see it hurt Yuki, too. The illusion that she had any share of a normal family life evaporated once more in that moment. Like a primal scene burned into her memory, she saw her father crouching down next to her, extorting a promise: "Everyone thinks you're my niece, and it's safer if we leave it that way."

"Do I have to call you 'uncle' or something?" she remembered asking.

"No," he'd said. "Just call me 'Dad' and let everyone assume you don't really mean it." And so he introduced her to his ways, and a lifetime of subtle subterfuge. He explained the dangers to her—obscure enemies, an old vendetta, hiding in plain sight—she didn't really understand it all, and even the Cardanos didn't seem to be in on the secret, even though she and her dad had lived with them for as long as she could remember.

"Do you have any homework, young lady?" Yuki asked, shifting gears, and maybe trying to recover some control over the moment.

"I did it at school... mostly. There's just some reading for History left."

"I wish you didn't spend so much time at that dojo."

"Do we have to do this again?"

"It's not a suitable place for you."

"It's my *favorite* place."

"*Karate* is just a hobby," Yuki said, slipping into Japanese. "You have more important things to do with your life besides rough-housing with a bunch of boys in a dojo."

Emily barely noticed the shift, having learned the language from Yuki alongside the English she spoke with everyone else. That fact by itself should have shown her the extent to which Yuki had taken the place of her mother.

"It's not like I don't keep up with my schoolwork, and my chores," she retorted. "Oh, c'mon. It's not that bad. I get straight A's. I'm gonna go to college."

"But what about friends, a social life? Do you even know any other girls? There's more to life than that damned dojo."

Emily rolled her eyes. Yuki had a point—she was a bit of a loner in school. But what did they expect, living way out on the edge of town like this?

"What am I supposed to do, then? Without the dojo, I wouldn't ever see any other kids." Emily's eyes flared up as she spoke these words.

"I'm sorry, Emi-chan. I don't mean to... it's just that... I know it's been hard."

"It hasn't been hard. Between you and Dad... I mean, you've been like a mother to me. It's not like I'm a deprived child." Yuki frowned and Emily noticed, but didn't exactly know how to smooth it over with her.

In fact, there was a lot about her Emily didn't understand. She'd heard about some sort of scandal involving Yuki's father in Japan years earlier. A scientist, he specialized in bio-engineering, or some sort of genetics research. Whatever it was, it must have been very cutting edge, since there had been a dispute about patent rights related to a discovery he'd made. It was all hushed up in the end, but the episode must have shamed him and he took his own life. Later, perhaps as an act of contrition, the company that claimed the patent turned it over to the Japanese government. Though Yuki never spoke of it, Emily had the distinct impression, from the little her father had told her of the matter, that Yuki's father had been falsely accused of industrial espionage.

Yuki seemed to be about the same age as Emily's father, though exactly how old was not easy to say. She had enormous energy, much more than could be expended in running the kitchen of a large, socially active household. She must have vast, secret hobbies, Emily sometimes mused. How else to account for all that vitality? Sometimes she teased her about it, needling her to find out what she really did with her spare time. But she could only push Yuki so far before she would turn a withering glare her way. Then it would vanish, and those familiar warm, dark eyes would reappear, smiling at her. Had there really been that much menace in her eyes? Or was it just a trick of the light? Sometimes, Emily couldn't really tell for sure.

In the end, Emily shared her dinner with Josefina—hot soup with chicken, a bowl of rice and seaweed, and a little bowl of *tsukemono*, though Josefina didn't care for pickled cabbage—while Michael discussed plans for a special event with Yuki. Afterwards, she went back to the apartment over the garage she shared with her father. She didn't tell him what Yuki had said, though perhaps the expression in his eyes showed that he already knew.

"It's dark enough," he said. "You ready to go?"

"I'm gonna change shoes," she said, and crawled into her closet. At the bottom of a stack of shoeboxes, pressed between the pages of a book she'd read in fifth grade, her fingers found another photograph. Foxing frayed one corner, and perhaps she'd hidden it, though she couldn't quite say why. It showed her face, eyes closed in blissful sleep, her head resting on her mother's shoulder, her real mother. According to the date stamp, she was ten weeks old, and all she could see of her mother was long, straight black hair pulled to one side to reveal the line of her neck and the curve of an ear.

"Coming, Dad," she replied when he called to her, and returned the photo to its hiding place.

CHAPTER THREE
BREATHING

Standing in front of her locker, in the southwest corridor of Bath County High School, Emily couldn't help chewing over what Yuki had said. As much as she craved independence, and as much as the weight of Yuki's words oppressed her, the truth of them hit home. She didn't have any girlfriends, and the boys at the dojo weren't really her friends either. They hardly spoke to her there or in school, for that matter... except for one of them, but she hadn't told Yuki about Danny yet. As for the rest of them, she wondered if she would even recognize them if she bumped into them in the hallway... and she seriously doubted they'd recognize her.

Cheerleaders laughed as they walked by, and one of them seemed to sneer at her. Football players cleared their own path, and the A/V kids got out of the way. To be recognized at school, or anywhere, what a change of pace that would be, even the not-so-friendly notice of the popular kids.

The shy girl whose locker abutted Emily's dropped some papers, and she began to fuss and fret. When Emily bent down to help her gather them up, she smiled nervously. "At least she knows who I am," Emily thought. "She probably dropped the papers to get my attention." A vain notion, she recognized it right away for what it was. But even if this girl wanted to be friends, what could they possibly have in common?

"Hi," Emily grunted, and then turned away, more flushed than she could account for. "I don't even know what a friend is," she muttered walking down the corridor toward her last class. "Maybe I'm really just a loner."

A group of Goths huddled by another locker caught her eye. "They're sort of like me, I guess, and they have each other." She stood nearby for a second, taking the occasion of a little congestion in the foot traffic to hover and maybe see if they'd say anything. The piercings and the makeup—even the boys wore eyeliner, and they all seemed to have dyed their hair black—it seemed so totally clownish. They wanted to be taken seriously, like they had some deep, dark secret, or something, but the costumes just made them look ridiculous.

Did she look ridiculous, too? She had black hair, much blacker than theirs, but she came by it naturally. *She* dressed like a normal person, t-shirt, denim jacket, camo-cargo pants, work boots or black sneakers. That's what she wore everyday, without even thinking about it. Yuki and Andie had tried on more than one occasion to get her to dress up for school, but she found the idea revolting. "At least, I'm not wearing a costume," she snorted.

~~~~~~~~

A few days later, sitting in the dojo, legs folded under her, she looked at the faces turned in her direction. Sensei often had her lead the breathing exercise. She wouldn't learn any new techniques in these classes, given her skill level—in private sessions, sensei would show her what remained in his cabinet of wisdom—but even in a large class, there was still something to learn by looking inside oneself in a moment of stillness. For most people, even achieving a moment of stillness was a significant accomplishment.

"Let's try the 'Iron Wire' to begin with," she said, and then rehearsed the movements with the class. Breathing slowly, in and out, she pushed her arms forward with a swooping movement, alternately relaxed and tensed, then turned palms down and stretched them to the side, as though she were pulling a string tight. Palms up, she brought her fingers together in front of her, as if she were balancing a staff on them. When her arms finally came to rest on her lap after a few more turns, she began the cycle again.

Usually she would begin to drift off, away from the dojo, or her bedroom, or wherever she happened to be, and find herself in a familiar place: a wooded glen, tropical, leopard shade flashing across her face as she walked the path. Her bare feet would crinkle the leaves and dirt, and she could hear the sound of running water in the distance, though she never seemed able to find it.

But today, for some reason, her mind kept bringing her back to the dojo, her eyes resting on one face or another. "Do I know any of these people?" she wondered. Of course, she knew some of the adults' names, mainly middle-aged men and women, but she had nothing in common with any of them. Their names were just tags—might as well have been pinned to the front of a *gi*—no invitation to discover anything shared with them. What about the kids her age? Surely she knew them.

There's that huge kid, Wayne something-or-other, and a couple of boys she recognized from the football team... as if she cared about team sports like that. Two girls in the back row, green belts, sophomores, she knew them by sight, though they'd never shared any classes with her, and likely never would after this year.

She didn't see Danny anywhere... and maybe that was a blessing. His name she knew, and maybe he counted as a friend, though she wasn't exactly sure. She'd gone to a rave with Danny Rincon a couple weeks earlier, and things didn't end so well. But under no circumstance did she want to give her father a chance to speak to him when he picked her up after class.

She didn't want to look at any of them anymore, since these reflections were becoming painful. It took an effort to close her eyes and let her hands rest on her thighs, and she tried to listen to nothing besides the sound of her own breathing. Of course, it never really worked like that. The sound of her breathing rode on top of the noise of her beating heart, and the blood in her veins. Eventually, it led outside of herself to the rise and fall of the other chests in the room. Her breath pressed against theirs, and beyond them to the walls of the dojo. If she'd had the patience, it might have carried her spirit even further, out to the street and the woods on the other side, and up to the covering clouds.

On any other day, she'd have followed the trend of her thoughts wherever it led, even if she really only wished to find her way back to the wooded glen. Second best, she turned her thoughts to the previous weekend, to seek comfort in the woods she'd just shared with her father.

Building the first lean-to had taken the better part of an hour. An abundance of fallen branches made it easy enough, though her father insisted on spreading dry leaves and branches all around in a broad perimeter.

"Think of it as an alarm system," he said.

"We're worried about burglars?"

"Don't close your eyes in the woods without opening your ears."

The stars kept her up late, a moonless night showing her glimpses of the Milky Way rolling overhead while her father slept. The next morning, she woke to his crunching down a raw breakfast, and a rabbit hanging from the lean-to.

"I didn't see you set a trap last night," she said.

"I hit him with a rock."

"A burglar?"

"Yup," he said, and laid a handful of something on a flat rock by the lean-to. "Eat up. There's a stream back that way. We head out in fifteen."

"Which way are we headed?"

"West by northwest. If you want to get some target practice, we have to get to the other side of those hills."

"What do you expect me to do with that?" she said, pointing at a pile of thorny twigs with what looked like rose-berries.

"Breakfast. They're good, if a little bitter."

"The bugs, too?"

George crouched down to get a better look, and pinched a small, brown beetle between two fingers. Without a second thought, he popped it in his mouth, and then pushed a twig aside to capture another, somewhat larger one.

"Here," he said, holding it out to her, legs still wriggling. "Your turn."

"You have got to be kidding," she snorted.

"I can't give you a Ranger badge if you can't live off the land."

"Fine," she said, after a moment and an angry stare did nothing to dissuade him. She put the bug in her mouth, and the worst part wasn't even the taste, since it didn't really taste like much. But the legs tickled the roof of her mouth and almost made her gag. She had to crunch it between her teeth to get it to stop moving so she could swallow it. He handed her a little apple, sour enough to take her mind off the bug. Once the puckered scowl faded from her face, he handed her the persimmon hiding in his pack.

"These are ripe," he said. "In fact, I'm surprised the possums haven't eaten 'em all yet. And there's wild strawberries by the stream. Let's go."

Scattered grumbling called her back to the dojo, and she opened an unfocused eye to see that the huge kid had sweated through his *gi*. He looked exhausted and quite mystified by the entire breathing exercise, and she supposed he had no notion what the point of it all was. Perhaps none of the boys did.

"Line up," Sensei said, having come up behind her at the front of the room, and then using Japanese terms, he announced a sequence of techniques: rising block-lunging punch-front kick, followed by a roundhouse kick and a double block designed to trap an attacker's arm. The sequence ended in a backfist to the imaginary attacker's face. Emily demonstrated each technique as he called it out, and like many *Shotokan* training techniques, it involved getting the class to march across the floor with each forward step.

"That's really the spirit of the style," she thought, circulating around the room, giving pointers to each student as they followed where Sensei's commands led them, from one wall to the other and back again. Black t-shirt and cargo-pants, a sports bra underneath ("…like I even need one," she would sometimes snort at herself, looking in the mirror disapprovingly after a shower), she cut an odd figure in a room full of white uniforms. Some of the boys had noticed, but they seemed to know better than to say anything about it to Sensei.

Focus drills followed, first punching a moving target-pad, then kicking a tennis ball suspended from a hook in the ceiling. They lined up and tried to hit the ball with a roundhouse kick, a complex move in which you begin moving your leg up and forward, but then pivot and open your hips to strike the target from the side. At waist high, most of the class had no trouble making contact. But, as Sensei raised the ball, accuracy declined, until at shoulder height few people could do more than graze the ball.

"You will rarely have an occasion to kick this high," Sensei said. "But as a focus and flexibility exercise, it can be useful. Eventually, you should be able to do something like this." He nodded at Emily and held out a target-pad at roughly the height of his head. She stepped forward and struck it twice, first with the roundhouse kick they'd been practicing, then, without pausing, she put that foot down and followed the motion through, pivoting into a high wheel-kick, catching the target with the heel of her foot. She ended up in a fighting stance, one foot in front, hands in guard position, facing the target.

"Notice her guard. Never lower your hands to maintain your balance in a high kick. If you can't keep your guard up, you can't kick that high." He nodded to Emily and she repeated the kicks, while he cautioned the class to watch her footwork. "Notice how she keeps one heel on the ground. If you lift that heel, you will not be grounded and your kick will be weak."

The rest of the class was spent working on kick combinations in pairs with target-pads. Afterwards, the two girls in the back asked if Emily would demonstrate the *nunchaku* for the class. "That will have to wait until Monday," Sensei said, nodding to the clock, and the line of parents waiting outside.

Emily overheard some of the boys talking about a camping trip they had planned for the weekend after next. "Maybe we do have something in common," she thought, and drifted over in their direction, half hoping they'd ask her to join them. The mere thought of springing such a suggestion on her father was delicious. Camping with boys—what could he possibly object to? Yuki's words also echoed in her mind, and she relished the prospect of announcing the trip in the kitchen. "See, I do have friends," she pictured herself saying.

"I'm going camping with my dad this weekend," she said out loud.

"We were out by the yellow ridge," one of them said, not quite registering the fact that Emily had spoken to them. "You know the place, right? We followed this stream down, and then two guys with huge guns came out of nowhere and chased us off."

"Guys with guns in the national forest?" the huge kid, Wayne, asked.

"These weren't hunting rifles either. One of the guys was almost as big as you."

"What were they doing there? It's not like it's private property."

"My dad said we'd probably strayed too far west. There's some big estate over there that backs on the forest."

"Sounds like it was probably Ethan and Jesse," Emily said in a little voice.

"Wait. That's your estate?"

"Well, it's not like we own it," she said, regretting that she'd said anything. "My dad's just the chauffeur to the family."

"But you live off McGuffin Road, don't you?" another boy said. "We were nowhere near there."

"It's a pretty big estate," she said, and then looked for a way to retreat and find her father.

"Hey, maybe we could go hiking out there with you," Wayne offered, as she backed away. "I mean, if you feel like having us along sometime."

"Yeah, sure," she said, and squirted through the front door just as the family car eased up to the curb. Glancing back, she saw a row of expectant faces along the front window, and waved at them before ducking into the passenger seat... and tried not to look at her father until they'd left the parking lot. In the rumbling of the car, she found an excuse not to say anything to him either.

"I have to go out of town tonight," he said after a few moments of silence. "I won't be back until Saturday evening at the earliest." This wasn't the first time he'd delivered this particular sort of bad news. Occasionally, he would leave the estate for a few days, if Michael Cardano asked him to, but never for longer than a week, and he never told Emily what he did on these trips, and she didn't ask anymore.

"Dad," she groaned, finding a second syllable in the word, "this was supposed to be our weekend."

"I'm sorry, Chi-chan. It's really out of my hands. Why

don't you go to the woods tomorrow without me? If I get back in time, I'll try to find you. Then we'll see how good you really are at covering your tracks."

"You'll never find me, old man." she retorted.

"I already know you're gonna climb Promontory Rock and hide there. Don't think I haven't noticed you casing that spot. You can't fool me."

"Fine," she said. "But if you don't find me by Sunday morning, you'll owe me big time!"

"Fine!"

"Fine!"

They rode home in silence the rest of the way. As vexing as this change of plans might be, she knew there would be plenty of pleasures for her out in the woods by herself... *and damned if he wasn't right about Promontory Rock.*

By the time they pulled up the drive, the sun had already set and Emily was hungry. Her father, it seemed, had already eaten. He put the car away and retired to their apartment over the garage, while Emily ate in the kitchen of the main house with Yuki and Josefina.

CHAPTER FOUR
SOFTWARE

Michael Cardano seemed to be an important man. He'd once held some minor posts in the federal government—a deputy to the Ambassador to the Philippines in the eighties, later he held an obscure office in the Pentagon, and then worked briefly for a well-known conservative think-tank. Most recently, he consulted for the State Department on Southeast Asian economies. He enjoyed an influence and importance that could hardly be accounted for by a perusal of the various official titles he had held. His acquaintances assumed he really worked for the CIA, or perhaps the NSA. That would at least account for the resources employed to secure an estate in the backwoods of Virginia someone of his professional attainments could hardly be expected to be able to afford. But in the end, no one inquired too closely into his finances, or his work.

"Mike, you're gonna have to turn 'em over to us," the

voice on the other end of the phone said. "You realize that, don't you?"

Michael reflected on the quality of the tone of that voice. Several million lines of code and a few hundred miles of fiber optic cable lay between him and the man on the other end. The code was written to ensure the security of the connection, dissolving the vocal noises made at either end of the connection into miniscule bits, whirling them into a billion randomized patterns and then, at the last moment, reconstituting them into a facsimile of the original vocal intonations. Most of the code was actually tasked with recreating as accurately as possible the sound of the original voice. The voice from the phone sounded like the man Michael knew him to be, and he could hear the tonal indicators of his emotional veracity. The sound was true to the voice. He hoped his own voice would sound as true at the other end of the line, since he felt the need to be able to control the shading of his voice, to shape the way he was perceived, and he didn't want the nuance he aimed to create to get lost in the code.

"You gotta be kidding," he snorted.

"Nope."

"You realize this is just more of Meacham's bullshit, don't you?" he said to needle the caller.

Silence.

"He's gonna flog this turkey all over the hill, and we both know it's bullshit. That's not how real soldiers work."

"Maybe you're right. So what?" the other man said.

"He's gonna get us all killed... or worse. That's what!" Michael muttered.

"That doesn't change anything. You still have to turn them over. Are you gonna bring 'em in, or do we have to come get 'em?" he asked menacingly.

"Fine. I need a couple of days. I'll have 'em there on Monday."

He hung up the phone, not waiting for a reply. The

man on the other end would accede to his request, that much he knew. But he was equally certain the teams would come down early, sometime on the weekend. They wouldn't wait for him. With a little luck, they wouldn't come down before Sunday, late in the evening, hoping he would have his guard down—which meant he needed to be ready to move on Saturday. A lot depended on Kane.

~~~~~~~~

Michael first met George Kane years ago in the Philippines. Working out of the embassy in those days, he occasionally needed a driver, sometimes even a bodyguard. But a bodyguard large enough to be worth anything would spook his contacts. So he ended up taking a lot of chances. Before one meeting, his boss arranged for a new driver, some kid from Subic Bay. He looked like a callow farm boy from Kansas or Iowa, who knows, maybe even Nebraska. Smallish, on the skinny side, he wore a Marine uniform, which seemed improbable. As he sat in the backseat of the sedan, it struck Michael that this kid wasn't wearing any rank insignia. Just fatigues. He'd assumed it was a uniform largely because the kid walked like a Marine. You didn't learn to walk like that in Kansas. But now he wondered who this kid really was.

Light banter got Michael nowhere. The folder Meacham sent over indicated the kid had bounced around the services a bit. He'd started in the army, apparently hoping to be a Ranger, but he didn't look like the physical type they favored. Somehow, he found his way into some obscure unit in the Navy—being large wasn't quite as useful on a ship. So here he was, working out of Subic, driving cars for the embassy, having washed out of some program or other. The Navy didn't quite know what to do with him, but Meacham must have seen something he liked, and he didn't usually make mistakes about people. About everything else, maybe, but not people.

On that first day, Meacham sent the two of them to meet a Chinese contact: Tang. Michael didn't really know much else about him, and neither did Meacham. He'd indicated a willingness to sell something concerning the North Koreans, though exactly what wasn't clear. The standard practice was to get a potential asset to commit to something, and that seemed to mean Michael needed to expose himself and take a chance, since he'd been developing Tang for months with nothing to show for it.

The route took them through a seedy neighborhood in Manila. Of course, at that time, every neighborhood in Manila looked seedy to American eyes, and it didn't help that Tang had insisted on meeting at an Italian restaurant, of all things. *Was he mocking him, or just trying to put Michael off his guard?* "Whatever you do, don't eat anything in there," he thought.

"You sure you want me to wait outside?" George asked as he pulled the car up in front of the restaurant. Another car, a gray Korean model, blocked the alley next to the restaurant, the driver leaning against the passenger side door.

"Yeah. Maybe you'd better. What do you make of that guy?"

"Too tall to be a local," George said. "Probably Chinese, maybe embassy staff."

"That's not promising. If Tang brought him along, it might mean he doesn't have the nerve to breach security."

"Unless he wants to do it right under his minder's nose."

Michael didn't care for either interpretation. Standing on the front stoop of the restaurant with one hand on the door, he noticed George approaching the other driver for a cigarette. *What was he up to?* It was too late to stop him, so Michael tried to focus on what he might have to promise Tang to sweeten the deal, and pulled the door open.

The glow from the kitchen and whatever late afternoon sun glared in through the dirty windows out front provided the only light in a dim room. From a booth at the far end of the room, a Chinese gentleman waved him over. It looked like Tang from that distance, but he couldn't be sure. Before he'd taken three steps, a strong hand reached around his face from behind and clamped a sweet smelling rag over his nose and mouth. Everything went dark, and felt much more compressed.

He woke up, feeling groggy and nauseous, in the back seat of his car. George held a cool, damp cloth over his forehead.

"Here, drink this. You'll feel better soon," he said.

"What the hell happened back there?" Michael wheezed.

"Things went south in a hurry. I had to get you out of there… fast."

"Where's Tang?" he asked, trying for some composure.

"Dunno. But those guys weren't there to deal."

"Shit."

Back at the embassy compound, Meacham filled him in. Tang was dead. Or there never was a Tang. It was hard to tell. The men at the restaurant had meant to throw Michael in the trunk of their car, and that would have been the last anyone ever heard of him. They probably expected Meacham at the meeting. Michael wouldn't have been of much use, since he didn't know enough. After they discovered their mistake, they would have disposed of his body.

The local police requested an interview the next day, which took up the better part of an hour. Alternately listless and officious, they asked a few questions, but seemed only half-interested in the answers. The following morning, an article appeared in the local paper about four dead Chinese. The police had no leads, it said. The men had been found in an alley behind an abandoned restaurant. The newspaper didn't mention the peculiar fact that someone had already taken fingerprints of the victims before the police arrived. At least, that's what George discovered by chatting up the driver, who'd been left to wait outside the embassy: all four men had ink on the fingertips of their right hands.

"That's odd," Michael said, after the police left. "What do you think it means?"

George said nothing.

"It's nothing to do with us," Meacham said. "Probably just the *Guoanbu* taking an inventory of their people at the embassy."

The mere mention of the Chinese intelligence agency made a shiver run up Michael's spine. Over the next few days, the Chinese ambassador made no public comment, but behind the scenes, his Cultural Attaché was screaming bloody murder. They may not have cared much for the lives of a few operatives, but being seen to have lost face could prove dangerous.

But what had really happened in that restaurant? Those guys were big… at least the two Michael saw. Bigger than him, so a lot bigger than George. When Meacham showed him the police report, he noticed it didn't mention any gunshot wounds.

George said nothing about the events of that day. Nothing about the restaurant. Nothing about Michael throwing up on the ride back. Nothing at all. Meacham had found him the perfect driver: a bodyguard no one would notice. Nothing about him drew anyone's attention. No one felt threatened by him. Unless, of course, they looked in his eyes, those blank, dead eyes. Empty, like the eyes of a Midwest farm boy… and then some!

~~~~~~~

Michael stared at the phone for a long moment, considering his options. Then he left his den and went down

45

to the basement, where he kept his private office. There were actually two basements under the main building, the lower one connected by passageways to the other buildings. It wasn't a huge underground complex, like you see in the old Bond movies. The lower basement was very discreet; a quick search of the compound might not reveal it, especially a search conducted in a hurry, perhaps under fire. It would be no good to hide down there for long during an attack, since a more deliberate search would eventually reveal it. But you might be able to use it to elude intruders for a little while, perhaps long enough to escape through the long, underground tunnel that led into the woods behind the main building.

The tunnel, by contrast, had been concealed much more carefully than anything else in the basements. It might take a full thirty or forty-five minutes to find since it didn't extend in a direction one might expect, namely to the fences, or any of the gates. Instead, it led further into the heart of the estate, a bit of misdirection that might enable someone who really knew the forest well to get away. At night, it would be almost impossible to track someone there.

The upper basement served mainly for storage, though in a few rooms the concrete floors had been carpeted and casually furnished, like a suburban rec room, with brighter light fixtures, a ping pong table, a pool table, a couple of couches and a TV. Michael also kept a small, private office down there, with the only computer terminal in the main house. The mechanicals occupied a room at the far end, and another room housed the mainframe and servers that ran all the electronics on the estate.

But there was no arsenal. It wasn't that kind of place. The security guards had the only firearms on the estate. Michael figured the enemy he was really preparing for would always be able to outgun him, so he saw no point investing his resources there. Instead, he focused on stealth and subterfuge, and, he hoped, better intelligence.

The second basement was much darker, barely even lit. To get to it you had to climb down a ladder hidden behind the bar. At almost fifteen feet below the floor level of the upper basement, it was little more than a cave, and even though it was completely unheated, the temperature remained a constant fifty degrees year round. Two dreary rooms, which formed a passageway connecting the main house to the garage, did not require more than sparse furnishings, a wooden table, a few chairs, and a crude bench. No need for electrical outlets, since the light fixture in each room was powered by batteries connected to solar cells on the roof. Michael never intended to spend any time down there.

~~~~~~~

Michael sat in his private office in the upper basement and reviewed his plans. He'd have to hide his family, and they'd have to spirit Yuki away from the estate, and Emily too, he supposed, and they'd have to do it quickly. Another part of the plan called for George to meet a couple of agency contacts at a safe house outside of Langley, so Michael could call in an old favor, and he worried that George might not be able to persuade them to trust him. Michael trusted George implicitly, because he had good reason to, but others often didn't. Why should they?

"It'll all have to go," he muttered. The house, the estate, everything—he might as well burn it down himself. "Andie's gonna be disappointed. Anthony, too, but he's young enough to get past it."

His thoughts turned again to Emily. This was the only house she'd ever known, and now that she was getting ready to graduate from high school, there was no time to build more childhood memories. "Did it really have to come to this," he asked, and turned his mind to other scenes.

There had been many more scrapes after the

Philippines, and George had saved his life a number of times… more than he cared to remember. Michael owed him everything, and never felt so safe as when he was around. He'd also protected George, concealed him, so it wasn't entirely a one-sided relationship.

The trouble started in Tokyo, where Meacham had sent them on a different kind of mission, shadowing a team of scientists working on a project that had become Meacham's new preoccupation: drug-enhanced soldiers. Years of research into the effect of psychotropic chemicals showed it was possible to enhance both the response time of the aggressor instincts, and the sensory acuity to actuate those instincts.

"It's a fool's errand," George had said when Meacham first proposed it. He almost never said anything, so this must have rankled him. Meacham didn't take it well.

"If we don't do it, our enemies will," he said, sounding more like a salesman than a statesman. "Think of it. A few units of predators could accomplish more than whole battalions. It could mean the end of conventional warfare."

"It's a fantasy," Michael remembered saying, but Meacham had already gone too far down this road to listen. "But even if they can make the drugs work, those guys would be too twitchy to be of any use."

"This isn't an academic conference. I don't need you to review the scientific merits of the stuff. Just make sure we get it, and nobody else does."

Their suspicions turned out mainly to be correct. Test subjects couldn't concentrate on mission-commands for more than a few minutes, and quickly became difficult to control. Soldiers like this would require constant battlefield supervision. But if they could be kept on task, they demonstrated great ferocity, and seemed utterly uninhibited by concerns for their own personal safety. Horrific side-effects dogged the entire project: most of the early subjects went insane, and several committed suicide. Other side-effects mimicked those of anabolic steroids: hair loss, megalocephaly, loss of libido, depression.

A breakthrough occurred when it was noticed that the worst side effects were greatly diminished in female subjects. Also, in the case of women, the enhancement of the aggressor instincts did not come at the expense of a greatly reduced attention span. Female soldiers seemed able to carry out complex missions lasting over several hours. The Tokyo group conjectured that it might be possible to manipulate the genetic code of males to mimic the neurological profile of females. These genetically altered males would then be able to benefit from the enhancements these drugs promised, while suffering greatly reduced physical and emotional detriments. They would be able to reverse the genetic alterations at a later date, or so the scientists believed.

"I don't care about that," Meacham said, when Michael reported the latest developments. "Stay focused on your mission."

"But this isn't the project you sent us down here for, a short-term enhancement. How many guys do you think will volunteer for something like this?"

"Let me worry about those details. Word is, the Chinese are interested, and they may already be on the scene. Don't let them get the drop on you."

"You can't argue with a zealot," he told George later. "He thinks America's military and economic future depends on this."

"He's only thinking of his own future," George said. "Baloney like this won't lead anywhere good for anyone who gets involved with it."

"Probably not, but we still have to keep the Chinese from stealing it out from under us, and I've made no headway with Dr. Kagami. Have you been able to talk to his daughter?"

George said nothing, at first. A geneticist in her own right, Yukiko Kagami knew the inner workings of every aspect of her father's research. She was his confidante, his partner and his colleague.

"Don't hold out on me," Michael pressed. "I know you've spoken to her." A low grunt signaled assent, or maybe annoyance, probably both. "Spit it out, man. What does she think?"

"She says what we've known all along: the project is bullshit. Her father managed to sell the Mori people on it, but he's no closer to making the drugs work then before."

For whatever reason, something about George struck a chord with Yukiko, and she trusted this *gaijin* with the empty eyes. It didn't seem to matter that he had come because of her father's work and represented everything she feared. Unlike the Chinese and the Russians, he understood that the Predator project was misguided, even wrong.

Michael and George spent the next two years working with Yuki, cajoling her, deceiving her, learning from her, understanding her, and in the end helping her... and it stretched Meacham's patience to the breaking point. But when a Chinese operative managed to infiltrate the lab, they knew it was time to act in a different vein, and on an accelerated schedule.

"We can't just leave her there," George said, the day after the Chinese managed to ransack the lab. "It's too dangerous. Whatever the Chinese got from the lab, it's not a working prototype, and now that Kagami's dead, they're gonna come after her."

"What are we supposed to do with her?" Michael remembered asking, not yet fully comprehending the nature of George's resolve.

"You know the Chinese will grab her—who else is left?—and it's not gonna be pretty, what they'll have in store for her. We owe her."

"Meacham's not much better. Maybe he won't torture her, but she'll be a virtual prisoner for the rest of her days."

"We need her to explain to Meacham why whatever it

was the Chinese stole has no value. But that means turning her over to him."

"No," George said, in a tone of voice Michael hadn't heard before, and which still rang in his ears. "You're gonna have to convince him. We'll get her to explain it to you. After that, we keep her under wraps. You can tell him she's dead, if you have to."

They spirited her out of Tokyo that night, before the Chinese could act. Yuki gave Michael a crash course in molecular genetics over the next two weeks, while they hid out in Hokkaido, and gave him the lab records to prove that the project was a failure.

"It's better if you don't know where we are," George told him, when he left for Manila.

"What if Meacham doesn't buy it? He might decide to come after us?"

"Then I'll have to take him out."

At the time, Michael recoiled at the thought, without exactly knowing why. But now, sitting in his basement, as he worked out how to tear down the façade of his life without letting his wife know the true extent of the danger, he almost wished they had followed George's 'Plan B' two decades ago.

As it turned out, Michael succeeded in persuading Meacham, and they didn't have to kill him. He didn't hear from George for over a year, and that was probably for the best. Later, he saw a report that Yuki had died in a car crash on Kyushu a few months after they parted, and that George had wangled a billet at the Marine Corps Air Station at Futenma on Okinawa.

Michael parted company with Meacham in Manila, and devoted himself to currency speculation, while taking a position consulting with the State Department. He'd always had a knack for making money out of money, and he knew he'd need a lot of it, if Meacham ever changed his mind about the Predator project. He settled in Hawaii, met and married the daughter of a Navy family, and waited to see what George would do.

The following spring, George showed up at his doorstep with Yuki in tow, who looked reassuringly alive. But there was something he hadn't expected: a small child had been added to their party. *Where had she come from?* At first, he wondered if George had found her in Hawaii, or on some other pacific island along the way. Clearly at least part Asian, or perhaps Polynesian, it hadn't occurred to him that she could be Yuki's daughter, convinced as he was that he could recognize a Japanese face when he saw one. When George said she was his niece, he believed it—his cousin's child, who he said had married a Korean woman while stationed outside of Seoul. According to this story, the mother died in childbirth, and as his cousin's health was failing, he'd offered to take care of the girl.

As the years passed, Michael found plenty of occasions to doubt the story of Emily's origin, but he was not inclined to challenge George over it. He owed him too much not to be willing to go along with it. In fact, he owed him so much he was about to dedicate all his energies to creating a new life for all of them.

In the ensuing years, Michael Cardano's career flourished, without anyone quite knowing very much about him. He moved from one mid-level government post to another, occasionally leaving government service for the private sector, later returning to another government post. Without making much of a splash, he amassed a considerable fortune, and a formidable network of shadowy connections... all because he knew Meacham, or someone like him, would eventually try to revive the Predator program. When that moment came, he would have to be ready; and now that moment had arrived.

CHAPTER FIVE
BACK IN THE WOODS

"About the camping trip...," Emily's father began, in that tentative way in which bad news tended to announce itself. He stood in the doorway to his daughter's bedroom, above the garage, and she leaned around her closet door to look at him. She'd already packed what she meant to bring in a little backpack: a light jacket, socks and underwear, a knife, a sling, and a rifle-scope she'd liberated from the guard shack by the front gate a few weeks earlier.

"No, Dad, you promised. I'm caught up on all my homework. There's no reason we can't go... just like we said. I'll go out tomorrow morning, and you can find me when you get back."

"It's not so simple anymore, Chi-chan. We're bugging out this weekend."

"Bugging out?"

"It's not safe here anymore. I'm sorry, but you need to pack whatever you can't live without. Keep it light, two duffles only."

"What's going on, Dad?" Her chin trembled as she said this, and she glanced at the stack of boxes in her closet and the photo in her hand. "Is it because of those men at the dance?"

"Yes, sweetheart, and it's only a matter of time before they come here. We have to move fast."

"Are we going to get Mom, too?" The thought of being reunited with her mother brought a rosey gleam to the tear in the corner of her eye. She turned to look at the photo one more time, and slipped it back into its hiding place. The hesitation on her father's face, when she looked his way again, made her nervous. "Well, Dad? If we're in danger, she must be, too, right?"

"We'll get her, don't worry."

"Are we going to Taiwan?"

"Not exactly," he said, glancing at his watch. "She's closer than that. I'll explain later, but I need you to pack now."

She thought about what he'd said after he left, and concluded that she didn't quite believe him. Something about his manner, the way he spoke about her mother... he was hiding something. But what could she do about it? Looking out her window, she watched him walk across the driveway to the main house, and in through the kitchen door. Emily scooped up her backpack and went downstairs, meaning to follow her father and get some straight answers.

But with one hand on the doorknob, she paused to consider... and then turned into the garage, opened a door behind one of the pickup trucks, and climbed down into the basement. The slope between the buildings meant that this basement connected directly to the lower basement of the main house. She came up behind the wet-bar and crept up the back staircase as quietly as she could manage, the echo of raised voices from the kitchen drifting down to her. She eased open the door just off the kitchen.

"You should have let me send her to Naxos with Andie and Anthony," she heard Michael say.

"No," her father said. "It would have been too

dangerous."

"Jesse and Ethan are with them. They can handle anything that comes up."

"Not if she's with them."

"George, I don't know what you're thinking. I sent the decoys to Hong Kong and Valparaiso. It'll be months, maybe years, before anyone thinks to look in Greece."

"If she's with them, Meacham will never stop looking."

"I don't get it. Who the hell is she, anyway?"

In the silence that followed, Emily recognized the question at the bottom of her own heart. Her father had taught her to lie to everyone about who she is, and it occurred to her that she didn't know the truth herself. She pressed her back against the wall to brace herself for what she might hear. In the passageway between the kitchen and the dining room, she considered once again the pictures of the family. Only this time the pictures were gone, lighter squares and rectangles where they had hung, and empty frames stacked on the sideboard, all the images of Anthony and the family having been removed, taken to Naxos, no doubt. But what of the pictures of her, the ones that had accidentally captured her playing with Anthony, but also the one of her with Yuki in the garden… did anyone think them worth saving?

"No, George," Yuki cried out, alarmed. The sound of her voice was an unwelcome intrusion to Emily's ears, if it meant she'd be denied the truth.

"She's my daughter," George said, and the words washed over her like a cool spring, bringing her a longed-for reassurance.

"That's not really a surprise, George," Michael said. "But how does that make her too dangerous for Jesse and Ethan to protect?"

"Those men at the dance…"

"I thought you decided they only wanted her for leverage. Have you changed your thinking on that score?"

"No," George said. "But it didn't end there. After what she did to them… it's not just us Meacham will be hunting."

The pounding of Emily's heart, the throbbing at her temples, drowned everything else out. If her father thought their present troubles were her fault, if only she hadn't gone to the dance, if only…

"George, please. Let us take her with us," Yuki pleaded.

"No we stick to the plan. I'm going to see Burzynski's man, and you and Michael need to get everything ready for your departure."

"And Emily?"

"She can wait in the woods, where she'll be safe, until I get back."

Emily could hardly believe her ears. Her father had been teasing her about the camping trip, but he really meant to send her out there anyway. And to what end? To leave her behind while the family escaped.

"Fine," she muttered, and pushed herself away from the wall of empty picture frames. The door clattered shut as she ran down the stairs and made for the ladder behind the wet-bar. Voices called after her, but she had no interest in listening to them anymore.

"Emily, is that you?" Yuki called to her, and footsteps followed after.

She slid down the ladder and let the trap door fall shut above her. In the main room, on her left, a heavy, steel door secured by a deadbolt, she pulled it open and hurried down the tunnel that led out into the woods, snugging the backpack to her shoulders as she ran. At the far end, over a hundred yards away, she burst through the underbrush concealing the entrance at the far end, without breaking stride, and proceeded at a dead run into the depths of the forest. No one would be able to keep up with her, not racing down the wood paths she knew so well even in the dark.

Not until she was thoroughly winded did she stop, and she hardly cared where she'd ended up. Crouching by a stream, peering into the reflected heaven that trembled with the current, her shoulders shook and tears rolled down her cheeks. Eventually, she found a shrub large enough to crawl under and sleep, shivering under her jacket, resting her head on the pack. She consoled herself with bitter recriminations, until her eyes closed for good.

"Maybe I belong here, a hermit in the woods, if I'm too dangerous for human company, if even my own father doesn't trust me."

Surviving in the woods wouldn't be difficult for her, at least until the weather turned truly cold. She hadn't prepared for a long stay. But her father had taught her how to hunt, how to fend for herself, even how to eat bugs. The notion of losing herself in the wilderness seemed strangely appealing, an adolescent fantasy of independence, and even the prospect of intense loneliness couldn't make returning home attractive.

The next day, Emily wandered far and wide, not caring which direction as long as it didn't point home. But wherever she went, she found places she'd already shared with her father. Over one hill, she rediscovered the spot where her father taught her how to shoot. In another glade, she'd learned how to use a sling, or to build a fire, or skin a rabbit. Birds had eaten all the persimmons, but she found some wild apples and autumnberries—the apples were face-scrunchingly tart, but the berries had just come into their sweetness.

She couldn't help thinking of the boys from the dojo who'd run afoul of the security staff, and kept an eye out for the cameras that sprouted from odd corners all over the estate. Mostly they watched the perimeter fences and walls, but a few aimed at the approaches through the woods. A constant theme of her father's survivalist games, avoiding the cameras, had amused her since she was little. It made her feel like a guerilla or a commando, stalking an enemy compound. She got to be pretty good at spotting them before they saw her, but her father always seemed to know where one would be, even before they came near it. At first, she thought maybe he could hear some faint whirring sound, though perhaps he just understood the security team who moved them every few days. Her own sense for the cameras wasn't based on a whirring sound, or any deep insight into the locations where they were placed. She simply began to see the terrain the way the cameras did. She understood them, or the people looking at the monitors at the other end of them. When the land looked a certain way, she knew a camera must be nearby.

Just before sunset, she found herself standing in a ravine at the base of Promontory Rock. She'd followed a stream that meandered among maples and elms whose leaves had only just begun to put on their fall colors. The rock projected from a cliff a hundred feet or so above where she stood, only partially visible through the leaf canopy. She found a path that snaked along cliff face before turning up a side slope and leading up to the back of the final pinnacle. The trees gave way to smaller oaks and mountain mahogany as she climbed until it finally thinned out to grass and a few shrubs around the rock itself. One large clump several feet from the precipice was dense enough to hide a small hollow within, and still had enough foliage to conceal her without the need for a lean-to or any other sort of covering. She could see out in three directions without much difficulty, and thick brambles prevented any silent approach from behind.

Of course, with all the dry brush, a fire was out of the question, and even if it wasn't, it went contrary to her instinct for concealment, and she was fully prepared to shiver through the night if she had to. Fortunately, it proved to be warmer than the previous night.

From her position, she could see bits of the estate through gaps in the trees: the front gate with its guard shack, the back of the main building and the southwest side of the garage. Rolling hills began to dip in to shadow to her west, gradually concealing a few small farm parcels just on the other side, while to the northeast, the Shenandoahs hung on to the last few rays a bit longer. To the northwest, miles of wilderness stretched out to the north, much wilder than the estate, startlingly beautiful from her vantage. The glow of a small town to the east gave a shine to the skirts of the evening sky. By midnight, even that had gone dark, since the town wasn't big enough for streetlights, or a shopping mall.

She watched as cars and large SUV's came and went much of the evening. On any other night, this would mean something important happening at the main building, maybe one of Michael's dinner parties. The magnification of the rifle-scope gave pretty good detail over most of the estate, not enough to resolve the facial features of the people bustling about the main building, but she could see there were a lot of them, and they were very busy. Of course, she could hear nothing from that distance.

Around three in the morning the bustle of activity died down, and a few minutes later she noticed what looked like the family car pull around to the back of the garage. It had to be her father, home a bit later than he originally said.

"Finally," she muttered. "I hope he doesn't think he's gonna find me."

She scanned the lawns and the forest paths closely for any sign of him—would she be able to spot him heading across the lawn from the garage toward the woods? Under the three-quarter moon, the garage stood out clearly enough against the glistening lawns, even with dark windows. Sure, a stealthy figure could probably dart into the woods without her being able to see. But that wasn't her father's way; he preferred the direct approach. She knew he would walk directly to wherever he thought she was, flush her out, force her to break cover and run. Then she would have to trade a well-meditated hiding place for one chosen in the moment. He might even let her see him coming, at least initially. Later, under the cover of the woods, he might choose a more indirect path, since a direct path would offer no real advantage there. Then he might pop up unexpectedly, just when you thought he had to be someplace else. So she kept her eyes moving.

"And what would he even want with me?" she muttered, though her self-pity eventually gave way to the thought that if he found her, she would be reunited with her mother. At least, that's what he promised yesterday… if she could still believe anything he'd said.

Her stomach churned as she watched the estate from on high, feeling very much like some sort of sentinel: shrouded in the silence she heard all around her. It gave her a feeling of calm that restored some little bit of her confidence—her gaze was powerful, she could see whatever would come, as long as she had the will to look, and if she could see it, she could face it. She concentrated on looking with all the intensity she could muster.

~~~~~~~~

Concentrating on her silent vigil got a lot harder when Danny popped into her mind. She didn't particularly want to think about him just now. *He didn't mean anything special.* But somehow, his face floated to the surface of her consciousness anyway. She mainly knew him from the dojo, had seen him around school, thought he wasn't as irritating as the jocks usually were. At least, he seemed cooler than the other football players, from what she could see. He'd approached her a few times, making idle, empty conversation. He made sure she knew he was the starting tailback on the varsity team, and maybe didn't notice how little that meant to her. She could see he was strong, though not as large as the biggest guys on the team, and he wasn't bad looking. Lots of girls would like to have his attentions, and when they noticed his interest in her, she could tell they resented her for it. "Who was she, after all?" she imagined them saying. "She's nobody, just some weird girl with no friends."

"Hey, loser," one of them actually did say to her one day, as she walked out to the bus line with her head down. "I hope you don't think you have a chance with Danny Rincon."

"What?" she said, not quite able to believe one of the cheerleaders would think of talking to her.

"You heard me. Stick to the Goths, or whatever freaks would want a scarecrow like you."

When Emily looked up, she was surrounded by three girls in short skirts and tight sweaters. One of them plucked at her denim jacket, and the girl who originally spoke glowered at her, hands on hips, sizing Emily up. Maybe she was right: what would someone like Danny see in her?

One of them put a hand on her shoulder, another reached out to push her, or maybe pull her hair. Emily turned to look at her, and pictured defending herself— maybe grab the girl's wrist and twist her down, force her face into the pavement, make her cry. The others wouldn't be able to do anything about it. She felt her face get warm as she ran through the possibilities, and the girl must have seen something in her eyes, because she pulled back, trembling. Her friends recoiled, too. "Freak," one of them said, but they left her alone after that. Danny joined the dojo the next day.

He was stronger than most of the boys in the dojo, and fast. He hit hard and had good balance. None of the other boys could get him down. *Shotokan* suited his aggressive instincts, and he picked it up quickly, especially the sparring. Within a few months, he was able to beat most of the other boys. Sensei seemed to think he had potential.

One evening, he asked her if she wanted to go to a concert at the local armory on the weekend. She'd just finished him off in the ring, and reached a hand down to help him up, expecting to see the usual look of perplexity and embarrassment. "This one's at least a little different from the others," she thought, when he asked her out.

Emily bristled when she heard Sensei snort behind her, as if he knew there was no way she'd say yes, and when she looked around the room, all the faces gaping at her seemed to confirm Sensei's view. "Okay," she said, at least partly for the pleasure of surprising them all. "Sure, why not?"

Telling her father about it later tempered her pleasure, since the look on his face reminded her of other anxieties.

"Absolutely not," he said, as they walked into the kitchen at the estate. "Don't you have homework, or something?"

"Dad, I've finished it all. There's no reason I can't go."

"I haven't even met this boy."

"What boy?" Yuki asked, when she stumbled into the argument, coming up the basement stairs.

"She wants to go to a dance," George said.

"That's wonderful," Yuki said, and though at any other moment Emily would have found that reassuring, just then she found it oppressive. When her father tried to disagree, and Yuki set her jaw, Emily slipped into the dining room, no longer wishing to be a part of the conversation.

"It's too dangerous," she heard her father say.

"No one even knows she exists," Yuki replied. Overhearing these words hurt more than she expected. She felt the truth of it cut through her like a knife, and reached for the back of a chair to steady herself.

"We don't know that for certain. Are you willing to take the chance?"

"I don't know, but we've cheated her of so much already, George."

The conversation had taken a strange turn, Emily recognized that much, and by far the most puzzling thing about it was the way Yuki said "we," as if she thought of herself as a partner in their little family.

Danny arrived that Saturday evening in an old pickup truck, and the ride to the concert was even more awkward than introducing him to her father, since neither of them knew what to say. A lot of garbled, semi-personal information came out of his mouth in nervous spasms. She didn't know how to respond, and wondered if other girls were this hard for boys to talk to. He wanted to impress her, she could see that much, but he seemed to have no notion of how to do that. He filled up the conversational space with irrelevancies: how he loved football and admired his coach, how he wanted to go to college on a scholarship, though he had no idea what he would study. She knew his parents were separated, and that he lived with his mom, an ER nurse at the local hospital. He told her how his dad came to all the games and yelled from the stands—finally something she understood—but he seemed reluctant to talk about the one safe thing they had in common, the dojo.

Inside the Armory, the music pounded loud in her head, so much bass that the melodic line could barely be heard. She preferred to be able to listen to herself, and the din made that impossible. But everyone swaying together, moving with the beat, that interested her. She could almost feel connected to all these people, an experience of a primal synergy, everyone open to the same suggestion. She longed to experience something communal, to share whatever they longed for. Of course, they were all really alone. The music had brought them all together, but in the end it kept them all isolated.

They danced together, their hands touching in the moment, and her hips grazed his. It was almost possible to see something different in him, if only it weren't so loud. In between songs, they were jostled by some other kids. They tried to move to the side, to make way, but the crush was persistent, and the air on the dance floor had become oppressive. Danny suggested they step outside to cool off. He got a couple of ices from a vendor by the door and they headed out to the patio.

The crowd had already clogged that space, too. Danny pointed to a bench on the far side where they could be alone.

As they crossed the patio, a large man in a leather jacket with a short stubble on his face asked her if she had any matches. "No," she said, sizing him up. He seemed too old for this music, but not as ancient as her father. Whatever his age, he didn't quite fit in. Perhaps he worked at the armory. His hands looked strong, and his eyes were bright, but unsympathetic, as if he meant to be intrusive.

Before they could sit down, the same man called out to Danny to watch himself. Just then, three men appeared out of the shadows, one shoving him against the wall, a second punched him in the stomach, doubling him over. As she turned to see, the man in the jacket grabbed Emily from behind and began to pull her around the corner, to the loading dock. She saw Danny manage to recover himself and take a swing at one of the men, striking him on the cheek. He swung another back into the wall and kicked at the third. He looked good doing it, but she could see he was in over his head. These men knew how to handle themselves in a scrap, how to take a punch; they'd been hit before.

Emily's assailant loomed over her by at least six inches, and must have had seventy pounds on her. Holding her in a bear hug from behind, he tried to keep her feet off the ground as he carried her away. Oddly calm at such a moment, she wondered what he had prepared for her around the corner, and let her body go limp. His hands and arms were strong, much stronger than hers, but as he took an uncertain step backwards, she shifted her shoulders ever so slightly. He tried to adjust his balance, and in the process he let her touch the pavement. She recognized her moment, and pushed off the ground hard, knowing he would react instinctively to oppose her effort, to keep her down. When he shifted his balance and leaned over her, she slid her fingers inside his right hand, grabbed across his palm and thumb, and twisted all the joints of his right arm out and away from his body. He found himself running as fast as he could face first into the side of the building. The pain in his arm must have been excruciating; hitting the wall would have seemed almost preferable to trying to resist her.

He yowled in pain, his face bloodied, his nose bent grotesquely to one side. Enraged and not a little disoriented, he lunged at her. Again, she didn't resist, and when he closed his hand around her shoulder for an instant, she pressed her hand behind his elbow and swung him around again, crashing him into one of the other men, heads colliding like pumpkins. They lay in a heap for a moment, stunned, blood oozing out of their faces, watching as she turned to the other two men.

One of them seemed to have had some karate training, and swung a roundhouse kick at her head. When she leaned out of the way, he tried to draw his foot back, but she hooked his ankle with her left foot and jerked him towards her. As she expected, he spread his arms in a vain attempt to regain his balance, and when she pulled his foot even further forward, forcing him into a perfect hurdler's split, he screamed in pain. She chopped him across the throat and let him fall forward onto his face. He gurgled and wheezed, struggling to breathe, and the thought occurred to her that she might have crushed his windpipe. "This isn't the dojo," she muttered.

The last man grabbed her ponytail from behind, no doubt thinking to control her with his other arm, and expecting her to pull away so he could yank her head back. Naturally, she pivoted into him, wrapping an arm over his elbow and under to twist the joint out at the same time as she forced his shoulder down. The pressure on his arm left him no way to extricate himself from her grip, and she was so close to his chest he couldn't move quickly enough to grab her with his free hand. The heel of her left palm smashed his chin, and she heard his teeth crack through his tongue just as his elbow snapped. He crumpled to the ground in tears, and looked up at her, not quite able to focus, as she slammed her knee into the side of his head.

She turned to the first two men, her cheeks warm from the rush of ferocity she had just unleashed. The one with the broken face, groggy but still more or less conscious, moved to pick himself up until he saw her eyes and shuddered. With a finger pressed to her lips, she pushed him back down until he lay flat on his back on the pavement.

Crouching next to his head, she said, "Don't make me hurt you," and flashed him a crooked smile, her head tilted to one side.

Bracing herself with one foot against the wall, Emily hauled Danny from where he'd gotten himself wedged in behind a bench. They had worked him over a bit, but hadn't had time to do much damage, and hadn't marked up his face. At least he would be spared a lot of questions at home. Emily propped him up on her shoulder to lead him back to the truck, and they pulled out of the parking lot a moment later, before the police arrived.

On the way home, she reassured him about what happened. "Just some thugs looking for trouble," she said. No deeper meaning in it. He'd been brave. Fortunately for him, he didn't see just how thoroughly she had rescued him.

Once he'd dropped her off, other things occupied her thoughts, things she would have liked to settle in her mind before talking to her father. Who were those guys, and what did they want? She wanted to believe it was just a random attack, but a nagging thought kept her wondering. That man had tried to carry her off, and he'd brought other men with him, well-trained men. That didn't feel random.

An even more troubling thought kept nudging its way into her consciousness. Had she reacted too fiercely? She wasn't concerned for those men. They had meant to do much worse to her, exactly what she didn't know, but she'd felt the malevolence in them, the absence of any humane sentiment towards her. At the same time, she remembered feeling the thrill of her own ferocity and wasn't sure she'd really been in control of it. She'd vanquished her assailants, but she couldn't help wondering if she'd lost sight of herself in the process. She'd never been in a real fight before—not just sparring, not a schoolyard scuffle. Those men meant to harm her, maybe even kill her, and she had prevailed, though she found the thought that she might have killed one of them alarming.

"That must be what it means to be in a fight," she muttered, trying to quiet her mind as she walked up the stairs to the apartment above the garage. "If someone puts your life on the line, he puts his own life on the line, too."

One thought offered some little bit of comfort: if she'd harbored any doubts about her ability to defend herself, to keep her wits about her, and to generate enough sheer aggression to prevail, to survive, those had been effectively dispelled. She could still wonder what this victory had really cost her. All of her training had not been directed toward fighting, or at least that's not how Sensei had always presented it to her. He spoke of deeper, more meaningful goals, spiritual goals, and the residual thrill—and remorse—of the evening threatened to eclipse those entirely.

"Tell me about them," her father said, once she broke the news, his eyes alight. "Did they seem in any way familiar?"

"They were trained," she said. "And they didn't belong at the concert."

"Like soldiers, you mean?"

"I don't know, Dad. They were kinda like the security guards around here," she replied. "You know, trained but indifferent. They didn't care about us. They weren't pissed or anything."

"Was that boy any help to you?"

"Nah. Not really," she snorted. "He probably won't remember much of what happened either."

"That figures," he growled.

"He did okay, Dad. He was outnumbered three to one," she remembered saying in Danny's defense, though she didn't quite know why she cared.

"Fine. But now you know what you can expect from him," he said as he stood up. "I've gotta talk this over with Mr. Cardano."

She didn't tell Yuki any of this, and she hoped her father wouldn't either, unlikely as that might be. News like this has a way of spreading throughout a household, and she shuddered to think what Yuki would say. In the end, Yuki said nothing about it to her, but Emily felt certain she knew everything from the way she looked at her the next morning. A cold, dark fury swirled in the back of her eyes. "At least she's not pissed at me," Emily thought, or rather hoped. "But if not me, then who?"

She saw Danny in school the following Monday. He looked embarrassed, uncomfortable, and didn't seem to know what to say to her. No police report ever emerged, and no official questions troubled either of them, which was a relief, though she wondered how that had happened. Danny's mother might have treated those men at the ER, but if she had, surely the local sheriff would have been notified. She figured no one had witnessed the fight—those men would have arranged the scene to ensure privacy—and it was even possible that they had limped off (eventually) without drawing any attention. Though the more she reflected on that little inference, the more troubling the event became.

~~~~~~~

This all happened in early October, almost three weeks ago. Why was she thinking about it now? Eventually, Danny came back to the dojo. He recovered his composure around her, talked to her again. She said nothing about the attack to anyone, partly because she didn't want him to be the butt of every joke at school, but mainly because she found the silence comforting.

Around four in the morning, she noticed a slight glow in the eastern sky, and wondered if all was well at the estate. She couldn't put her finger on it, but something didn't feel right. Peering through the scope, she expected to see some movement, at least, at the guard posts. But there was none. Smoke floated above the central chimney of the main house, and she couldn't think of a reason to have that fireplace going this early.

She half expected to spy her father making his way along the stream, but she saw no sign of him either. If it had been him arriving in the family car a few hours earlier, he would have found his way at least that far by now—earlier in the evening, she would have added, "…if he's even looking for me at all." But something about the present scene chased those adolescent ideas from her mind.

"Where is he?" she muttered, feeling very divided about what to do. Climbing down and scouting the estate buildings might bring her right into his hands, and after yesterday she still wasn't comfortable with that idea. But something else, something vague and unsettling, made her distinctly uncomfortable about holding her position on the rock. She decided to pack up her equipment and climb down now, while there was still some darkness left to cover her movements.

CHAPTER SIX
GETTING OUT THE DOOR

Michael had to hurry. The people on the way to his house would be in an ugly frame of mind by the time they arrived, so he knew he had to spirit everyone away before then, even the security guards. They were just contract employees, after all—he couldn't leave them behind to be killed—and he'd already sent his wife and son away.

He'd begun arranging their disappearance as soon as he heard about the attack at the concert. Andie and Anthony had been living in a small house on the island of Naxos in the Aegean Sea for the last two weeks. But he'd worked very hard to make it appear they were in Hong Kong. Every scrap of paper or digital information anywhere in the Border Control systems of several countries indirectly implied this, though he had been careful to make it look more obviously like he wanted the authorities to think they were really in Valparaiso. He stationed a female operative in an apartment in Kowloon with a small boy "borrowed" from a local orphanage. She was under instructions to flee to Panang at the first sign of trouble, deposit the boy in a safe house there, and leave a trail that would dead end in Kuala Lumpur.

A clever sleight of hand like this one would distract his enemies for a few months, maybe even a year, which might be just long enough. He figured they would lose interest in his family before then, but he also knew Meacham would hound him and George as long as they lived. The security guards would not be worth pursuing, since they knew nothing. As long as they were not on site when the tactical teams arrived, they would be safe enough. He gave them all cash bonuses, put them on a chartered bus for Las Vegas, and hoped their discretion would protect them.

George was a different story. He knew way too much, at least as much as Michael himself, which meant no place could hide him for long. Michael had already successfully hidden him for almost seventeen years as it was. Of course, Meacham probably expected him to keep George nearby, but as long as he thought the Predator program was worthless, he had no interest in either of them; they'd all been safe as long as Meacham believed that. Now he no longer believed it, and Michael assumed he had seen intelligence about a Chinese program, since he'd seen some ambiguous intelligence about this, too. The Chinese might have succeeded where Dr. Kagami had failed, or perhaps they merely labored under a renewed suspicion that Kagami really had succeeded... though it hardly mattered which it was at this moment, given the need to get on the road quickly and quietly.

"We may have to leave without him," Michael said, looking at his watch. In the desolate night air, with almost everyone gone, the estate no longer felt like home. He looked down on the top of Yuki's head as they stood next to each other on the driveway and tried to recalibrate his plans, since the two of them were more vulnerable than ever. "There's no time. He can meet up with us later."

"We're waiting," she said, in a tone of voice he couldn't recall hearing before, and when she turned to face him, the look in her eye chilled him. The peculiar combination of sorrow and determination he found there made it clear that resisting her wishes on this point must fail. He shivered and averted his eyes.

He was used to George's insistence on protecting her, and attributed it to a chivalric impulse; George always did have a bit of the paladin in him. Since they'd had a share in bringing the turmoil into her life, he felt obliged to set things right, at least to the extent that was possible. Michael reflected on how strange it was that after all these years he had never quite fathomed her feelings for George. As far as he knew, they might secretly be husband and wife. That they'd become more than just friends over the years was easy to see. Some sort of spiritual bond connected them, and it found a focus in Emily, as if Yuki fancied herself a stepmother. Protecting Yuki was the main purpose of this evacuation, and he was prepared to risk everything to do it, which made it deeply frustrating not to understand her motivations at this precise moment.

How exactly Emily fit in was an even more vexed question. Of course, Michael had long since come to the conclusion that she was really George's daughter, even if he couldn't quite bring himself to challenge the story that she was only a niece, or a cousin technically, at least not directly to George's face. The mother must have been some camp follower, or perhaps a Nara courtesan—that would account for George's reticence to open up about her. Michael had even entertained the possibility that Yuki was her mother, but the timing of her birth didn't quite fit that notion, since she and George hadn't been that close in those days, and it was impossible to broach the subject with her without committing some mortal breach of etiquette. So little did he really understand about Japanese culture that he assumed the suggestion would have outraged Yuki. No, the path of least resistance was to assume that Emily's mother was a prostitute. In self-congratulatory compensation for this inference, he'd even begun to think of himself as a sort of uncle to Emily, and as soon as he learned of the attack at the concert, Michael offered to send her to Naxos with his family. But, as infuriating as he could ever be, George refused.

"I have a plan, George," he'd said, at the time. "She'll be safe there, much safer than on the run with us, I promise you."

"I have to keep her with me," George said. "It won't be safe on Naxos… not if she's with them."

Michael remembered his surprise at this response, since he'd expected at least some recognition for the generosity of his offer. The family connection between them, however he chose to interpret it, seemed to mean more to George than whatever safety Michael could provide for her on Naxos. Emily had a certain enigmatic magic about her, he saw that easily enough, and Anthony saw it too. She babysat him, and he was absolutely devoted to her. When she took him out to explore the forest, he'd follow her for hours, and when they returned, he'd want to go out again. If she ran across the lawns, he couldn't resist running after. Of course, Michael could see the girl was a pretty tough customer. After all, she'd handled a team of mercenaries all by herself that evening at the concert—*and exactly how had she managed that?*

As he pondered the situation, Michael was reminded of a birthday party for a five year old, and how he'd meant to catch her by surprise, hoisting her high above his head and tickling her mercilessly, like a good sort-of-uncle. Somehow she'd squirmed her way out of his grip and fallen to the ground. All that was normal enough, if a little bit scary. She landed on her feet, thank goodness, but on the way down she turned her face directly towards his, and he still remembered the look in her eyes, calm, collected—no sign of childish panic—perhaps even fierce. She was unique, he had to give her that, though it hardly explained George's behavior.

"What do you think is going to happen to her here?" he remembered asking, as he thought back once again to that puzzling conversation with George. "She'll be on the run all the time. It'll be miserable for her. And if there's trouble and she gets separated from us… what then?"

"She can handle herself," George muttered.

As he thought over that conversation, and compared it to what George had said that evening in the kitchen,

Michael's perplexity about the girl seemed to verge on a sudden clarity: *If she really is his biological daughter, does that mean Yuki is her mother?* He didn't dare ask, even though such a conclusion would make sense of much that still puzzled him. George would be right to think Naxos wouldn't be safe, *if she was Yuki's daughter,* since if Meacham learned of her existence, he'd bend all his resources to the task of finding her, in order to use her as leverage over Yuki. What was worse, even if it weren't exactly true, Meacham would probably still jump to that conclusion.

Michael had planned to get the four of them out of Virginia, to a hideaway in the mountains of northern New Mexico. But with George's insistence on keeping Emily with him alone, he needed a new plan, simpler perhaps, but with a slightly different cover story: two people instead of four, until they met up again. He always felt safer with George than without, and he found it difficult to know how to plan on not having him there.

Still thinking about that conversation, he looked down at Yuki, and weighed once again the likelihoods concerning Emily's identity.

"Fine," he said, now fully back in the moment. "Then we've got some work to do."

Yuki nodded and climbed the stairs to the apartments over the garage, while Michael went down to his private office, and each of them prepared the scene for their departure. He burned boxes of papers in the furnace, the ones he wanted really destroyed, but he set up a fire in the living room fireplace on the main floor for other papers he meant to be only partially burned. Yuki rolled the clothes George and Emily would need into two large packs and left them next to the garage door. Then she tried to create the impression of a hasty departure, strewing clothes everywhere.

She'd prepared a huge meal earlier for the security guards, including *bento* boxes to take with them on the bus. But she'd made much more than was necessary, and left the kitchen a mess, food and pots and pans everywhere, dirty dishes piled high in the sinks and on every surface. She even left the freezer door ajar and cooked a kettle of water dry on the stove. To an intruder, it would look very much as if they had all left in a great hurry, certainly not able to make careful preparations.

One last task remained for Yuki: to prepare food for Emily, assuming George could find her—and now it looked like she'd need to make enough for George, too. She put together a couple of *bento* boxes of pickled vegetables, tofu cakes and rice, stuff that would keep without refrigeration. Then she took the last of the sticky rice, rolled it into several *onigiri*, each with a pickled plum in the center, and wrapped in seaweed. She sprinkled toasted sesame seeds, before putting them in a plastic bag. At first, she thought of leaving the boxes and the *onigiri* on the end of the counter, where on any other day Emily would be sure to find them. But in light of the incident the evening before, she realized that wouldn't do, and walked out to the garage to squeeze them into the packs she'd placed there for George and Emily.

When the family car lumbered up the drive and came to rest in front of the garage, Michael rushed out to see what had happened, and Yuki watched apprehensively a few yards away. After an unnervingly still moment, the driver's side door swung open and George stepped out, looking weary and care-worn.

"Just like we feared, Burzynski never showed," he muttered. "Porter was waiting with a couple of heavies."

"What happened?"

"They're in the trunk. It seemed unwise to leave them behind."

"What'd you do with the packet?"

"I left it there, in case you're right about Burzynski. He should know where to look. But Porter was definitely not interested in the data. He only wanted Yuki," George snarled.

The news that Burzynski had not come sorely disappointed Michael, since his plan had involved disclosing the truth about the Predator program to certain elements within the CIA. The packet contained all the important data from Dr. Kagami's lab, along with the results of some further investigations Yuki had carried on in the intervening years. There were no breakthroughs, no wonder drug an ambitious agent could use to catapult his career forward. But Burzynski could use what was there to fend off Meacham in any hearings the House Intelligence Committee might hold, and thereby solidify his own position. If only he was interested. That he'd been unwilling to meet George was not encouraging. Even more so that he had turned it over to Porter.

Michael had figured Porter was ready to break free from Burzynski and make his own move, and that meant he would have no use for data purporting to show that such a program couldn't be salvaged. For him, only a positive result would be of interest, and that would inevitably entail taking custody of Yuki. Porter's vision of the future, had no room for George, or himself. It was almost a relief to think of him now, stuffed inside the trunk of the limo, though Michael was sure he had more connections than the two men lying there with him. There would be others interested in his fate, maybe even Burzynski himself.

There was also a little bit of comedy in the offer to Burzynski. Besides the data, and Yuki's analysis of what it meant, he had also dangled the estate itself in front of him. Michael knew Burzynski wanted a facility he could use as a shadow power base, and the estate would certainly be suitable for such a purpose. Five thousand acres backing on an immense forest preserve would make for a lot of privacy. What Burzynski might not know was that the estate already belonged to the CIA. Michael had managed to obscure the agency's own records concerning a fifty acre parcel of land at the south end of the George Washington National Forest, and of course the agency had concealed the fact of its ownership in all public documents. He then added to it a much larger adjoining parcel from the National Forest unbeknownst to the Forest Service. In fact, he had amassed an immense holding at almost no cost to himself, relying entirely on the inability of federal agencies to adequately control their own papers. He always knew once he left, the forest component of the estate would revert to the Forest Service. They would merely discover some papers that had seemingly been misplaced, and then reassert their authority over this section of the forest. None of the estate buildings had been built on Forest Service land. As for the CIA, it might never recoup the loss, or even learn of it.

This was a high stakes game, playing one covert power broker against another, but Michael could see no other path through the current situation. The only way to take their attention off Yuki and George, and himself, was to get them to turn their attention on each other. All things being equal, it was probably better for everyone if Burzynski prevailed, rather than Meacham. Best of all, however, would be if they destroyed each other.

"We're ready to go. We've just been waiting for you," Michael said. "But there's been no sign of Emily."

"I'll find her," he said, with very little conviction in his voice. "Don't worry about that."

"And then we meet in New Mexico, right?"

George nodded, though Michael's mind could hardly process the calm he exuded under these circumstances, and especially not to be able to find the one thing in this world he seemed to prize above all else.

Michael pulled a large, black SUV around to the kitchen door to load a few boxes in the back, while George hauled the bodies to a woodshed behind the garage. There wasn't much time, and Michael guessed he would start a fire in the shed. It wouldn't be hot enough to destroy the bodies completely, but it would probably mask their identities for a

JACQUES ANTOINE

while. Perhaps he also meant to use the blaze as a signal to
Emily. When George came back around the corner of the
garage, Yuki ran up to him.

"Where is she?" she shrieked, striking him on the chest
with both hands.

From where he stood, peering through the window of
the SUV as he arranged things in the back, Michael saw
George's face go pale, head down staring at his shoes, like a
schoolboy caught in some mischief. Yuki's onslaught made
him take a step a backward. As far as he knew, this was more
emotion than either of them had ever betrayed in front of
anyone before.

"She'll come back," he said, nodding to the woods and
trying to wrap his arms around her. She pushed him away,
and Michael rolled down the passenger side window to
listen.

"What were you thinking, leaving her out there?"

"I'm sure she's on her way back," he said defensively,
trying to sound confident. "She'll be here soon. If not, I'll
pack the dirtbike and go after her."

"If anything happens to that girl…" she snarled, and
turned back into the house.

Michael took the opportunity to finish loading the last
of Yuki's things into the back of the SUV and motioned to
George to bring her out. "There's not much time. We gotta
go now!"

Anyone could read Yuki's reluctance to leave without at
least seeing Emily, which fairly glowed in her face and the set
of her jaw, and George's attempts to reassure her did not rise
to the level of persuasion, nor did Michael's supportive facial
expressions. In the end, Yuki accepted the necessity of
leaving right away, if only because she understood that
Michael's arrangements depended on decisive action. When
she finally settled into the front seat, and rolled down the
window, she looked George in the eye and growled: "Find
her. Keep her safe."

"I will," he said.

~~~~~~~

Michael drove off with Yuki, and George stood watching them from the driveway for as long as he could still see their taillights. They passed through the main gate, turned right and disappeared behind the front hedge. Eventually, they would head over to Route 64 and then go west through West Virginia and Kentucky, changing vehicles several times along the way.

George went into the garage and rolled out an old dirt bike, and concealed it in the woods behind the main house, along with the packs Yuki had prepared. His plan was to put Emily on the back and ride out along some old logging trails through the forest, slip into the Monongahela Forest in West Virginia, and switch to a car he had already stashed in Mill Creek, a little town on the edge of the park. Now he just had to find her.

A glow in the east worried him, since it meant it was approaching five am. The thought crossed his mind that he might not find Emily before Meacham's men arrived, and he'd have to fight it out. If only she had the sense to stay hidden in that case.

"Yuki's right," he muttered.

He'd blundered, leaving her out into the woods by herself, preferring another errand to that one. He should have chased her down as soon as they'd heard her outside the kitchen, though he wasn't really sure he could catch up to her, not in the woods, not in the dark. But one thing he did know with full confidence, that to let her go with Michael and Yuki was an unacceptable risk—he would never put everything that mattered to him in one car if he wasn't in it, too... and maybe not even then. If he hadn't been able to return from the meeting with Porter, he needed to know she'd be safe, at least for a little while, and he knew she'd be

JACQUES ANTOINE

safe in the woods. No one would find her out there—"Hell," he snorted, "I can barely track her anymore." But after that, she'd be on her own, and the thought harrowed him.

George had imagined the worst contingency and tried to prepare for that. But now that things didn't look quite so dire, he began to feel the difficulty of his situation. If only he had more time, several hours perhaps, he could try to find her, though with every weekend spent in the woods she had gotten harder to track. As things stood, he couldn't tell if he had even ten minutes.

He went into the main house and set fire to the drapes in the living room, splashing gasoline over the furniture and around the room from a large can. If Emily saw the smoke from the house, and the glow from the burning woodshed, she might think something was wrong and come back. It was a desperate move, but he had no other way of getting her attention. He only wished the fire would spread faster.

Back out in the driveway, he kept a lookout for Emily, scanning the tree line at the edge of the north lawn for any sign of her. Out of the corner of his eye, he spotted movement in the hedges to the left of the main gate.

"No way that's her," he said, "not from that direction."

Meacham's tactical team had arrived. He froze, ramrod straight, and when the woodshed fire flared briefly, flashing a brighter light across the lawn momentarily and possibly providing some cover behind the flare it would cause in their night-vision glasses, he took a chance and ducked behind the garage. If only they hadn't seen him, he might be able to seize some slight advantage. Meacham probably sent two teams of four, he figured. They'd be heavily armed, probably body armor, too. Thankfully, the terrain provided insufficient elevation for a sniper. He had no need of night-vision gear, since the blazing fire in the woodshed, and the fire beginning to peek out of the windows of the main house, cast enough eerie light to see, especially give that the estate was familiar ground for him. But with the dawn

80

approaching, he knew he had to act soon.

A shootout with these guys would be much too risky, even if he had a gun, since Emily might get caught in the crossfire. He figured they would focus on the main house and not allow any diversion to distract from their primary mission: subdue the inhabitants and apprehend Yuki and Emily. But maybe he could use that against them. He figured his best chance was to lure them into the main house as quickly as possible.

He knocked over some garden tools, a rake, a wheelbarrow, a bucket, all to create a clatter, and ran quickly to the front of the main house. Bullets whizzed past him on all sides, and he felt one graze his side just as he burst through the front door. It didn't feel like a serious wound, but it burned like a hot poker resting just below his ribs. He tumbled into the dining room and felt a blast of hot air on his face. The living room was pretty hot now, the drapes were in full blaze, and the upholstered furniture near the outside wall had begun to burn. The bookcases would catch fire soon.

One team would come in through the front door. With a little luck, they would be forced, at least for an instant, to focus on the fire in the living room. The other team would circle around to the kitchen entrance, with an eye on the garage. He needed to find a way to get the second team into the house before Emily arrived. At least then she would have a chance to size up the situation before encountering them.

CHAPTER SEVEN
IF YOU CAN'T STAND THE HEAT…

By the time Emily found her way to the edge of the forest she had already seen the fire in the woodshed. From her vantage on Promontory Rock, she had only suspected something was wrong, but now she could see that nothing at all was right at her home. She'd caught a glimpse of a black SUV turning out the front gate, but couldn't see who was driving. Then she saw her father standing in the driveway, alone, and felt the urge to run to him. Despite the emotional turmoil of the last two days, he was still the one constant thing in her life, no matter how stormy it got. But the smoke billowing from the first floor windows of the main house froze her for an instant. That's when she noticed the sickening glow peeking through the kitchen windows.

It felt strange not to see any security guards, as if the estate were deserted. She also spotted something much more ominous: suspicious activity in the hedges off to her left. Several men who didn't belong there moved as quietly as they could manage through some dense and noisy underbrush… and, as luck would have it, they seemed not to have noticed her yet. She circled around to her right, always remaining concealed within the verge of the forest.

She positioned herself behind a spoonwood bush at the point in the north lawn where the woods came closest to the estate buildings, about thirty yards from the corner of the garage. All the pink flowers it had sported in the spring were long gone, but the remaining foliage provided sufficient cover for her in that light. From this position, she had a very clear view of her father, crouching against the corner of the building, peering over a low shrub toward the far hedges. "Thank goodness, he sees them too," she thought with a palpable feeling of relief.

Just then, she saw him scatter some tools with a clatter and burst from behind the shrub towards the main house. She wanted to call out to him, to urge him to keep hidden, to keep quiet, but the men hiding in the underbrush had already seen him, too, whoever they were. He ran as fast as she had ever seen him go, and he only had to cover twenty yards to reach the cover of the house. She didn't hear the muzzle report of any gunfire, but the sound of bullets ricocheting off the corner of the front portico was unmistakable.

When she saw smoke seeping through the second floor windows, she figured the house was lost. She wanted desperately to run after her father, to find him and see if he'd been hit, to warn him about the fire if he hadn't already seen it, and most of all to wrap herself in his arms. But something made her hold back, a voice telling her to wait just a moment, to see what those men would do next. They didn't seem to know she was there, and she might need that advantage.

A moment later, several men burst from the tree-line, all carrying guns, bristling with equipment, and she watched them run toward the house. One group came from the far side, and still had to cover about fifty yards of open lawn by the time she spotted them. A second group came from her left and approached the rear of the house, slowly and more cautiously than the first group. She shifted her position further to her right, trying to find a spot as close to the kitchen door as she could manage without drawing their attention. This brought her to a position near the blazing woodshed as well. She discarded her backpack and got ready to run. Her jacket was dark brown, but she knew the khaki pants and orange tank top she had on under it weren't ideal camo, so she would need the cover of the fire.

She watched as the first team reached the driveway, firing as they ran. With a signal to the men approaching the rear, they entered through the front door. The second team scouted the garage briefly, then moved toward the kitchen door. She knew once they made it to the kitchen door, their lines of sight would make it impossible for her to approach the house unseen. She had to act now—no more time to wait, no more deliberating. She moved quickly, running in a semi-crouch toward the corner of the house near the kitchen, keeping the woodshed between herself and the last position where she had seen the second team. The brightness of the flames prevented them from seeing her, but it also kept her from seeing precisely where they were. But if they hadn't been aware of her presence before, she figured they wouldn't be looking for her in the fire now.

A noise from the house sounded like muffled gunfire, then a crash and the sound of breaking glass. She peered as far around the woodshed as she dared, and saw the men by the garage dash toward the house, some peeled off toward the front, but at least two burst in through the kitchen door. Emily used their movement to mask hers, and followed them in hoping not to attract their attention. When she cleared the door a moment later, she saw a full on gun battle, two men in the kitchen laying down a steady fire into the public rooms of the house and even more gunfire returning their way. A third man had sustained a significant leg wound, and the first two men tried to help him out of the line of fire, without halting their own pattern of fire. None of them seemed to notice her.

The familiar sight caught her eye once again, the wall of family photos—they were gone, of course, and this drove the point home: the family had already left. The next thought inevitably seared her mind: "What about my photo?" She could just glimpse the freezer door, since it was propped open, and the picture of Yuki holding her hand in the garden wasn't there. She brushed a tear away and drew the only conclusion she could bear: she hadn't been forgotten.

Emily's first thought was to launch herself at the men shooting into the rooms where she assumed her father was. But the gunfire was too hot to make it worth the risk. If she were shot or killed, she wouldn't be any help to him. Her next thought was to make her way to the back staircase and down to the basement. From there, she could come up at the other end of the house where she might be able to make herself useful.

As she slipped behind the open freezer door, she glanced once more at the magnet that usually held her photo—*Yuki and Josefina would never leave that door open*—and slipped down the back stairs. When she cleared the staircase and entered the furnace room, she peeked through the doorway into the rec-room, and saw her father walking unsteadily from the other end of the basement. Blood had soaked through the left side of his shirt, and she couldn't keep from running to him, with barely enough self-possession not to cry out when he pressed a finger to his lips. She threw her arms around him, wanting nothing more than to hold on as tightly as she could. But when she felt him wince, she slid around under his right shoulder and helped him stand. With the relief of seeing her, he seemed to breathe a little easier. *Now, to get them both out of there.*

"Quickly, Chi-chan, downstairs," he said in a sharp whisper.

"Okay, Dad. What's going on upstairs? Anyone else up there?"

"No. We're all that's left. Come, quickly."

They slipped behind the bar, and she lifted the trap door covering the ladder to the lower basement. Once they were down, Emily lowered the door back into place over their heads, holding the string that pulled the rubber mat into place on top. It wouldn't conceal their escape route for long, but it might buy them a few extra minutes. The sound of shooting grew dim, as far as they could hear in the lower basement, and then died away altogether. The tactical teams, or what was left of them, must be regrouping.

"What's happening, Dad?"

"No time to explain. Thank goodness you came back."

"But who's doing all the shooting up there?"

"I tricked them into shooting at each other, which bought us a little time, but I think they've figured it out. Now we need to get out through the tunnel before they make it down here. Hurry, Chi-chan."

"I'm on it, Dad. Let's go!"

Unfortunately, the enemy was already there, somehow—*But, how?*—a man in black tactical gear burst from behind the steel door leading to the tunnel, which must have been left unlocked. George saw him just as he raised a gun up to fire. He knocked the gun to the side, slapped the man hard across the face, stunning him for an instant, and shoved him back into the tunnel door, slamming it closed with considerable force. If there was anyone else in the tunnel, this would contain them until he could settle with this first attacker. The man sprang up with a huge knife in his hand, and lunged towards George.

Emily watched, paralyzed in shock, as her father fought off the attacker. She desperately wanted to help him, but found herself rooted to the floor, staring as he parried the lunging blade; and she watched as his left arm moved in a lazy circle around the man's right hand. It had an almost hypnotic effect on her, and on the man with the knife, too. She couldn't quite see how it happened, how her father gained control of his opponent's arm, but he twisted the arm out and away, slapped the man's face again with his right hand, and sent him sprawling backwards in a complete flip. He stood over his attacker, holding his wrist as he pressed a foot to the side of his face; and when the man reached for the gun, which lay just within reach, George pulled up on the arm sharply and stomped down hard on his face. He stopped moving.

The blunt violence of her father's skills shocked Emily. She had never seen him in a fight before, and she found watching him both thrilling and terrifying. Her mind spun as she tried to grasp the scene: she knew he didn't have the luxury of fighting from out of the stillness of his *chi*, since he had too much to lose: he fought to keep her safe... and he was bleeding out of his side. He'd found the most direct way to dispatch this man, to prevent him from firing his gun, or alerting the men upstairs, not to mention whoever might be behind him in the tunnel. Emily now felt she understood her father perfectly, and appreciated him as never before.

George picked up the gun, tore open the door and fired several rounds into the tunnel. When the light from the muzzle flairs didn't reveal anyone, they concluded that the tunnel was clear. Emily heard voices from upstairs—they must have found the trap door. It would only take a few seconds for them to force it open. She dragged the dead man into the tunnel and pulled the door closed, hooking him to the handle by the strap of his rifle, and letting the barrel catch on the doorframe. Then they ran as fast as they could to the other end and out into the woods, where the sky had just begun to show blue.

It took only a moment to find where George had left the motorcycle, collect their packs, kick over the engine and speed off into the woods, going much faster than Emily felt was safe, strictly speaking. But she felt the same urgency her father did, wanting to be out of sight or hearing when the tactical teams emerged from the tunnel.

They rode for a couple of hours through the forest, hardly ever coming out from under the canopy of trees. If anyone was looking for them from above, they would be practically invisible. They stopped a couple of times to rest, and to give George a break from the jostling of the ride. His wound had begun to bother him, and Emily saw that blood had soaked all the way through his jacket.

"Dad, we gotta get you some help," she pleaded.

"We have to keep going. There *is* no help around here."

"How far is the nearest town?"

"Chi-chan, it's another thirty minutes to the car."

"Dad, you can't make it that long, can you?"

"I dunno. I think you'll have to take over from here. You up to it?"

"Trust me, Dad. I can do it. Clutch with my hands, shift with my feet, right?"

"Oh, Lord," he snorted.

Fortunately, Emily turned out to have a better understanding of how motorcycles work than she let on. After a few rough bits at the beginning, she found her comfort-zone. Her father wrapped his arms around her and held on for dear life, as Emily sped off, going as fast as she dared, along wide paths and narrow ones, occasionally scooting along a shallow stream, until finally they came into an old growth stand. The brush on the forest floor thinned out, and Emily shifted into third gear, crested a hill, and they burst out onto an older, broader logging trail. Strangely, in the midst of the crisis, she couldn't remember experiencing a pleasure quite like this one, as if she'd entered upon a new phase of her life, one offering new responsibilities and challenges, and breathtaking dangers. She spun out third gear going up a hill and nudged the gearbox into fourth coming down the other side.

By the time they got to Mill Creek, George looked much weaker, and alarmingly pale. Emily tried to dress the wound with a first aid kit from the trunk of the car. The wound wasn't large, and the bullet seemed to have missed his ribs, and most importantly it seemed to have entered and exited. She could only hope it hadn't injured any organs. But he had lost a lot of blood. Once she'd stopped the bleeding, she helped him find a comfortable position in the back seat of the car, and followed his directions to the interstate, where they headed north toward Pittsburgh. At a steakhouse in Morgantown, Emily got takeout and George ate what he could in the back seat and explained the plan to her.

"We go north through Ohio and Michigan," he said. "They'll expect us to head south, then west."

"Where are we trying to go?"

"Montana, for now. We're gonna lay low in the wilderness for a few weeks, maybe a month or two, and there are lots of cabins around the Kootenai National Forest. We should be able to find an empty one in late October."

"And after that?" Emily asked, now beginning to recognize the familiar patterns of her father's mind. This plan was just like him: elude an enemy who expected him to move quickly by moving as slowly as possible, without remaining completely still. Everything would be direct and deliberate, nothing rushed, nothing decided in haste, and yet still be utterly elusive. He would make the enormity of the country his ally instead of his obstacle. Emily understood the plan perfectly.

"Once things cool down, we'll head south to New Mexico and meet up again with Michael and Yuki there."

~~~~~~~~

Later, as they bucketed up Interstate 79, George lay across the back seat and pondered their situation. He knew Emily had been keeping an eye on him in the rear-view mirror. He felt his strength ebbing, and the world had begun to look grim through his dark eyes. Whatever else might happen, he couldn't leave Emily without telling her the truth.

He'd been looking for the right moment to tell her everything for the last few years. She wasn't a child anymore—not exactly an adult yet either, but she might have to become one in a hurry. He'd hoped for a sunnier moment than this one, if only he had more to choose from. She would be pissed at him, he knew, for all the lies, but he'd had his reasons. He just hoped she would see the wisdom of his schemes and precautions, too. Fortunately, the truth he would tell her had a happy side as well.

Emily pulled the car into the Grove City Airport parking lot, a sleepy spot this time of day, and as good a place as any to give her father a rest from the ride. He propped himself up on a bag and reclined against the back door, his face pale as a sheet.

"Dad, you look…"

"I know, Chi-chan, it looks worse than it is."

"You must be bleeding internally. We need to get you to a doctor." She tried to force a smile, but he wasn't fooled, and he needed to change the subject.

"There's still time," he said. "Open that up." He gestured to one of the packs in the front seat. "I need to talk to you about something in there," he said.

Emily looked in the pack and pulled out Yuki's rice balls. "Wow, this is just what we need, Dad! You didn't make these, did you?" She handed him one and took a bite out of one herself. Those were definitely not what he expected to see come out of her bag. Still, he decided to get right to it.

"Your mother always knows what to make for you," he chortled.

Emily laughed. She was glad to hear a lighter tone in his voice. It took a moment for her to link his words to his voice and manner. She turned her eyes directly into his, trying to read his face, and let everything register. He saw her eyes flash, and winced. The thought of the pain he'd brought into focus for her shook him to his core.

"What are you trying to say, Dad?"

"I'm sorry, sweetheart. I should have told you sooner. I wanted to. But it just didn't seem safe before."

"Tell me what, Dad?"

He could see the storm brewing in her heart clearly enough. The signs were easy to read in her watery eyes and the tremble of her lips.

"I've been deceiving you all these years about your mother," he began nervously. "Her name is not Mei Li. She is not Taiwanese. That was all a lie." He paused for a moment before going on. "Yuki is your mother."

She sat speechless for a few moments as that last statement hung in the air. Finally, she burst out: "Daddy! What possible reason could you have for not telling me? Why didn't Yuki tell me herself? All these years..."

She yelped in rage and frustration, and George felt the shame of having caused it, as well he might. He knew he'd cheated her of something, even wronged her. Did his reasons, his worries about obscure dangers, have any weight compared to the pain she felt right then? Nothing he could say wouldn't seem like a craven excuse. Even so, he had to say something, to tell her what, if anything, about her life was true. His hesitation choked him.

He let out a long sigh and began to tell the tale beginning with Michael's assignment in Tokyo. He told her all the things Michael, knew. Then he told her about Yuki and him. She was born in Okinawa, at the base hospital; they'd been married a few weeks earlier. Then he explained her grandfather's research to her.

"That sounds disgusting, Dad," she said, her eyes on fire. "Isn't that some sort of crime? Like a war crime or something."

"Yes, it is bad," he said. "Like an atrocity without an official category yet."

"And Yuki... I mean, Mom... what did she have to do with this?"

"No, sweetheart. Your mother was always opposed to his work. But she had to protect him from the people it attracted, and that meant working in his lab. He was her father, after all."

There was more he told her, things even Michael didn't know. The Chinese learned her grandfather had shifted his efforts from seeking a gene mutation to support the Predator drug to developing a mutation that would achieve similar ends independently of the drug. He believed he could design a virus to implant the mutation in an adult subject. It would take effect in a few days, and might even prove to be reversible. That, at least, was what the Chinese told themselves.

"Was he insane?" she muttered. "That's not possible, is it, what he was trying to do?"

"I don't think so," George said, with as much conviction as he could muster. "As far as we know, he never actually pursued the idea in his work."

He wished he could offer her even more reassurance, knowing well enough that if such a thing were possible, the risk of the virus getting loose in the general population ought to dissuade any sane person from carrying on with the project.

But there was still more, perhaps the most important part of all from his point of view. The files Yuki gave to Michael and Meacham said nothing about the new mutation. She'd left them in the dark. The Chinese must have heard a rumor about it from an informant higher up in the Mori Corporation, but none of the files they'd managed to copy had any information about the mutation. Still, they became convinced her grandfather had hidden the design of the mutation, or even the mutation itself, in his own body. The routine autopsy done after his death would not reveal any anomalies on the genetic level. The Chinese stole tissue and blood samples from the remains before the cremation, and studied them for years, but found nothing.

"You mean they think Yuki knows how to design the mutation… or maybe she is the mutation?"

George nodded his head slowly. "Maybe now you can understand why…"

"Why you lied to me for all these years? Because if they found out about me, Yuki would be in danger, is that what you mean?"

"It's even worse than that, Chi-chan. They might conclude that you..."

"...that I'm the mutant?" Emily paused to think through everything she'd just heard.

He knew the Chinese would stop at nothing to get Yuki's child if they ever learned of her existence. She was pregnant when they fled to Hokkaido, and from that moment on, he bent all his efforts to conceal Emily's true identity from everyone... even from Michael. After the attack at the concert, George began to think she was in much more serious danger. She had begun to attract the attention of some very dangerous men. He couldn't be sure if they knew who she really was or just meant to use her to get to Michael and Yuki, but he was damned sure he wasn't going to take any chances. That's why he insisted keeping Emily with him rather than letting her accompany Michael and Yuki to New Mexico—thinking they were each safer apart than together.

"Those men at the concert, Dad, did they think..."

"I don't know what they thought."

"The men who came last night, the ones who shot you, were they looking for me?"

"If I had to guess, I'd say they were probably looking for your mother; and the mercenaries at the concert may only have wanted to use you to force your mother to go with them."

George studied his daughter's face as she listened in stunned silence. So many painful questions swirled through her mind, but the theme that recurred most forcefully in the jumble of her thoughts was "Who am I?" It wasn't hard for a father to see this.

"It's not true, Chi-chan," he said in a tone of voice intended to reassure her. "There never was any mutation. It was just a casual notion of your grandfather's. He never pursued the idea in his work. You are just our little girl."

"But how did I get to be so good at fighting?" she asked in a shaky voice. He knew how devastating this thought could be, that the thing she loved best was just a product of some monstrous mutation.

"No, honey. You're good because you're a tough chick. That's all," he said. "You're just a normal kid, like any other. There is no magic pill, no special gene, no short cuts. Just a lot of hard work."

"But if all these people think I'm some sort of freak…"

"All the world thinks you're my niece, with no special connection to Yuki. But if our secret's out, then we're gonna have to approach things a bit differently from now on."

He let her think about that for a moment, and then asked her to examine the papers in her pack. She rummaged through it and found a lot of cash—a little over thirty thousand dollars—a safe deposit box key to a bank in West Virginia, a birth certificate, a social security card and several passports.

"Who's Michiko Tenno?" she asked, holding a birth certificate that recorded the live birth of a baby girl seventeen and a half years ago on a US military base in Okinawa, Japan.

"That's you, Chi-chan. It's the name we gave you when you were born."

"Tenno?"

"It's a very old name from your mother's family. It was your great grandfather's name, and now it's yours.

"But it says my father is George Walker."

"It's still me, sweetheart, don't worry. We didn't want any paper trail connecting you to either of our names, Kane or Kagami, in case anyone checks. Walker was my mother's maiden name."

"This is very strange, Dad."

"I know, sweetheart. But we did it to keep you safe, and it's worked for seventeen years. Whatever else anyone may say, Michiko Tenno is who you really are. That's a valid birth certificate. You were really born there. And the passport and Social Security card that go with it are perfectly safe and legal."

"What about these other passports?"

"The red one is from Japan. Open it." Inside she found a birth certificate recording her birth at Chubukyodo Hospital in Okinawa City. When she looked up at him, with a quizzical look on her face, he continued. "These are valid documents, too. Your mom insisted that you should also be an official citizen of Japan. It's completely safe and legal. You can go anywhere as Michiko Tenno. It's up to you which one you want to use. "

"Can I really be both?"

"Yes. There's no law against dual citizenship. But if you look closely, you'll see that the birth certificates don't agree about exactly where you were born. You might not want to draw attention to that discrepancy."

"What if I don't want to be Michiko Tenno? Can't I just be Emily Kane. I kinda like her," she said with a mischievous smile.

"I like her, too," George said. "No official records support that name…"

"Even my school records?"

"Except your school records, and you may have to fix that, if you ever get back to Virginia… but I'd be honored if you still used my name."

"What about these other 'Emilys'?" she asked, flipping through several other passports. "Emily Hsiao and Emily Chung, who may be either British or Canadian, and this one says Emily Kane, born in Hawaii, and the birthday makes me… eighteen years old."

"Those are fakes, good forgeries. They'll fool most Law Enforcement types, and get you through Border Control in low-tech places. But if you're ever arrested and those passports are scrutinized closely, they'll just get you into more trouble."

George gave his daughter very precise instructions about how to use the fake passports, about how to find her way to New Mexico, where to find her mother, what was in the safe deposit box. He told her as much as he could in the short time he had

~~~~~~~

Trying to digest so much information made Emily dizzy. Her father had just turned her life upside down—as if the men with guns hadn't already done that—and it felt alternately thrilling and disorienting. Everything she had grown up believing about herself and her family, such as it was, had just been snatched away from her. But in the cacophony of ideas in her mind, one comforting thought pulsated at the heart of all the confusion. Whatever else might turn out to be false, she knew without a doubt that Yuki loved her, and now she knew why. She traded an abstract dream of a mother for the absolute truth of her real mother, the mother who had been there her entire life. Her mother loved her! Mei Li hadn't cared enough to take her with her when she ran out. She cast that canard into the oblivion it deserved and embraced the mother who so palpably loved her. But it cost her dearly.

"Help me," she cried out the window as she pulled up outside the ER of Kane Community Hospital. "He's hurt."

"Remember what we agreed," George croaked from the backseat, as a pair of paramedics hurried to the side of the car.

"No, Dad," she said through watery eyes, leaning over the seat back to help him up. "Don't make me."

"It's the only way to stay safe," he croaked at her.

"I think he's been shot," she told them.

At reception, she reported finding a strange man lying along the roadside in the Allegheny National Forest, and handed over his Veteran's ID card. A Sheriff's deputy thought it was probably a hunting accident.

"Abdominal GSW, through and through," one of the

paramedics called out as they wheeled him into the ER. George was unconscious. "Haemodynamically unstable."

"He's hemorrhaging," a man in surgical scrubs said.

"Will he be alright?" Emily asked one of the paramedics.

"Do you know him?" the deputy asked. The blood throbbed in Emily's ears at the sound of this question.

"No," she said, and tried to suppress the quiver in her voice.

"If we have any further questions, where can we find you?" the deputy finally got around to asking. Emily repeated the story her father had worked out for her, that she was staying at the Hilltop Suites.

George Kane died that night, having never regained consciousness, leaving his daughter alone in the world, in the town of Kane, Pennsylvania, on the edge of the Allegheny National Forest.

"This is just perfect," she said with a whimper, when the nurse told her the news.

She remembered the morbid little joke he made about the name of the town: "Two Kanes enter, one Kane leaves." At the time, she'd hoped he meant she was entering as a Kane and would leave as a Tenno, but even under that construction, she couldn't bring herself to laugh at it.

When the Sheriff's deputies arrived on the scene, they asked a lot of questions and got very few answers. George had schooled her well. The passport she showed them identified her as Emily Chung, Canadian citizen, who said she was on the way to Philadelphia to visit relatives. No one doubted she was exactly who she appeared to be, a bewildered, vulnerable eighteen-year-old. She could see that her father's surmise had been correct, a rural Sheriff's department would not have the resources to penetrate the darkness surrounding his death.

After the noise died down, Emily persuaded one of the nurses to help her make arrangements with the local funeral home to have the stranger's remains cremated as soon as the investigation was closed, which she imagined would be soon. The last duty of a child, and even this had to be done furtively, under the cover of a lie. If only this could be the last lie she'd have to tell for her father.

Later that afternoon, she drove back to the interstate and turned south. She understood her father's escape route, north then west to safety. It was a good plan, and a perfect expression of his character, but it did not suit hers. She turned back toward her pursuers, figuring that if she was the target, going to New Mexico might bring them to her mother that much sooner. As much as she wanted to be with her mother at this moment, she had unfinished business in Virginia.

CHAPTER EIGHT
BACK TO THE WOODS

Emily retraced her steps to Mill Creek, and found the spot where they hid the dirt bike. She meant to return to the estate, and there was no way to approach it in a car without drawing attention to herself, given all the cameras. But first, she needed to gather the most important things from the various bags in the car and fit them into her pack, which she then strapped to the back of the bike. It was too dark to ride through the forest, so she slept on the ground near the car. The next morning, she rose early, changed clothes, ate the last of the *bento* and rice balls, and headed off into the forest. The logging trails were easy to follow and she had a pretty good memory for the route they had taken thirty six hours earlier. If she made good time, she could be back to the western edge of the estate by nightfall.

The emotional register of this ride was almost entirely the reverse of what she had experienced on the ride out. Then, she sat behind her father, arms wrapped around him, or he sat behind her enfolding her in his arms. They rode with the sunrise at their backs at heart-pounding speed, eluding dark forces with deadly intent, racing toward a bright, uncertain future. Now she was heading straight for the darkness with grim determination, intent on wresting the future of her choosing from its clutches. She rode by herself, nothing to hold onto but the handlebars of the dirt bike, and roared up and down the logging trails, sometimes cresting hills, or racing alongside creek beds, occasionally bursting out onto an exposed ridgeline. The scenery thrilled her. The trees still wore their autumnal regalia and, under the canopy, the sun painted everything in shades of red and yellow.

She rested under a tree just below one of the highest ridges and surveyed the landscape. In the early afternoon light she could see the terrain for miles around, laid out like a harvest quilt, alive with color. A thin, small warmth stole into her heart as she thought back over the events of the last two days. She'd lost her father just the day before, but she had found her mother, or at least recognized her for who she really was. She wept with sorrow and joy at the same time. She was loved; she had lost. The great absence of her heart, the mother who had abandoned her, had been cast out by the infinite affections of the mother who had always been there, watching over her. This revelation had cost her dearly. It was a heady mix of emotions, and she felt almost overwhelmed by it.

The thought of the enemy who lay ahead brought her out of this reverie. A part of her knew she would eventually have to confront them some day, and that part wanted to unleash the dogs of war, however foolish and self-destructive it might prove to be. But the better part of her didn't want to dedicate her life to vengeance. That was not her father's way. He had devoted his life to protecting her from them, and he hadn't done it just to leave an avenger behind. To honor him, she needed to turn her life to sunnier purposes. It was easy to imagine herself killing them all if they forced her hand, but she hoped they would let her alone. She didn't want their deaths, or hers, to be her defining moment.

But, then, why go back to Virginia at all? The question

lingered, and she had no clear answer. She'd made no friends there, and now she had no family either, other than Sensei. Why not head west, as her father had urged, and make a new life with her mother?

"I've been nobody for too long," she muttered. "Whoever Michiko Tenno is, I can't fabricate her on the run. She has to be who I already am."

Satisfied with this resolution, or at least a little less uneasy, she got back on the bike and rode on.

~~~~~~~~

Around dusk, she spotted the familiar shape of Promontory Rock in the distance, and pressed on, going as fast as she dared on the narrowing trail. She had hoped to arrive before nightfall to avoid turning on the headlamp, but fortunately, the nearly full moon provided enough light to move pretty quickly for a little while. Eventually, the logging trail dead-ended and she had to continue on hiking trails, most of which had been thoroughly carved out by mountain bikers, so it was pretty easy going at first. Soon these gave way to smaller walking trails, and then she found herself riding through the underbrush itself, branches slapping at her as she passed. Riding along riverbeds gave some relief, or even through them wherever it was shallow enough, and the little bit of clear sky overhead made it possible to see. It was now too dark under the forest canopy to ride safely. Finally, she came upon the familiar stream, and followed it to the base of her favorite cliff. She stashed the bike in the bushes, fished the riflescope out of her pack, and climbed to the top.

Lying on her belly on the rock, she saw no sign of any activity on the estate. The main building looked gutted from here, but the garage seemed intact, and the family car was still parked out front. There were no police cars or fire trucks to be seen. *Had the Fire Department even been called?* Perhaps the house had just been allowed to burn itself out. It would be almost impossible to spot any tactical teams on the grounds in the dark from this distance. She would just have to chance it, since she needed a few things from the apartment over the garage. It seemed reasonable to assume whoever had attacked them had already done a thorough search of the main house and taken anything they thought might lead them to Michael or his family. Thinking of the story her father told, she figured they had probably been looking for any signs of an active lab on the estate. Emily hardly knew what they actually could have found, she realized, but she was pretty confident they wouldn't have been interested in what she had come back for. She needed clothes and shoes—but in a different style than she was used to—some camping equipment, as well as some papers... and her school books. She needed the materials to restart her life as Michiko Tenno.

The residual warmth of the day faded and the night air made her shiver. "It's now or never," she said, and climbed down from the rock. She retrieved her pack from the bike, hoisted it on her shoulder and ran along the familiar paths toward the main house. In the depths of the forest, not far from the beaten path, she heard the whirring of a camera panning. *Were they still operating? Was anyone watching at the other end?* She reacted instinctively and ducked under a large juniper, whose loose, low branches provided ample cover. The camera hadn't picked her up, she thought, but she would have to be alert.

At the edge of the woods, she scanned the north lawn before giving up the cover of the trees. Other cameras sprouted from several new positions, and they were definitely operating. She spotted four of them, all placed so as to scan the grounds away from the buildings. No doubt, there would be a few more on the other side of the house watching the main gate and the front drive. But they didn't seem to be set to cover the buildings themselves, which meant if she could slip past them, she could move about the garage freely.

Once inside, she went straight to her room, and gasped to see how it had been ransacked. The contents of her drawers lay on the floor, and everything in her closet had been torn off the hangers. The shoeboxes she'd so carefully stacked in the back of the closet were nowhere to be seen, and she began to feel tears on her face. She could admit to herself now why she'd returned—because she wanted a photograph. As embarrassing as it sounded, she felt that to reclaim her life would require at least one icon, one star to navigate by. Her heart raced at the thought that it might have been destroyed or confiscated by those men, and she groped under the clothes scattered around the room.

"It's not here," she cried. "Please, let it be here."

Emily searched all over the floor with no luck, crawling and craning her neck to peer under the bed and behind the chest of drawers. She sat up and leaned her back against the wall, trembling in a way she'd not expected. One last clump of clothes and shoes caught her eye, trapped in the space between the door and the wall. She rolled onto her side to be able to reach it, ruffling through it with outstretched fingers, until she glimpsed a shiny edge, obviously a photo, one corner bent back. She seized it, pressed it to her face, and then rubbed it on her shirt to dry the tears off. The hair, the curve of the neck, the shape of the ear, it all seemed so obvious now.

"Why didn't you tell me?" she sobbed. "You could have trusted me."

Of course, she knew the answers to these questions now, and rehearsed them for herself. But the logic of her parents' precautions had no power to move her. She stopped to consider whether her anger really referred to her mother, and a darker voice spoke from the depths of her heart, reminding her of the men who'd attacked the estate, and the more obscure forces that had driven her parents to such desperate measures. These were the people who merited her anger, the voice told her, even if she couldn't quite bring them into focus.

"Kill them all," it said, and Emily trembled to hear it.

Should she act on such an impulse, if the opportunity arose? Her heart raced as she groped for an answer, and she tried to steady herself by pressing both palms into the floor, feeling too weak to move for the moment. She picked up the photo and gazed at it again, this time contemplating the serene expression on her infant face, eyes closed, resting on her mother's shoulder. A long, slow breath filled her up, and as she let it out she listened again for the quiet of the forest and the babble of the stream she never seemed to be able to locate.

Finally, she heaved herself up, climbed the stairs to the attic and brought down two large duffles. Back on her knees, she scraped together all the socks and underwear on the floor into one, as well as whatever she could find of her shirts, pants and shoes. Then she went down to the basement passageway and made her way to the storage closet under the main house, hoping the fire hadn't gotten all the way down there. Given the new cameras, she didn't think she could risk a flashlight, and there was no power in the upper basement. As luck would have it, however, the floorboards had been mainly burned away over the rec-room, even though everything else seemed to be intact, and the moon managed to shine through. In the storage closet, they had ransacked everything, leaving the contents of drawers and boxes strewn across the floor. But they weren't looking for the same things she was: Andie's clothes. Emily figured she wouldn't have taken her fall and winter outfits to Naxos.

She thought about wearing her mother's clothes, but dismissed the idea with a snort—they would never fit her. Yuki was at least six inches shorter, and at least thirty pounds lighter. Andie, on the other hand, was about her height with a similar build. Emily might be a bit slimmer, because she was so much more physically active, but that wouldn't matter much. The important thing was that Andie had a completely different style. Lots of long elegant things, form fitting pants, and loads of really nice shoes. Emily grabbed whatever she could find and stuffed it into the duffle bags. She paused over a box of underwear.

"Andie has really nice stuff, so soft and smooth," she thought. "Totally not what I would ever think to wear."

She grabbed a fistful, and then another: bras, panties, shirts, stockings, whatever. Just as she was about to go, she noticed a turquoise wig, and grabbed it too, zipped the duffles closed and made her way back through the passageway to the garage.

Her dad kept a pickup truck at the far end. She tossed the duffles in the back, as well as her dad's sleeping bag and a two-person tent, then went back up to the apartment and collected her school things and the keys to the truck. Her dad kept the papers for all the vehicles in a cabinet in the garage. It had been rifled through, but must not have been of any interest to anyone except her. She found the paperwork for the truck and the motorcycle, and stuffed it in the glove box. Last of all, she got a screwdriver and removed the license plate from the back of the truck. She didn't know if this was a useful precaution—they may have gotten all this information already—but on the off chance they hadn't bothered, she saw no reason to let the cameras pick up the plate number as she was leaving.

The garage door slid up with a minimum of clatter, and even though the truck was heavy, she managed to get it rolling, until the slight slope of the driveway began to work in her favor. She didn't want to alert anyone who might be watching until the last possible second. She eased up a moment to allow the moon to pass behind a cloud, and once everything had grown much darker, one last heave got the truck rolling again and she jumped into the driver seat. With the ignition in the 'on' position, she pulled the side mirrors flush to the side of the truck and steered down the drive. So far she saw no obvious signs that an alarm had been triggered. The gate would be closed, and probably locked—either way, she didn't want to risk stopping to open it—she aimed for a spot about twenty yards to the right of the gate, where the hedge was thinner, with no trunks, just small branches. It might just be wide enough for the truck to squeeze through. She eased the shifter into second gear, gave the gas pedal a tap and pulled back sharply on the clutch pedal. The engine lurched and then sprang to life, and she turned off the pavement, put the gas pedal to the floor and plowed through the hedge. Branches snapped and screeched along the side of the truck, but she crashed through with no significant damage. There didn't seem to be anybody waiting on the street side, so she turned right and sped off without headlights.

Three miles along the south end of the estate, far from the lawns, where the forest loomed thickly over the road, she located a stream culvert running under the road. It took only a moment to pull the truck off the road and out of sight. She entered the forest at a dead run, following the stream bed for a mile or two, which led her directly to the base of Promontory Rock. A quick kick-start and the dirt bike sputtered back to life, and carried her down the streambed back to the truck. Since the bike was a little too heavy to lift by herself, she backed the truck up against the embankment and let the tailgate be her ramp, then secured it on its side in the bed.

Emily Hsiao spent the night in a motel in Warm Springs, having paid in cash. After a moment's hesitation leaning on the bathroom sink, she worked up the nerve to cut her hair—shoulder-length, just long enough to be able to gather it into a pony tail, but short enough to wear it loose without much annoyance. As she looked at the pile of black hair on the bathroom floor, she thought of Yuki. Her mother would cry to see it, almost eighteen inches worth of hair, all jet-black and perfectly straight. Then she thought of what her father had said about how these people might be looking for a gene mutation *in her*. She swept up all the hair and put it in the dumpster behind the building.

She woke up Tuesday morning, rummaged through the duffle bags and put on some of Andie's clothes. Just some cotton pants, a white cotton blouse and some light shoes. She barely noticed how they looked, but she was amazed by how they felt. The shoes were so light and comfortable, so unlike the sneakers or hiking boots she usually wore. The pants and blouse felt like half the weight of the blue jeans or cargo pants and t-shirts or sweat shirts she used to favor. The most striking thing, however, was the underwear. She'd only worn sports bras for the last few years, and this felt so much better. *Andie has really great clothes.*

She ate the continental breakfast in the lobby, loaded all her stuff into the truck and went to school.

CHAPTER NINE
SCHOOL DAYS

At school the next morning, everything seemed normal, which she found surprisingly disorienting. Of course, she'd only missed a day of school, and as she walked up the front steps, she kept one hand in her pocket, touching the note she'd forged from her father to the effect that she had to miss school on Monday because of a family emergency over the weekend. When she handed the note over to Mrs. Telford, the school secretary, no alarm bells went off, no questions were asked. In fact, no extraordinary official notice was taken of her, or her absence: just another bit of ordinary school business. Bells rang, teachers yelled, kids shuffled from classroom to classroom, lockers opened and closed, big kids picked on little kids, and everyone ate lunch. How odd normality felt in the aftermath of the most momentous weekend of her life. Events had shaken her to the very core of her being, and she had emerged on the other side intact, whole, but with new enemies of frightening dimensions, as well as a new sense of her own identity, and underneath it all, she felt stronger than she had ever felt before.

Yet no one seemed to notice. The girls who resented

her, still resented her… though they seemed to look at her differently. In fact, they were staring.

"Whoa! You look different," she heard Danny exclaim as she stood at her locker. She turned her head and contemplated him in puzzled silence… and she saw in his face that he wondered if he had offended her. She hadn't ever invited him to talk to her like she was a girl before. Had he crossed a line? Should she call him on it? She smiled feebly through her own perplexity, and he seemed to understand.

"No, I mean you look fantastic," he tried again.

She blushed a little—"Thank God, he didn't notice."—and then it occurred to her that he was seeing her new self, Michiko. She enjoyed his attention, strange as it felt to her, and she tried to articulate the sensation for herself. His gaze was almost analogous to how she felt wearing Andie's clothes. The reflection allowed her to recover some composure.

"You know, I just felt like making a change," she ventured nonchalantly. Would he believe her show of indifference? He seemed to.

"Your hair looks cool. You goin' to the dojo after school?"

She hesitated. Concealing herself in the ordinariness of school was perplexing enough. But at the dojo, she might have to tell something of what happened to Sensei, and she didn't feel ready to do that. What could she tell him, after all? The facts were so extravagant as to seem preposterous. As soon as she tried to imagine herself describing the events to him, she couldn't help seeing how absurd it all sounded, even to her.

"I dunno. Maybe. See ya later, okay?" She turned away and walked to her next class.

"I like your shoes, by the way," he called after her. She smiled to hear it. Maybe he wasn't so hopeless after all.

At lunch, she had to go through the line, since there

hadn't been any time to prepare something to bring with her from the motel. She began to see all sorts of domestic tasks devolving to her: meals, laundry, driving, shopping, etc. No one else in Virginia would or could do them for her. This thought showed her that a motel was not an adequate solution, and neither was camping in the woods. She needed to find a regular abode.

She got the rice and succotash, refried beans and a cheese enchilada. It was an uninspiring meal, to say the least. Usually she brought a *bento* box from home, something Yuki cooked up for her. Rice and curried lentils, maybe, or tofu, some pickled ginger on the side, maybe some *daikon*, or some *kim chee*, and her favorite, *onigiri*. It was all very strongly flavored, and probably healthier, or at least a lot less greasy than the meal that lay before her today.

She sat alone at a table in the corner and looked down at her tray, sampling the rice and beans, and poking idly at the enchilada with her fork. Danny came and sat at her table a moment later. He'd begun to sit with her at lunch these last few weeks, though he hadn't quite figured out how to speak to her with any degree of comfort since the concert. No one else even had the temerity to approach her on most days. If it was raining and the patio was unusable, it would be more crowded inside, and other kids would have to squeeze in at her table. But today, for some reason, Billy Codrow plumped down across from her, and Wayne Turley came in right behind him. She knew them all from the dojo, but Billy and Wayne had never sat with her before.

"Hey, Emily. Nice look. It's like a whole new you," Billy offered, uncertain how it would be received.

She smiled at him graciously, perhaps a little bemused at the new attention being offered to her. He was on the football team with Danny, one of the cornerbacks on defense. She sized him up: not very big as football players go, not even much taller than her, but she suspected he was speedy, and probably quite agile. In the dojo, he hadn't made as much progress as Danny. He did everything quite stiffly compared to some of the others, and needed to work on stretching. As a result, like most boys, he ended up focusing too much on the strength and speed exercises, since these came easiest. His dad was a dentist and his mom managed the office for him, which meant he generally dressed better than Danny—newer shoes and sharp outfits.

"Thanks, I'm trying something new," she replied.

"Mrmmph," grunted Wayne as he tried to stuff two tacos in his mouth at once.

"What did you say?" asked Danny.

"You using that pudding?" Wayne demanded.

"What the hell, man... I was saving that," Danny shot back, half in jest.

"It's goddam tapioca. You hate that. And it came with your pizza for free," Wayne roared. "Give it here."

"Yeah, yeah. Whatever."

Danny slid it across the table, and Wayne made as if to devour it in one huge gulp. Then he shifted rhetorical gears and pretended to savor each tiny spoonful, pinky pointing skyward. "Exquisite. Velvet lumps, good nose, vanilla aroma with just a hint of cinnamon," he diagnosed. "Savorous!"

They all laughed... even Emily. She'd never really paid any attention to what boys said to each other before. Her previous experience, narrow as it was, had led her to believe they never said anything worth listening to. But here she was laughing along with these three. They were probably her closest friends, and she felt she hardly knew them. Of course, this new Emily seemed to have totally captivated them. Until now, she knew they'd found her an intimidating figure, maybe even a little scary. She tried to be friendly, to the extent she knew how, but she always felt herself clipping off her conversations with them, as if she didn't want to risk letting them get close. And now, here she was, sitting with them, laughing at their jokes, and when she looked around the room, she saw all the kids staring at their table, like something strange and new had happened. She wondered if Billy and Wayne felt the same way. Did they think of her as some sort of weirdo? Is that why they'd sat with her?

She looked at Wayne, sitting across the table, as she often did at the dojo. He was enormous, probably more than six and a half feet tall, and well over two hundred fifty pounds. When he first joined the dojo, he was chubby, and slow, and had no stamina. But he'd stuck with it, and lost some of the weight, maybe sixty or seventy pounds, and he always seemed a little more limber than people expected. And his katas were among the best in the class. He seemed to enjoy the precision aspects of *shotokan* most of all. As he lost weight and his stamina improved, the other kids in the dojo began to realize just how strong he was, too, and they began to call him the Rock.

Everyone liked sparring with him, since he was careful not to hit too hard, and it was hard to miss such a big target. Of course, those little touch strikes that score points didn't reflect what the reality of an actual fight with him might be like. He could take a punch, and it was really hard to make a dent in him with just fists… which was exactly why Emily didn't like sparring with Wayne. She didn't do touch strikes. She would knock you down, knock the wind out of you, make you take it seriously when you threw a punch or a kick her way. She didn't hurt anyone in the dojo, but her opponents knew what it felt like to hit the mat.

Once, sparring with Wayne, she snuck a reverse punch past his guard and nailed him right on the solar plexus, and he hardly noticed. Anyone else would have been gasping for breath. Of course, two moves later he lay flat on his back tapping the mat. That was an eye-opening lesson for her about the relative density of her opponents. It also taught her to worry about really hurting him: would his joints be able to sustain the pressure of moving the rest of his bulk if she applied a joint lock? His sweet temper exacerbated the dilemma for her, since she wanted him to know she thought of him as a real opponent, even though she always looked for ways to take it easy on him. She hoped he didn't notice.

Hey, Emily, you goin' to the dojo after school?" he asked. "We missed you yesterday."

"I dunno, Wayne," she replied. "I got a lot of stuff to take care of this afternoon. My dad had to go to the Philippines with his boss. That's why I wasn't there yesterday," she lied.

"How long's he gone for," Danny butted in.

"Until spring. He might be back for graduation." The lie began to get sticky.

"Emily, that's like six months, man. Whatcha gonna do for six months?"

"I know. It kinda sucks. They've pretty much closed down the estate. I'm all alone out there, except for the gardeners. I'm looking for a place to stay in town. I'm eighteen now, so it's all legal," she lied again. Fortunately none of them had the slightest notion when her birthday actually was.

"Hey, Danny. Doesn't your mom need someone to rent out the room above your garage?" Billy asked.

"Hey, yeah! Emily, that would be perfect for you. It's got its own laundry and a little kitchen type area.... Yeah, but she probably wants too much for it," Danny added dejectedly.

Anyone could see what the prospect of Emily living closer than next door would mean to him. It could hardly be less than rapturous, especially this new, non-intimidating Emily. So there was obviously no way in the universe he could imagine this working out. But Emily's ears perked up nonetheless.

"What's she want for it, do you think?"

"I think it's two fifty a month, but utilities are included. Can you swing that much?"

This could hardly seem like less than an astronomical sum to him, as they all knew, since he rarely had even fifteen bucks in his pocket at one time.

"That's just about right, actually. My dad gave me a bit more than that to live on while he's away," she said, almost truthfully. "Do you think I could come by later to look at it with your mom?"

"I can call her after school, if you want. Or you can see her when she picks me up at the dojo," he offered, hoping to lock her into coming to class tonight.

"I've got my dad's truck while he's gone. I can give you a ride home."

Danny called his mother at the hospital, the first chance he got, to ask her about it, with Emily hovering by his shoulder. She heard his heart pounding in his voice, and the voice on the other end—what she could hear of it—sounded dubious. "Another teenager," she imagined Mrs. Rincon thinking, as would only be natural.

But Danny's mother had already met her, on the night of the concert, and Emily thought it had gone well enough. She'd been her usual reserved self, and if that didn't suit Mrs. Rincon, there wasn't much she could do about it. Maybe Andie's clothes would make her look somehow more responsible. Actually, she had no idea what would impress an adult trying to rent out an apartment over her garage. One thing that might be on her side, she imagined, was the likelihood that they needed to rent the place soon, if they were strapped for money.

The rest of the school day passed uneventfully. Emily could see her new look attracted attention, more than she wanted. She thought it might be a good idea to tone it down a bit tomorrow… if only she had some idea how to accomplish that, other than returning to her usual camo. In fact, she had no idea what she was doing to attract even this much attention. This new life would take some getting used to.

Going to the dojo that afternoon turned out to be a relief. Sensei shot her a knowing look, but made no inquiries, even though he could hardly conceal his curiosity about her new look. She went to the back to change clothes before class, and that was unusual right there. Ordinarily, she wore street clothes in class, but Andie's clothes were hardly suitable for a workout, so she dug a t-shirt and running pants out of a duffle bag in her truck and wore those. She changed back into Andie's clothes after class.

Tuesday classes usually featured a long breathing and meditation session, and she'd been looking forward to it all day. For the first twenty minutes or so, she found a profound relief from just losing herself in her breathing. She began to see the extremity to which the stress of the last few days had brought her, and felt herself breathing it out and away. The noise of her mind gradually died down, her thoughts slowed, allowing her to approach each one separately, to turn it over in her mind and contemplate it.

There, at the bottom of her mind, she discovered once again the connectedness of her experiences, the unifying principle of which could only be her own personality. She saw how Emily Kane and Michiko Tenno really were the same person—only external circumstances had changed— and how she could go forward as Michiko and still retain everything Emily had achieved. She would continue to go by Emily in school, so as not to create a public connection in the minds of her teachers and classmates between her dangerous identity and her safe one. At some point, she'd have to figure out how to change her school records to reflect her new name before graduation, so she could use those records to enter college as Michiko. But for now, she would remain Emily.

Her mind drifted through memories of her childhood, playing with her dad and Yuki... no, her mom. That last thought burst across her consciousness like the morning sun, blindingly bright. She almost laughed out loud, and it upset her breathing. It took a moment to regain her composure, and in the process she caught a glimpse of Wayne in the corner, sweating profusely, completely at a loss as to the meaning of this exercise. He flashed her a look, smiled his big, goofy smile at her, and she snorted, almost burst out laughing again. The rest of the dojo caught it, too. Soon everyone was laughing.

Sensei came storming in from the back room to see what was going on. He'd never had a problem letting Emily run exercises like this one. She smiled at him sheepishly and shrugged her shoulders, as if to confess that she was at the center of it all. She knew there was no point going on with the exercise, and he tried to hide a smile.

"Okay, fine," he barked at them. "Floor exercises, then sparring."

He marched them back and forth across the dojo, shouting out instructions, directing them to practice punches and kicks, combinations and evasions with each step. The last exercise was knife sparring. They didn't use real knives, of course, only rubber knives. Sensei demonstrated several techniques for the class, and then had them take turns practicing together in pairs. A punch or kick landed counted for one point, knife contact counted for two, as did disarming your opponent.

Emily was paired with Billy, and with his quick hands and good balance, he was pretty good at this game. She left her knife on the mat, preferring not to use it in knife sparring. One lesson her father taught her, which she never forgot, was that it is almost always better not to have a weapon in your hands, not even a blade. As he would say, "the best weapon is the one in your opponent's hand." Obviously, this didn't apply to guns, unless you could get close enough.

Billy posed a good challenge for her, holding his knife blade pointing down towards his elbow. This allowed him to use punch techniques with the knife in his hand, since each strike could be used to slash at her at the same time. But the technique was also vulnerable to inside blocks, which Emily took advantage of, blocking him several times in a row, each time pivoting inside his attack, grabbing his wrist below the knife, twisting his arm up and around, and taking the knife from his helpless hand. One time, instead of wresting the knife from his hand, she forced him to hold it, raised his arm and stepped through, then twisted his arm down behind so that he'd have to stab himself in the ass—it was all quite embarrassing.

The next time, he switched to a forward grip with the blade protruding from his thumb and forefinger, a better technique for stabbing motions—hard to defend against because the attacker's hand remains free to slash through an inside block, but vulnerable to a down block or grab. The first time Billy lunged, she slid back into a crane position, then slid forward to seize his wrist with both hands from above and yank his arm upwards. He winced from the pressure on his wrist and dropped the knife. If she had pulled up as sharply as she easily could have, she would have broken his wrist.

Billy tried one last time to get past her defenses. He knelt down to retrieve his knife, and suddenly lunged upwards from below, no doubt hoping to catch her by surprise. But Emily was ready for him... sort of. Her mind flashed to the scene in the basement tunnel, her father's left arm swinging in a lazy circle around the lunging blade. Her arms moved like her father's, before she quite recognized what she did and, for his part, Billy seemed transfixed by the movement and stood motionless as she grabbed his wrist from below, twisted it in towards his body and then sharply upwards. Billy gave out a little yelp, half from pain and half surprise, as he felt his arm pulling his entire body into a flip. He might have been able to resist, but that would have been much more painful. Letting his body follow the movement created in the joints of his arm was the clear path of least resistance. Emily saw that if she held onto his wrist all the way through the maneuver, she would surely dislocate his shoulder. She released his wrist, and sent him sailing across the room. Fortunately, he landed on some mats stacked in the corner and avoided serious injury.

"Omagod," she shrieked, and ran over to help him. "Billy, I'm so sorry. I had no idea.... Are you okay?"

"That was amazing," Billy gushed. "How on earth did you do that?"

"No. It wasn't," Emily said. "You could have been seriously hurt. I'm really sorry."

"I'm fine, Emily. Don't sweat it."

Actually, Billy was more than fine. He was ecstatic. Emily looked him up and down to make sure he hadn't broken anything, and then noticed everyone in the dojo staring at them—at her really—with blank expressions, mouths agape. What were they staring at, she wondered, the strange technique she'd just done, almost unconsciously? Or were they just staring at her, at the way she paid attention to Billy? It occurred to her that she'd never really paid attention to any of them like that before—shrieking and running over to check on someone, or even making a mistake she'd have to apologize for.

"What kind of fool am I becoming?" she muttered. "Is this what having a friend means?" This was a new experience for her. It's not like she didn't care about them before. After all, she taught them all kinds of stuff—kicks, holds, sneaky backhanded strikes. But through it all, she always managed to keep them at a distance, like they were more subjects of her observation than actual friends.

When she glanced at Sensei, she could see his thoughts ran in a slightly different direction, as if he recognized that technique. He had never taught it to her, and now that she'd actually done it, she saw how aggressive it was, almost cruel, using the opponent's mass and leverage to wrench his joints apart. Had she not released Billy's wrist at just the right moment, he would have been lucky to get away with only a dislocated shoulder. She felt very fortunate to have recognized it in time, and smiled to think how fortunate Billy was, even if he didn't realize it.

The thought dawned on her that Sensei had trained her father, and that he must have recognized what she'd done, too. But he hadn't taught things like that to her, and if he wouldn't, for reasons she couldn't quite fathom, she wondered what he'd think of her for coming up with such a technique on her own. Of course, he might simply assume her father had showed it to her, and in one sense that wouldn't be incorrect.

The more she thought about it, the more the entire scene had her completely perplexed. The man in the tunnel had been distracted by the seemingly lazy movement of her father's arm, and so was she... and the same thing just happened to Billy. She waved her hand in front of his eyes and he froze. The move came out of her spontaneously, unplanned, unconscious. She wanted to think it had stuck in her mind because of its graceful curves and the illusion of serenity. But another thought bothered her: perhaps she was drawn to it because of its extreme cruelty.

"Is that what's really inside me?" She found it all very unsettling, and breathed a sigh of relief when Sensei announced that class was over for the evening.

In her anxiety, she changed back into Andie's clothes as quickly as she could, and then found herself having to wait outside by the truck for Danny. Sensei motioned her back to the office and asked a few vague questions about "things." He clearly didn't know how to ask what he really wanted to know: was everything okay with her and her family? That he feared something had gone wrong was easy for her to see, but she had no idea how to begin an answer, so she kept him at a polite distance.

"I can't really talk about it right now," she said. "But I'm fine. Please, don't worry about me."

"Where did that last move come from?" he pressed, and she hardly knew what to say. She didn't dare lie to him about this.

"I think it came as if out of a dream. I don't understand it any better than that."

In a way what she said was the truth. But it was also designed to conceal as much as possible about her current circumstances from Sensei. He would find out soon enough that things had changed at the estate. Then he would have to ask even more personal questions. He'd known her since before she was born. Maybe he was the closest thing to a friend her father had, since she didn't quite know how to describe his relationship with Mr. Cardano.

She knew Sensei would not be able to let the matter drop, especially since the whole town would find out what had happened soon enough. There would be questions, an investigation, perhaps even suspicions about her own role in those events. She hadn't committed any crime, she'd done nothing wrong. Still she began to see it was not going to be so simple to step back into her previous life. In order to make the transition from Emily to Michiko, on which her entire future safety depended, she needed precisely not to become the center of attention of the whole town. If everyone in Bath County knew her by both names, the people who had killed her father would always be able to track her. This was definitely not the moment to explain everything to Sensei. But she would not be able to put that moment off for much longer.

"Sensei, I need time to think. It's all very confusing to me right now. I'll tell you all about everything in a few days. Okay?"

He nodded and gave her a half smile. Danny came out of the dojo and together they went to see his mom about an apartment.

CHAPTER TEN
YET ANOTHER GARAGE

Emily and Danny's mother, Laura Rincon, spoke for about half an hour, once they had shooed Danny out of the apartment. It was just a big room with a bathroom and walk-in closet on one end, and a tiny kitchen and dining table on the other. Two large windows faced out over the driveway toward the street, and a smaller window on the opposite wall looked out over the neighbor's backyard. The kitchenette occupied the corner next to the back window, just inside the entry door. A twin bed stood out from one wall, in the nook created by the bathroom and Walk-in closet, and a long, old couch and lamp stretched under the front windows. The staircase led up the right side of the garage and could be seen from the main house through the kitchen windows. The landing at the top was large enough for a couple of lawn chairs.

"It's small," Emily said, "but clean. I like it."

"Where exactly are your parents?" Mrs. Rincon asked.

"My dad's traveling in Asia on business."

"I thought your dad was just a chauffeur."

"He is, but he is also sort of a bodyguard. His boss likes

to have him along on trips like this one." It was a relief to be able to say something that was true enough, since she was wary of saying too much, of getting caught in a lie... especially in front of people she hoped to live with.

"What about your mother?" Mrs. Rincon pressed on.

"I don't know where my mom is. I've never met her," she said defensively, hoping for a little sympathy, and to get her to back off.

This remark was less true, but given her bizarre circumstances, it wasn't exactly a lie either. She had never met the woman who, until the last few days, she thought was her mother. But she also had to worry about being consistent in what she told everyone around town. Some careful planning of her story would be necessary, if she was going to fit in among these people, not just for a few days or weeks, but for as long as a year. She needed to *come* from this town, if she was going to go anywhere else in a normal, ordinary way. That meant having a coherent story they could tell each other about her, not to mention what they'd tell anyone who might come around asking about her.

In Danny's case, the problem was perhaps even more acute, since he was a friend, and becoming more important to her every day. When the truth about her father's death came out, she did not want to be thought to have lied about it. But the lie about her mother was safe. No one in this town need ever find out Yuki was her real mother. If everything went as Emily hoped, no one in the world would ever connect Michiko Tenno to Yukiko Kagami.

"Oh! I'm sorry honey. I didn't realize," Mrs. Rincon said, embarrassed for having intruded into this girl's private pain.

"It's okay, Mrs. Rincon. I'm used to it."

Mrs. Rincon sighed. She would not be able to press her any further now.

"And you're eighteen?"

"Yes," she lied, innocently, but with the documents to

back her up.

"You want the place through May?"

"Yes, though I might want to stay through the end of the summer, if that's okay with you." Mrs. Rincon hesitated for a moment, but then relented.

"We don't really need a lease, I guess, for a month to month arrangement. Are you sure you can really afford the rent?"

Mrs. Rincon's jaw dropped when Emily counted out twenty-three one hundred dollar bills and said: "That should cover everything through the end of May."

"I guess I owe you fifty bucks then. I'll get it to you tomorrow, if that's okay." Laura handed her the key, looked at her for a moment, and then turned to go. She stopped at the door and turned again to say: "Why don't you come over for breakfast in the morning before school."

The next day after school Emily went to the DMV and took a driving test as Michiko Tenno. She passed the written test and had an appointment for the road test Friday afternoon. After she passed the road test, she sold the truck registered to George Kane to Emily Hsiao. She'd have to take the test in her other identities, too, she supposed, which would probably require going to another town where she wouldn't be recognized. Creating a paper trail for her new identity in Bath County, Virginia, was looking to be a tedious affair. Later she would convert the paperwork on the dirt bike to Emily Hsiao as well. It wasn't safe yet, she judged, to attach her real name to any of these vehicles.

Eventually, she would have to transfer the title and all of her school records to Michiko Tenno. This was a subject her mind returned to frequently. She didn't know quite how she was going to do it, but she was pretty sure she needed to wait until just before or just after graduation, since she didn't want anyone at Bath County High School to remember her as the girl who changed names in her senior year.

On Saturday, she went to the dojo early to talk to

Sensei. She hadn't planned out exactly what she would say to him, and hoped it would come to her when she looked him in the eye. He was alone when she got there. Students wouldn't begin to arrive for another twenty minutes or so. She went into the office.

"Emi-chan, it's good to see you, as always."

"Hi, Sensei," she said tentatively, almost sheepishly. She took a deep breath, let it out slowly, looked him in the eye and went on. "There's so much I have to tell you. Everything is different now. I don't know where to begin." Her voice quaked.

"Emily, what's wrong? What is it?"

"My dad is dead."

There, she'd finally said it. Someone else who knew him had heard it. Now it was a fact in the world. Tears formed in her eyes, trembled there for an instant, then rolled down her cheeks. It was now an inescapable fact for her as well. Up to this moment, she had been able to avoid confronting the reality of it, since it had been obscured in her consciousness by the blinding awareness that Yuki was her real mother, that she had not been abandoned. But now the full weight of the event came crashing down on her, and she began to feel ill, as if she would throw up. She staggered over to the wall, put her back against it and let herself slide to the floor.

"Oh, Emily," he cried out, and knelt beside her. "How? When?"

He stopped talking after a moment and just sat next to her. He had no comforting words. Just mute sympathy. They remained in that posture for several minutes, though it could have been days, or weeks, as far as she could tell. Students began to trickle in to the main room for class, and Sensei peered around the office door.

"I have to go out there in a minute. Will you be all right in here?"

"No. I've gotta do something. Meet me here late, say one o'clock, and I'll show you what happened."

He nodded and went out into the dojo. Emily slipped out through the front door once class started. No one noticed her, except Wayne.

She drove about twenty minutes east to the town of Goshen, to the Goshen Public Library. Her father had given her a thumb-drive containing a program for making encrypted web phone calls from a public terminal. He warned her to be careful about using any terminal that might be traceable to her, and not to use any location more than once, since he wasn't absolutely confident in the encryption program.

She was pretty sure Mr. Cardano and her mother would be in New Mexico by now, if they had made it there at all. She had fought every impulse to use the thumb-drive before now, not wanting to make them break cover before they had gotten dug in, so to speak. But the conversation with Sensei showed her exactly how much she needed to hear her mother's voice.

The library's terminals were in a glassed-in room at the far end of the first floor, and as luck would have it, the room was empty. With a little fiddling, she managed to launch the program and selected the first number it offered her. After a minute or two, it connected her, through a very circuitous series of digital diversions, to a disposable phone in Michael Cardano's pocket. After three rings, she heard his voice.

"George?"

"No, it's me, Emily. I need to talk to Yuki," she replied nervously.

She heard the stunned silence on the other end. He must not have expected her father would let her use the thumb drive. Yuki's voice came through the headphones next, and she practically melted to hear it.

"George?" Yuki asked uncertainly.

"No, Mom, it's me. Dad is dead." She blurted it out as if it were a hot coal in her mouth. Tears ran down her face, and she wondered how Yuki would take the news. The line went silent for several seconds. "Mom, are you still there?"

"Chi-chan, are you safe?" she cried out. "Where are you?"

On hearing those words, Emily felt a warm feeling rush over her. Her mother had used the pet name her father used for her. No one else ever called her that. Maybe no one else even knew about that name, or what it must refer to. But, of course, her real mother would know it, too. How much self-restraint had it required to keep from using it for all those years? In this, as in so many other things, Emily began to wonder at her mother's fortitude.

"Mom, I'm safe. Dad was wounded as we were leaving the estate. He died outside of Pittsburgh. Is it okay to say where I am on this connection?"

Yuki turned to Michael and asked. "As long as she's calling from a public terminal, yes," Emily heard him say in the background.

"I'm in Virginia. I've gone back to school."

"No, No, No! You have to come out here right away. What on earth are you thinking? You're not safe there. They'll find you. It's much too risky." With these words, she started sobbing, and Emily heard it.

"I'm sorry, Mom. But this is the only way. I can't run from those men for the rest of my life, always hiding, always pretending. I have to make a life for myself that isn't built on a lie, and I mean to do that here." Emily knew she was right, but she also knew her mother would never accept it. She heard Michael tell her mother they had to end the call in one minute. The pain was like nothing either of them had ever known before, to hear each other's voices, to have so much to tell each other, and to have so little time together.

"No, Honey. Please no. I can't afford to lose both of you. It's too much," Yuki sobbed out loud.

"Don't worry, Mom. I'm taking precautions, being real careful, the way Dad taught me," she said, trying to be reassuring. Yuki sighed audibly on the other end. "Dad gave me all the papers, the passports, the money. I've got a new place to stay, in town. And, Mom, I've got friends!"

She almost giggled as she said that last bit, still remembering the pain of their last argument about her social life, and how she'd stewed over her mother's words for days. What a relief to find out other kids wanted to be friends with her, that they could be fun, and that opening up to them, if only a little bit, wasn't nearly as scary as she'd expected. Who knows, maybe they had been fascinated by her all this time? Yuki didn't answer, but Emily didn't have time to consider the impact of her news.

"I've got one question, Mom. I need to know if I can trust Sensei."

She knew her mother had never really approved of Sensei, though she never quite cared before. Now she needed to know if that judgment concerned more than merely not wanting her daughter to be more girly, or lady-like or whatever. But if there was more to it, if Sensei had some involvement in the attack—as bizarre as that sounded—she would have to rethink her plans.

"Yes, you can trust him," Yuki said, after consulting with Michael, his voice echoing reassuringly in the background. Emily breathed a sigh of relief. "But don't tell him more than you have to."

"I'll call you again in a week. I love you, Mom!"

She cut the connection and waited as the program cycled through all the registries on the ISP's servers, erasing its tracks. Leaning back in her chair, arms stretched behind her head, Emily smiled through her tears, and reflected on the wonder of talking to her mother. She'd heard Yuki's voice, but it was her mother who wept with her.

Emily put the thumb drive in her pocket and walked back to the truck. On the way back to her new apartment, she stopped to eat at a little diner in Goshen, taking a booth in the back, away from the windows. While she waited for a soup and salad, she rested her forehead on the table and began to realize how exhausted the conversation with her mother had left her. She needed to rest up before meeting Sensei.

Back at the apartment, sleep came over her almost as soon as she lay down on the couch, and when she awoke the clock showed midnight. She changed into dark clothes and a jacket, put the rifle-scope in her pocket and went downstairs to roll the dirt bike out of the garage. With one foot on the left foot-peg, she pushed off and swung her leg over the seat, coasting the bike down the driveway and halfway along the block before popping the clutch to kick-start the engine. It was probably an unnecessary precaution, but the habit of keeping the noise of her departure to a minimum would not be denied.

She found Sensei in the parking lot of the dojo in street clothes: jeans and sneakers and a light jacket. It wasn't perfect camo, but it would probably do as long as they kept well concealed. He climbed on the back of the bike and they sped off out of town, cruising past the main gate to the spot along the edge of the forest where the stream emptied into the culvert under the roadway. They concealed the bike in the underbrush just inside the forest and picked their way along the streambed. If she had been by herself, she would have run the distance to the base of Promontory Rock. But this wasn't Sensei's forest, and she didn't think he would be able to move that fast in the dark.

She positioned them on the top of Promontory Rock and surveyed the estate under the light of a moon a little more than half full. She handed the rifle-scope to Sensei, and he gasped when he saw the gutted main house. But there was more to see this time: several large, dark SUVs with blacked-out windows parked in the drive, their headlights trained on the house. A number of shadowy figures in dark clothes could be seen carrying sacks and boxes out of the basement and loading them into the vehicles. Finally, three men wheeled out what looked like a large refrigerator and loaded it into a van.

"What is that?" Sensei asked.

"Looks like the big computer in the lab at school, only bigger, a server, or something."

"What the hell happened here?" Sensei growled. "Who are those guys?"

"I can't really tell from here. They're dressed like the guys who invaded the estate last weekend… but I think it's more complicated than that." Emily told him about the attack at the concert a few weeks earlier, and the plan to evacuate the estate that it triggered. "I don't know what happened to everyone else," she said, bearing her mother's warning in mind. "By the time I got here, it was just my dad, and men with guns—they looked like soldiers, sort of—they were everywhere. He fought them off and we escaped through the forest. But his wounds…"

He rolled over and looked up into the sky for a few moments, groaning with each breath. At least now, he understood Emily's distress and the extremity of her situation, and she hadn't revealed anything that might endanger her mother. They made their way down to the streambed and back to the road.

On the ride back to town, with Sensei hugging her from behind, she wondered what sort of conversation her mother must be having with Mr. Cardano. After that phone call, Emily knew she would have to tell him something, and since there was no one else to trust, or anyone left either of them trusted more, she would probably tell him everything her father had told her. How would he take the news, especially the parts that concerned her identity, and the nature of her grandfather's final project?

CHAPTER ELEVEN
A MEETING ON THE ROAD

School was closed the following Thursday and Friday for parent-teacher conferences. Of course, there would be no conference for Emily, nor was one needed, since she was a good student. As enigmatic as she appeared to her teachers, especially in the last couple of weeks, they could want nothing more from her as a student. She loved math and science, chemistry this term, but also history, and the teacher noticed her special curiosity about the history of Asian-Americans. He remarked to her once that it must be because she was partly of Chinese descent, and she didn't disabuse him of the error. Until recently, she shared the confusion.

The long weekend offered her the opportunity to insulate herself from a few more details of her former life. Early Thursday morning, she crossed the mountains to Harrisonburg, the next large town west of the Shenandoahs, and pulled the truck into an auto detailing shop to get a new coat of paint. A trivial change perhaps, but she figured subtle shifts like this might just provide a crucial margin of safety.

The one huge hole in her precautions was the fact that she insisted on going to school everyday as Emily Kane. Even if her family's enemies didn't know she was Yuki's daughter, if they simply took the trouble to inquire at the school, they would know immediately that she was George Kane's daughter. That in itself might make her seem worth pursuing, but it was a chance she was determined to take. She had to continue to be Emily Kane for a few more months, even as she laid the groundwork to become Michiko Tenno at the right moment.

"Forest Green," she said to the shop manager, imagining situations in which she might need to hide in the woods.

"Pinstriping?" he asked, and she shook her head. "My man, Hector, has a good eye, a real artist."

"Just the paint, thanks."

After a bit of chit-chat with one of the mechanics, she rolled the dirt bike out of the back of the truck and rode back to Warm Springs, taking a scenic route through Buffalo Gap, then across the mountains to Deerfield and south on Marble Valley Road to Goshen. The thrill of coursing through the wind at top speed made her shoulders tingle, autumn foliage in full color on perhaps the last weekend she could enjoy it, and the late morning sun setting the trees on the eastern ridgeline alight. She let her mind race on ahead, up and down the mountains on either side of the road. A few miles outside of Deerfield, she saw a pair of motorcycles in her mirror that seemed familiar, and remembered seeing a similar pair outside of Staunton on the other side of Buffalo Gap. She accelerated sharply, rounded a bend, and turned down a Forest Service road on the right to see what they would do.

It turned out to be a winding dirt and gravel road, a bit rutted on one side from recent rains. Hugging the left edge, she followed it south for a quarter mile, down a narrow valley between two ridges. As soon as she cleared the second turn, and before the motorcycles would be able to see her if they found the service road, she pulled off and sped up what looked like an old hiking trail. Stopping just below the ridge overlooking Marble Valley Road, under the cover of a large juniper, she cut the engine and watched the road. About a quarter mile past the Forest Service road, she spotted the motorcyclists next to a black van stopped in the road, apparently conferring.

If she was the topic of conversation, were these more of Meacham's men? She watched as they turned around and found their way to her turnoff. The van pulled on to the shoulder and waited while the motorcycles left her field of view. From her position, Emily could see both the van and the dirt road. After a moment, the motorcycles rode past the trail she had taken, and she wondered how long it would take them to realize she hadn't gone further down the road. Meanwhile, nothing stirred at the van.

She had a decision to make. It would be easy enough to evade these men, but then she wouldn't find out what they wanted with her. If they had first marked her in Harrisonburg, this might be the best course. But if they knew about her apartment over the Rincon's garage, or that she was attending school, then she was no longer safe, and neither were her friends. She could let them find her, take them on and see what she could find out about them. Though she hardly knew how to go about interrogating them, other than using pain-compliance holds. How many times had her father told her about his experiences in the military… and a recurring theme was the ineffectiveness of pain against trained soldiers.

It would be risky to engage them, but she had a substantial advantage in that they were likely to underestimate her. Also, she would want to make sure they didn't spot her from a distance. At close range, she might be able to control them, maybe prevent them from using a radio or a gun. But she had to take care not to kill them, since that would probably attract even more attention from whatever organization sent them. In the end, she decided it was more important to find out who they were and what they knew about her.

She scanned the Forest Service road and saw that the motorcycles hadn't returned yet. Then she looked down at the van and saw no activity there. "The moment is now," she muttered, and rolled the bike down the hill without starting the engine. She had to crash through some underbrush here and there, since there was no continuous trail on this side of the ridge. At the bottom, she left the bike behind some trees and watched the men in the van. She could see two in the front seats who appeared to speak only to each other without making any gestures to the back of the van, and hoped that meant there weren't any others. The direct approach appealed to her, maybe because it was her father's way, so she walked out of the woods, careful to stay in the driver's blind spot, crossed the road and tapped on the driver's window. Startled, he jumped in his seat at the noise, eyes wide and mouth open, staring at her, perhaps trying to decide whether to chat casually with a pretty girl on the side of the road, or burst out of the van and take her into custody. At last, he rolled down the window.

"You guys lost?" she asked pointedly.

Though he was probably not much more than thirty, that still seemed old to her. The man in the passenger seat made a move to get out, but the driver motioned to him to stay put. She had guessed right, there were no other men in the van. Bulges under their jackets told her they were armed, but they wore official looking clothes, jackets and ties, which suggested they weren't simply criminals. Perhaps something like a conversation was possible, but she felt the need to keep it brief, since the return of the motorcycles might upset the odd equipoise that hung in the air... and then serious violence might ensue.

"Look guys, I know you're following me. What the hell

do you want?" The driver said nothing for a moment, still dumbfounded. Finally, he figured out how to respond.

"I'm sorry, Miss, I can't disclose the details of an active investigation," he ventured, with obvious diffidence.

"An investigation. Good. Now who the hell are you? FBI? Let's see some ID," she demanded with a sneer, since she had a pretty good idea the FBI didn't work out of dark vans with guys on motorcycles.

"I can't disclose that, Miss," he replied. "But we want to talk to you about the events of a couple of weeks ago on Michael Cardano's estate."

"Fine. Let's talk. What did happen to the estate? Did you guys burn it down?" She wanted to put him on the defensive, maybe find out what he really knew about her before revealing anything.

"You were there, weren't you? Why don't you tell us?"

"Just who do you think I am?" she asked with a mocking tone.

"You're the chauffeur's daughter. You lived there. What did you see that night?"

"Who's asking? You gotta give something to get something," she said defiantly.

When he didn't respond, she turned and strode across the road toward the trees. The driver clamored out of the van with his gun drawn.

"Stop right there!" he yelled.

Emily turned to glower at him over her shoulder, and caught a glimpse of the other man getting out of the passenger side, gun also out. The driver took three long strides toward her, until his gun was only a few inches from her face.

"On the ground," he barked, as they stood in the middle of the road.

She looked him in the eye, saw a flicker of uncertainty, and ignored him. As she expected, he took his left hand off the gun and reached for her shoulder, probably thinking to pull her to the ground, and confident his gun gave him a commanding advantage. She let him pull her toward him, but instead of falling backwards, she pivoted toward him, slapping his gun hand across his chest, and glaring directly into his face until he flinched and averted his eyes. Before he could react, or even comprehend what was about to happen, she seized his wrist and elbow, twisting his gun hand down and around. When she pulled sharply upwards, he resisted, but her hands were stronger than he expected. Finally, the pain in his elbow became too great, and he had to allow himself to be bent over into an awkward crouch. The twisting movement accelerated and rather than merely being forced to kneel, he found himself flipped onto his back, his right arm bent into an extremely awkward pair of angles. She placed her foot on his neck, twisted the gun out of his hapless hand and pointed it at his chest.

When the second man came around the back of the van, he didn't expect his partner to be already disarmed and helpless. He raised his gun and rushed forward shouting "Drop the gun!" She tilted her head and looked at him with an insouciant smile, gave the driver's arm a slight twist with her left hand, and when he howled in pain, she hissed "Gun down."

They stared at each other for a brief moment, until she twisted the arm one more time and the first man howled, "Do what she says!" His partner eventually complied, though not without some consternation and a brief show of bravado.

"Whatever you say, girl," he said. "But you're asking for a world of trouble."

"Kick it over there, and sit down next to the van," she said.

A moment later, she stood over both men and demanded wallets and IDs. She found nothing informative in their pockets, no official credentials, and their personal information meant nothing to her. She threw their wallets and keys into the trees behind the van, then looked the driver in the eye and said, "I wasn't there when the attack happened. I don't know who did it. Don't bother me again, unless you have something to tell *me*." She turned to walk back across the road.

"Wait... wait, okay... you win. Three of our agents were killed that night. We found their burned bodies in an outbuilding, maybe a woodshed. We need to know what happened."

This was puzzling news, to be sure, even enough to fluster her, since it didn't quite fit in with the events she saw from the woods. But she couldn't contradict it without admitting she was there.

"I can't help you," she said, and began to walk away.

"Wait," he called out. "Here, take this." He tossed her a tiny phone with only one button. "Call, if you want to talk. The man who answers will be able to help you."

She looked at the phone skeptically for a moment, put it in her pocket, and stepped quickly back to her bike. Glowering back at the two men, she tossed their guns into the underbrush before speeding off down Marble Valley Road. She looked back a few times, but saw no sign of pursuit.

Emily knew what sorts of danger the phone might pose. Whatever else she did, she knew not to bring it home with her, since even if it wasn't tracking her now, she figured they could use it to track her as soon as she activated it. What's more, she had no idea what to say to whoever answered on the other end. She needed to talk this over with Mr. Cardano, and decided to ride down to the community college in Clifton Forge to use their library, since she didn't want to risk using a computer in the Goshen Library again.

Back in the stacks, in a deserted section of the library, Emily booted up the program on the thumb-drive at the first terminal she found. She selected the second number on the list the program presented to her, since Mr. Cardano would have destroyed the first phone already. He answered on the second ring.

"Emily, is that you?"

"Yes, Mr. Cardano. I have to talk to you. Is my mom there?"

"She's in the other room. Shall I get her for you?"

"No, not yet. I need to talk to you first," Emily said, and then told him about the meeting on the road, about the men in the van, and the phone they gave her. "Do you know who those men were?"

"Yes. They must have been Burzynski's men." Michael quickly explained who he was and guessed what he might want. He told Emily about her father's meeting with Porter, how he killed him and his men, undoubtedly in self-defense, and disposed of the bodies in the woodshed.

"If I call him, can I believe anything he says?"

"It doesn't matter, Emily. He has no information you want. He just wants to know if his men were killed by Meacham, and to find out what he wanted at the estate."

"I think I have to talk to him, no matter what. They'll just keep looking for me until I do."

"You're probably right," Cardano said. "But you must be careful what you tell him. Let him think his men were killed by the assault teams you saw that night, and that you don't know who any of those men were. You're just an innocent bystander who wants to know what happened to her father, okay?"

"Yes, I understand. Thank you, Mr. Cardano."

"Emily, from now on, please, call me Michael. You are an impressive young woman, and I am honored to know you," he said, in a grand gesture. She felt a little flushed.

"I'll call back tomorrow. Tell my mom I love her."

After she broke the connection, she pulled up the website for the university in Charlottesville on another terminal, and after examining some campus maps for a few minutes, she left the library and headed over to the mall across town. In an isolated corner of the food court, she pulled out the phone, and took a deep breath as she looked at its one button. No light or dial tone indicated its status. At length, she pressed the button, but still heard no sound. A few seconds later, a man's voice came out of the speaker.

"Hello, Emily," the man said. "I understand you have something to tell me about the events of the other night."

To hear her name used familiarly by someone she didn't know, and had no reason to trust, she found profoundly disturbing. But since she figured this was the effect he aimed to create, she decided not to conceal her revulsion from him.

"I've already told your men I wasn't there. What exactly is it you want from me?" she asked, in her best imitation of a petulant tone.

"Perhaps I can be of some assistance to you, maybe with finding out what became of your father."

"What happened to my dad? Where is he?" she demanded, with all the passion she could muster. She hated talking about her father in this way, bandying his memory about with people who she thought could not care less about him or her. But she imagined he would approve, if it gave her a useful advantage over her adversaries.

"Maybe we ought to speak face to face. I could come down to Goshen if you like," he proposed, and Emily tried to suppress a gasp, and hoped he was merely guessing. The thought that he might have been able to track her earlier phone call from the library in Clifton Forge unsettled her.

"No, someplace else," she said, in the defiant tone of a child, anxious to see if he would name Warm Springs next, and thereby reveal how much he knew about her living arrangements. But trying to get him to tip his hand was like fencing in the dark, and she had the distinct feeling he was more skilled at this kind of swordsmanship.

"You better tell me where you want to meet then," he said, pushing past her little test. She waited a moment before replying, hoping to create the impression that she had not had time to work out a place to meet in advance.

"Meet me at the university," she said, "on the patio outside Newcomb Hall, tomorrow at noon. Wear red plaid pants, I'll have an orange ball cap on."

She hung up without giving him an opportunity to argue. She removed the battery and sim card, wiped any fingerprints off the phone, wrapped it all in a napkin and smashed it under her shoe on the floor. Outside in the parking lot, she searched for any sign of Burzynski's men, any vans or motorcycles. She saw nothing, but as a precaution, she circled the entire mall parking lot twice before heading home.

CHAPTER TWELVE
OUT WITH THE GUYS

Just as Emily pulled into the driveway, she noticed Danny, Billy and Wayne sitting on the front porch, looking rather like they had spent the better part of the afternoon there. Though as soon as they saw her, they all came tumbling off the side and ran up to greet her.

"Hey, Emily! Where've you been all day?" Billy crowed.

"Emily, we've been wondering where you were. What have you been up to?" Wayne bellowed.

"Just running errands, guys. What have you been doing? Holding down the porch the whole damn day?" she snorted.

"You hungry, Em?" Danny asked. "How about we all go get some pizza down in Covington?"

Emily looked at him, her headed tilted slightly to one side, not quite sure what to make of the way he'd shortened her name. "That's what friends do, right?" she thought.

"Whoa, that's a great idea," Wayne blurted out, always ready for food of any kind.

"Yeah, let's make an evening of it. This is the weekend after all," said Billy. "Whaddya say, Em?"

"Yeah, that does sound good," Emily replied, not quite as surprised that he'd picked up on Danny's liberty with her name. "Who's driving?"

"I got my mom's SUV for the evening," Billy said.

"I'm gonna go upstairs and change. I'll be down in a bit," she said.

After a quick shower, she changed into one of Andie's outfits, grabbed a leather jacket and headed back down to the guys. She found Danny's mom talking with the boys when she got there.

"Don't you look nice, Emily," Mrs. Rincon said. "Keep these boys out of trouble, okay?"

"Don't worry, Mrs. Rincon, I'll take care of 'em."

The pizza place they finally found in Covington turned out to be a popular hangout, jammed with teenagers all looking at the same long weekend. The music boomed, and the conversation washed along beneath it like the tide, louder at moments, and quieter at others, to fit itself into the pattern of the music. The pizza was only so-so, Emily thought, but she felt that same peculiar synergy again, as she had at the concert, the same palpable paradox: even when they craved companionship, they remained somehow isolated from one another.

"It's a sort of human truth," she said, too quietly to be heard.

She leaned back into the cushions of the booth to observe her friends, and the kids in the booth opposite, and another group at a nearby table. The converse of that paradox struck her: in order to be together, they also had to be apart; even to have something of themselves to share, they needed to hold something back as well. The more intense the rite that brought them together, and the more entirely they tried to give themselves over to the group, the more resolutely they would hold something of themselves back. She imagined the extreme case, the bacchanalian revel in which the revelers lose themselves entirely. But the self they give to the revel is impersonal, generic, while the truly personal self is preserved entire and apart.

Teenagers in a pizza joint, they spoke of the same things that were on the minds of teenagers everywhere: cars, friends, school, college dreams, the urge to get away from home. Emily found she only shared an interest in some of these topics, and sat quietly listening to her friends' aspirations. Billy's parents wanted him to go to Charlottesville to study pre-med, but he just wanted to go somewhere and not get stuck in the track his father had taken.

"Pre-med would be okay for starters," he said. "But I definitely don't want to be a dentist."

"What do you want to be?" she asked.

"I don't know… just not a dentist. Maybe a veterinarian," he offered after a moment.

Wayne's mother wanted him to go somewhere, anywhere. She made a modest living as a real estate agent, but the interest income from an insurance settlement allowed them to live comfortably. She had no particular ambition for her son, and she probably spoiled him a bit. Emily knew his father had been an insurance salesman, who'd been killed in a car accident a few years ago, and for whatever reason Wayne just wanted to stay near home. She figured either he felt an urge to protect his mother, or to be protected by her. And it seemed natural, or at least inevitable, that he had no idea what he wanted to study.

Like Wayne, Danny was simply adrift. Emily expected he would go to some school, eventually. He hoped to get an athletic scholarship, since without one his parents probably wouldn't be able to afford the tuition. But he didn't seem able to lift his imagination beyond the practicalities of paying for college to decide what he wanted to study. Emily feared he would end up like those kids who never really study anything, the ones who go to school everyday, but never apply themselves. Did Danny just want to follow his friends to college and pretend to be a student? She hoped that wasn't true, but he seemed directionless whenever he talked about college. It occurred to her that he might be pre-occupied with the wish that his parents would get back together again, a wish she could sympathize with.

"What're you gonna do after graduation, Em?" Wayne asked.

She thought about it for a moment and realized she hadn't turned her mind to this question at all in the last couple of weeks. All her thoughts had been focused on survival, and on the loss of her dad, and having found her mom, and then about graduation. She was so focused on not allowing her parents' enemies to ruin her life that she'd hardly even been able to imagine what she wanted that life to look like. They all looked at her intently, waiting for a sign.

"I dunno. I'll probably travel around a bit over the summer, before school starts in the fall," she said cautiously.

"What schools you thinking about?" Billy asked.

Emily could have rattled off the usual list of schools, but she realized she had not been able to talk to her mother about any of this stuff. She knew her mother wanted her to go to college, study a science, be like her. Isn't that what all parents want? But she only knew vague generalities about what her mother wanted for her. Would she have to formulate her aspirations without any input from her?

"I dunno, really. I'm going up to Charlottesville to check out the university tomorrow. Maybe I'll end up there," she said blithely. The excitement this report produced in her friends caught her completely by surprise.

"Hey, I'd like to go too, Em," Billy burst out. "Whaddya think, let's make a day of it."

"Me, too," chirped Wayne and Danny almost simultaneously.

"It'll be like a mini road trip," Danny added.

The boys all laughed, but Emily doubted the wisdom of

letting them tag along. Of course, she couldn't let them anywhere near her meeting with Burzynski, but she figured it would be easy enough to lose them merely by insisting on checking out the library. Boys have little patience for that sort of thing, she knew well enough. But she'd also have to find a way to steer them to one of the other food courts on campus. "No, it's a crazy idea," she thought. "I can't let them tag along." It was one thing to risk her own life, but she couldn't bring herself to risk theirs, especially if they had no idea of the danger.

"Guys, I've got an errand in Harrisonburg in the morning," she offered, to discourage them. "Maybe I should just go alone. We can all go to Charlottesville another time." She could see they were crestfallen.

"There won't be another weekday off before Thanksgiving," Wayne said. "I don't mind going with you to Harrisonburg. We can meet up with you guys in the afternoon."

"We can all go to Harrisonburg," Billy objected. "What're you doing there anyway, Em?"

"I'm getting the truck repainted. It's supposed to be ready tomorrow morning," Emily replied evasively. "Plus there's other stuff I gotta do." She began to see how difficult it would be to extricate herself from the boys' plan. "Look, I have to leave before eight to get everything done, and I've got an appointment at the admissions office at the university at eleven thirty. Why don't I meet up with you guys at like one thirty by the library?" She knew they wouldn't like the sound of getting up that early… and she turned out to be right. Once that ugly detail emerged, they became much more compliant.

As they were leaving the restaurant, they happened upon a tussle in the parking lot. It didn't seem to have anything to do with them—just some tough kids from Covington High acting out. Emily scanned the parking lot to see if anything looked out of place. Had they been marked by Meacham's operatives? Or Burzynski's? Could this be some sort of setup? She didn't see any suspicious vans, or cars or motorcycles, no older guys in dark suits. She saw only teenagers, and breathed a sigh of relief.

In the time Emily spent scanning the surroundings, Wayne had waded into the middle of the brawl. As if by magnetism, he'd been drawn into it... or perhaps it was just one of the perks of being the biggest guy there. Emily watched as he got shoved a bit, and shoved back. Maybe she didn't need to intervene.

Then one guy tried to punch him in the face, and Wayne blocked... and just as he'd been trained to do, he followed the block with a short, quick strike to the chest. His assailant staggered back and crumpled next to a car. Everyone went quiet, and a stunned silence filled a long moment, until suddenly all the boys turned on Wayne, regardless of which side they'd been fighting on before. He was outnumbered, at least seven to one, so Danny and Billy rushed in to help. Standing together, the three of them made a formidable team. Wayne was huge, and pretty much immovable, and the other two were trained athletes, strong and quick. And they'd all had some karate training. They knew how to hit, how to block, and even how to take a hit.

They had one other thing in common: Emily was there. She knew they wanted to be brave in front of her, to show her what they could do, and it probably didn't hurt that they knew she could probably bail them out if they got into real trouble. Emily understood. She stood to the side and watched, figuring she owed them that much.

Out of the corner of an eye, she noticed a few other girls standing nearby, watching the scene, too. They glowered at her occasionally, and she supposed they were wondering if they should try to hassle her. "How different their feelings must be from mine," she thought, since she admired her friends for their courage. They entered the fight to keep people from getting hurt. But she guessed that these other girls had provoked the original brawl in the first place, and now watched with satisfaction at how easily they'd been able to manipulate the boys. The very fact that all of them had so quickly turned on Wayne showed they felt no deep commitment to fighting each other.

"What you looking at, bitch?" one of the girls snarled, clearly trying to provoke something. When Emily ignored her, the girl stepped toward her, trying to look tough.

"I said, what...," the girl started up again, by this time standing directly in front of her. Emily looked her in the eye darkly and cut her off in mid sentence.

"Don't you have anything better to do, honey?" she said contemptuously.

The girl reached up to grab Emily's hair, no doubt thinking there was no way this girl in her pretty clothes was going to be able to stand up to her. A quick glance at the other girls showed that this was the ringleader, the tough chick, out with her friends. Emily caught her hand, twisted it down, then up. The girl writhed in pain and sank down to her knees on the pavement, struggling not to cry. She tried to yell, "Let me go!" as loud as she could, but hardly any sound could escape her mouth through the pain. When the other girls tried to come to her aid, Emily glared at them and shook her head; they understood perfectly and retreated. Then she leaned over the girl, helpless beneath her, and hissed: "This will get a lot worse for you if you stay."

Eyes wide with fear and pain, the girl whimpered something inaudible and tried to squirm out of Emily's grasp. Finally, she released her and the girl tried to edge away without completely standing up. Emily took a threatening step toward her and growled in a feral voice, "Run." The girl jumped out of her way and scurried back to the restaurant, visibly shaken, and her friends followed along behind.

Preoccupied with their fight, the boys hardly noticed what transpired among the girls, but Emily was at last the only spectator left. She mused on the difference in how boys and girls fight. Boys fight for dominance, she thought, which means that at some level they understand that they must preserve their defeated enemy. Otherwise dominance will not have been achieved. But girls fight to injure or eradicate. They have no use for a defeated enemy, which makes them much more malevolent than boys, she concluded.

The boy Wayne originally punched in the chest finally recovered his breath and picked himself up from the pavement. He had a look of focused anger in his eyes, and Emily noticed the knife in his hand. When he worked his way around to Wayne's blind side, she moved to intercept him. Before he had a chance to react, a short kick to the back of his right knee crumpled him to the ground. As he went down, she grabbed his right wrist and twisted it out and away from his body. She wrested the knife from his hand and tossed it into a nearby dumpster, then released him with a sneer. He sprang up in anger and made a move to grab her, but Danny stepped between them and spat out, "Why don't you try me, tough guy?" Meanwhile, the other boys saw that the girls had gone, and ran back to the restaurant. The boy who had the knife spat on the ground and slunk away towards his friends. "I thought so!" Danny snorted triumphantly, and when they all looked at each other now that they had the parking lot to themselves, they laughed out loud for a moment, and then piled into Billy's SUV.

On the ride home, the boys regaled each other with accounts of their exploits. "Did you see how I blocked that guy?" Or "Did you see how I took care of that nasty looking dude?" "That was amazing how you dodged that guy's kick!" "Yeah, he almost fell over from missing me!" "I couldn't believe it when you blocked both those guys into each other!"

Emily noticed how they didn't think to vaunt over injuries or any pain they might have inflicted. They didn't seem to understand fighting in those terms, even though their adversaries clearly did. She knew there was no glory in hurting an adversary, only in defeating him, and she was pleased to see that they felt the same way. She'd only come to know these guys by chance, but they were all such fine young men. When circumstances pressed upon them, they looked inside to see what to do, and the guidance they discovered there was essentially good.

She recognized the character of people who do the right thing just because it *is* right, and it was little short of marvelous to her that they had found each other. She'd have liked to think it had come about merely by chance, but she couldn't help wondering if it reflected some sort of destiny, or perhaps just the unseen operation of their natural sympathies. They might as well have gravitated toward each other naturally, not randomly or magically.

Billy dropped off Emily and Danny around eleven, and then drove Wayne home. As she approached the stairs to her apartment, she became suddenly much more circumspect, and looked for any sign of intruders, but saw none. She went into the apartment and changed into a dark sweatshirt and sweatpants, and once the lights had gone out in the main house, she came back down the garage stairs with a sleeping bag under her arm. A dark spot in the backyard, behind a couple of overgrown rhododendrons, served her purposes, since from there she could see her staircase and the top of the driveway between the leaves, while remaining pretty much invisible herself. She thought of it as a precaution, just for one night, in case Meacham or Burzynski knew where she was, and after her encounter that morning, it felt necessary. She woke up at dawn, climbed the stairs, showered and prepared to face the day.

On the way back down, and before she could get to the dirtbike, Mrs. Rincon called from the backdoor of the main house to invite her in for breakfast. Emily placed her helmet on the counter and sat down in her landlady's kitchen to share coffee and toast with her... and learn how Danny had told his mother all about the plan to go to Charlottesville before he went to bed.

"Emily, thank you so much for encouraging him to go. He needs to start making plans soon."

"Oh, it's nothing, Mrs. Rincon. We're all going, Billy and Wayne, too."

It amused her to describe it this way, with such cavalier enthusiasm, since she had tried her best to discourage any of them from going with her. And to top it all off, here was Danny's mom thanking her anyway.

"I don't believe that for a second," Mrs. Rincon insisted. "If it weren't for you, I'm sure none of them would be going. You've been a very good influence on them all. I know Danny would kill me for telling you, but he's been much more focused on schoolwork since you moved in."

Mrs. Rincon practically beamed at her, which Emily found just a little oppressive. She knew the guys depended on her in lots of ways they perhaps were not aware of, and she probably depended on them, too, but she didn't want to be responsible for them beyond that. Once again, she found herself torn between wanting to release herself into the joys of normal social life, and feeling the need to hold herself aloof from her friends in order to confront a danger no one else saw gathering around her.

"You're being too kind. I'm sure he has his own reasons."

"Well, maybe. But I'm sure you figure in those reasons somehow. Can I get you anything else?"

"No, thanks," said Emily. "I've got to get on the road if I'm gonna meet those guys later. Thanks for breakfast!" she chirped, as she headed out the kitchen door.

In the driveway she hoisted her backpack on and swung a leg over the seat. Thinking about possible eventualities in her meeting with Burzynski, she'd packed a change of clothes and a few accessories. She also had the paperwork for the truck in her pocket, as well as a couple thousand bucks, with

149

an eye to the prospect of swapping the truck, or selling it to one of the mechanics at the shop in Harrisonburg, in case that became necessary.

She kicked over the engine and sped out of the driveway and down the street.

CHAPTER THIRTEEN
STUDENTS EVERYWHERE

By the time she arrived in Harrisonburg, at a quarter to nine, the auto detailer's shop was already a beehive of activity. She walked around back to the bays and saw Hector, the mechanic handling her truck.

"Is it ready?" she asked. "The green F-150."

"Oh, yes, it's definitely ready," Hector replied. "Come on, I'll show you."

He led the way back to the yard where seven or eight vehicles were lined up, all sporting shiny new paint. There was her truck holding down the end of the row, in Forest Green.

"That'll do nicely," she said, already picturing how it would blend into all sorts of hiding places. Hector motioned to her to look at something in the cab of the truck.

"Miss, we found this inside the rear bumper during the final inspection this morning." He handed her a small transmitter with a short pigtail antenna, and a magnetic base for attaching to the metal parts of a vehicle. "We weren't sure if you wanted us to re-attach it, and I didn't want to break it."

151

"Oh, yeah. That looks like one of my dad's anti-theft gizmos. I'm sure it hasn't worked for a while." She stuffed it into her pack.

"Well, he sure did a good job hiding it. I was surprised my guys didn't find it when they removed the bumper during the first pass. But there it was, plain as day when I checked it over this morning."

"The paint looks great," she said, trying to hide her relief. She hoped Hector's account meant Burzynski's men had installed it after she dropped the truck off yesterday, and might not know where she lived.

"Have you thought about my offer?" Hector asked. "I could really use a bigger truck, and yours is in pretty good shape."

"Yeah, I know. My dad was real careful about stuff like tune-ups and oil changes."

The day before, Hector had offered her a swap for his little four-wheel-drive pickup plus some cash. She put him off then, but the news of this transmitter gave her second thoughts. And she realized that if Meacham or Burzynski had done this, it would mean they had checked the registration, and her identity as Emily Hsiao was no longer safe. The little truck was barely big enough to hold her bike in the bed, but it had an extra panel in the tailgate that folded out to become a ramp. That would certainly come in handy... and it would just be a lot easier to conceal a little truck than a big one.

"I can up the cash to five hundred," he offered hopefully. It wasn't a good deal. His truck seemed to be in good mechanical shape, but the interior was chewed up and the radio was busted. To anyone else, those would have been decisive considerations, but to Emily they meant almost nothing.

"Let me drive it around the block to test it out," she said.

He handed her the keys and she drove off. In that end

of town, marked by warehouses and railroad sidings, she recalled seeing a large shipping complex with a lot of long-haul trucks backed up to a loading dock. She parked at one end of the lot and walked along the dock, pretending to look for someone in particular. On hearing a driver say he was heading out west that afternoon, she quietly attached the transmitter inside the front bumper of his rig, walked back to the little truck, and drove off.

On the way back to the auto shop she slammed on the brakes and skidded to a halt, then popped the clutch a few times, and decided it was in good enough shape, though the four-cylinder engine seemed a little underpowered to her.

"You have the cash and title on you?" she asked Hector when she got back. He went into the office to get it.

"You cover the cost of the paint on the F-150 and you've got a deal," she told him.

He winced at her demand, but finally accepted. It was still not a particularly good deal for her, but she had other considerations.

"Leave the plates," she said. "I'll turn them in for you later today. You can do the same for mine." As it happened, she didn't actually care what he did with those plates, connected as they were to a registration and identity she would likely never use again.

With her bike in the back, she drove directly to the DMV and settled all the paperwork for the new truck. A self-satisfied smile spread across her face for taking care of this loose end so efficiently. It wasn't even ten yet. One last task: before heading over to Charlottesville, she climbed into the back of the truck to inspect the bike for tracking devices. There aren't a lot of places to hide one on a dirt bike, but still, she wanted to be sure.

After the business with the transmitter, Emily became rather more preoccupied with disguising her trail. Instead of driving directly to the campus, she parked the truck at a shopping mall a few blocks away. A short ride later deposited her at the Rotunda, where she stowed the dirt bike, before tracing a circuitous path to the admissions offices, which were in the complex behind Newcomb Hall. Once there, she ducked into a restroom, changed into one of Andie's outfits, and pulled an oversized school-logo hoodie over everything. She tied her hair back into a low ponytail and put on a pair of large sunglasses. Camo complete.

In this guise, she walked around Newcomb Hall, familiarizing herself with the layout of the building and examining the crowd, looking for anyone who didn't fit in. Most of the people she saw looked like students. They carried backpacks full of books, and talked like high school kids, only cooler. A few older people could be seen here and there, custodians, kitchen staff, office workers, all easy to spot by their dress, as well as their demeanor. They seemed preoccupied with doing a job, or not doing it, which marked them off pretty obviously from the students. One last distinctive group she took to be the teachers. Older than the students, but resembling them in other ways: they dressed a bit more conservatively perhaps, but carried backpacks or satchels full of books, and were similarly oblivious to their surroundings.

No one Emily saw set off any alarms, but she wasn't deeply confident she could spot a trained operative. It was a relief to see that the students looked a lot like her. They dressed more or less like her, and didn't look significantly older. She could probably lose herself in a crowd here in a pinch. Since it was almost noon, she decided to go to the upper terrace to survey the patio for a man in red pants. A few students milled about, but she figured the real crowd would emerge when classes let out at noon. She began to sense that hers was a hungry vigil, and decided to go down to the food court for something to eat. It would be a good cover and make her look more like a student.

A few minutes later, she walked out of the food court carrying a salmon teriyaki bowl with rice, and a bottle of water. Lots of students buzzed about among the tables on the patio, which was still warm enough for eating outside, at least in the sunny areas; no empty tables remained. But along the edge on the far side she spotted an older man looking foolish and annoyed in red pants, sitting by himself. She walked up blandly, asked if he minded sharing the table, and sat down without waiting for an answer.

"Hello, Emily," the man said. "It's good to meet you finally."

"Those aren't plaid pants," she replied coolly.

"That's not an orange ball cap," he said in an aggressive tone.

"You're not the man I spoke to on the phone yesterday," she said decisively and stood up from the table. "I'm tired of playing games. Let me know when you guys are serious about talking." She turned to go.

"Wait… just wait…. He'll be here in a second," said the man in the red pants. A moment later, a tall gray haired man in a tweed jacket walked over and sat down, slinging a backpack full of books onto the table. He waved the first man away, and Emily realized Burzynski had come up with a similar idea about camouflage on a college campus.

"Well, it really is good to meet you, Emily," he said in a voice she couldn't help but recognize. "I've heard a lot about you."

"I don't know if the feeling is mutual," said Emily. "Where's my father?" she asked as urgently as she could.

The man examined her very closely, as if he were trying to read her, and she didn't feel her sunglasses presented any obstacle to his gaze. She took them off and stared directly into his eyes, intent on letting him see the full depth of her irritation with him.

"I don't know yet. But maybe we can still help each other," he said, which mollified Emily for the moment. At least he hadn't lied to her… yet.

"I can't help you… and I don't know why I should even

try. How do I know it wasn't you who burned down my home?" she asked pointedly.

"Well, it wasn't. But I don't know how to convince you if you won't take my word for it," he said. He took a deep breath before continuing. "But, okay, I'll go first. I'll trust you. We found the burned bodies of three of my agents at the estate. We don't know how they got there or why they were killed. But they were supposed to meet with Michael Cardano earlier that day in DC." Emily gave an audible gasp for his benefit. "So you *do* know something," he said. "Were you there?"

"No!" she said vehemently. "Well, not exactly. I was camping in the woods behind the estate. My dad was supposed to try to find me. It's a game we play." Burzynski couldn't conceal a wistful smile. "From where I had set up camp, I could see the estate buildings, and I was watching for my father with binoculars. I didn't see him come home." She tried to simulate a catch in her voice.

"What else did you see?" he pressed.

Emily gulped and said, "I saw a lot of shooting, and then the house was on fire. I didn't see how it started. There were at least two groups of people. Some guys in suits were shooting from the area around the house. A whole lot more guys in black military style uniforms coming out of the woods on the north side were shooting back. I didn't wait around to see how it ended."

"How were you able to see the guys in the black uniforms at night?" he asked warily.

"It was a full moon that night, and the damn house was on fire! There was plenty of light," she replied testily.

"Sorry, I just had to be sure."

"Great! You're testing me. You obviously have nothing to tell me. There's nothing more I can tell you. Unless you find my dad, please leave me alone," she said angrily. She stood up, as if to go.

"Wait. Don't go just yet." He paused and looked her up

and down. "You're holding something back." She stood silently, wondering what he was thinking of. "You must know what happened to Cardano and the rest of the estate staff," he continued. "Were they there during all this?"

"I have no idea. By the time I was watching, there was no sign of them. There's still no sign of them. I'm on my own, trying to hold things together, and I don't need you bothering me anymore. You obviously have no information for me," she said, now in genuine anger.

"I'm sorry, I really am. I'll be in touch if I find out anything about your father," he said, as he stood up and abruptly walked off.

Emily watched him for a while, but decided not to follow, since she wasn't likely to find out anything about him that Michael couldn't simply tell her, and it seemed more important to preserve the impression that she was naive. But what impression did *she* have of Burzynski? He didn't seem deceptive, and he didn't say anything she knew to be a lie. Also, his sympathy with her plight seemed genuine, but she had to remind herself that he was trained in the art of deception. He may just have been better at lying than she was at detecting his lies.

Back in Newcomb Hall, the crowd of students had thinned out a bit. She went into a quiet restroom on the second floor to modify her outfit, on the off chance Burzynski's people were still tracking her. She took off the hoodie and stuffed it into her backpack and pulled out a sleek leather jacket to wear over one of Andie's outfits. Looking very stylish, a quick check in the mirror, a few final adjustments, and she noticed a tall, blonde woman enter behind her. Too old and too focused to be a student, probably not a member of the faculty either, for analogous reasons; she looked very fit, as if she had been through a rigorous training program.

Emily turned to leave, and the woman reached out to her shoulder as if to squeeze by in a confined space. It might have passed for an innocent gesture, but for the fact that the restroom was quite roomy. A glint of something shiny, metallic, in the woman's hand caught her eye, and she acted on a quick, almost instinctive impulse: a quick, upward block of the wrist and a sharp blow to the solar plexus. The woman staggered backwards several steps, then gathered herself to lunge once more at Emily, this time with no attempt to conceal her aggressive intentions. Now the needle in her hand was easy to see—the woman held a syringe and meant to inject her with something. Emily slapped the hand towards the woman's own chest, kicked her quickly in the right knee, and as she fell to the floor kicked her a second time, hard, on the side of the head, sending her spinning into the corner of an open stall, face down. Emily leapt on top of her, and controlled the hand with the syringe by twisting the wrist back and up behind her.

"Who sent you?" Emily hissed into her ear.

The woman, groggy and disoriented, didn't answer.

"What's in the syringe?"

Again, no answer, but she groaned from the pain in her wrist and elbow, and probably the throbbing in her head, too. This woman was very tough, and Emily felt the struggle to conceal how much pain she was experiencing.

"Fine," Emily said. "Let's stick it in you and find out." Emily moved the needle closer to the woman's ribs.

"No! No, no, no, please, no," she pleaded, suddenly wide-eyed and alert.

"Who sent you?" Emily asked again.

"I can't tell you. They'll kill me," she pleaded. Emily gave the wrist a slight further twist. "I can't..." A single tear ran down her face, and Emily jabbed her slightly with the needle. "No! please, don't kill me."

"What's in it? Poison?"

"Yes," she admitted.

"Who sent you?" she hissed once again. "Don't worry. I won't tell anyone you told me," she added with a sneer.

"I can't..." Emily jabbed her a little deeper. The woman let out a muffled shriek. Tears now streamed down her cheeks. "Don't kill me. You're not a killer. You can't do this."

"Why not? You had no hesitation about sticking it in me."

"You're right," she confessed, and went limp. "I'm sorry." The woman took a breath and uttered the name Emily already knew well enough: "Meacham."

"Why?"

"He doesn't want you talking to Burzynski."

"I don't *know anything*. That's what I told that other guy. Why can't you people leave me alone," she said in genuine exasperation. "How did you find me here?"

"We followed Burzynski."

"How many are with you?"

"Two men, downstairs."

Emily removed the syringe from the woman's hand, squeezed it out into the toilet and threw it across the floor. The woman breathed a sigh of relief, until Emily twisted her on to one side, pulled her face upwards and stared into her eyes for a long moment. She flinched, terror written across her face.

"You came here to take my life. I let you keep yours. Don't try me again," Emily whispered into her ear. Then she stood up, picked up her pack and walked out of the restroom, and breathed out her own relief at not finding anyone waiting outside.

~~~~~~~

The woman lay still on the floor for a few minutes, gathering her thoughts. A trained, professional operative, she knew how to handle herself in a fight; she'd faced fearsome adversaries, killed men and women, and no longer remembered how the pang of conscience felt. But this time hadn't gone like all those others. Once the pain faded, she mainly felt anger—with herself, with Meacham, with everyone—and shame. A callow teenager had deflected her attack effortlessly, thrown her aside like a rag doll. She never had a chance.

Strangely, the one person she wasn't angry with was the girl. It might have provided some consolation to think she was a trained professional, and considering the magnitude of her skills, and the fact that she seemed completely unflustered by the attack, it wouldn't have seemed unreasonable to anyone else. But when she looked into the girl's eyes, she didn't see a pro. At the bottom of those black eyes, she saw a placid, innocent spirit, and a profound sense of shame welled up inside her, something she hadn't felt in years. If that were all she'd seen, it would have been impossible to imagine any purpose killing the girl could serve. The moral repugnance of what Meacham had ordered her to do began to stink in her nostrils.

In that same moment, jammed between a toilet and the tiled wall, she'd glimpsed something else in the girl's eyes, a strange and familiar spirit. But the spirit she remembered was far from placid. If anything, she'd have called it cruel, dangerous, violent… even murderous. Somewhere, at the bottom of the girl's eyes, she sensed it, and it frightened her, not only because this time it took the form of a quiet fury, but also because of the dimensions it assumed. Like a storm that hides behind a calm, the hairs on your arms bristle at the electricity that gives it away, an unimaginable force seemingly held in perfect equilibrium. It was an intoxicating combination, and terrible.

She scraped herself off the floor, one hand on the toilet until she was sure she could stand—an impulse to vomit gripped her momentarily—and staggered over to the sinks to throw some water in her face. The mirror showed a red mark under one eye that would shade into a purple bruise in a few hours, and a long scrape that caught the side of her nose and mouth. She touched a lump on top where her head had contacted the base of the toilet.

"That's bad," she muttered. "Have to do something before it gets any more visible."

Failing to complete the mission was bad enough, but if the rest of the team saw the signs of the beating she'd taken… well, the consequences weren't worth thinking about. The scene could still be salvaged, even if the mission couldn't, though she'd begun to consider giving herself a new mission.

Until now, the assignments had always come from Meacham, and she didn't ask any questions, even though she had long been aware that both Meacham and Burzynski were operating outside any lawful authority, each making a bid for power in the covert operations community. Agents like her had gone along for the ride, in part for the thrill, but mainly because they had their own ambitions to gratify. Whatever else she'd learned when that girl's foot contacted the side of her face, she no longer knew what ambitions of her own the current trajectory of her career served.

"Bring the body-bag," she growled into a radio in the purse she'd retrieved from where it had ended up under the sinks. At the bottom of her bag, she found the silencer and twisted it onto the end of a Ruger .22, then reached up to disable the light fixtures above the entry door. The plan had been to zip the girl into a body-bag and send it down a trash chute at the end of the second floor hallway to be retrieved later. When the knock came, she pulled the door open, careful to keep her face in the shadow.

"I put her in the janitor's closet," she said, tipping her head in that direction, and holding the Ruger semi-auto behind her hip. Two men in dark suits and close-cropped haircuts stepped past her.

"What happened to the lights?" one asked.

"Tactical advantage," she muttered, and when they turned to look in the closet, she put two rounds in the back of each head. "You guys are so fat," she groaned, and shoved them into the closet, then paused to collect the empty brass.

~~~~~~~

Looking over her shoulder the whole way, Emily walked to the other end of the second floor hallway, down a back staircase and then turned towards the food court. She spotted two men in dark suits loitering conspicuously by the main staircase, and froze for an instant, until one of them put a hand to an ear, and then motioned the other one to follow him upstairs.

"Meacham's guys," she said, and kept on walking.

Outside the front entrance, she crossed over to the Admissions offices in an adjoining building, picked up brochures and application forms, and found a moment for a conversation with one of the admissions counselors about various programs offered in the history department. Even Emily was surprised at how easily she could shift gears: one moment a death-struggle with an assassin, the next a convivial chat about college possibilities.

A brisk walk across campus brought her to the library a good fifteen or twenty minutes before the boys were likely to get there, which gave her time to find a terminal nestled in a lonely spot among the third floor stacks and call Michael to discuss the events of the morning. He was stunned by the news, but as horrifying as the attack was, it suggested Meacham either did not know about the mutation, or more likely had no idea of Emily's relationship to Yuki.

"There's probably cause for relief in that," he said.

"Please don't tell my Mom, okay?"

He grunted and said, "She's right here. I'll put her on."

Yuki fumbled with the phone and gushed at her for a few minutes, desperate to know every detail of her life, every desire, every sorrow, every joy, and Emily knew there'd be no way to satisfy her mother, or herself for that matter, in the few minutes they had left before she'd have to end the call. But one subject might be important enough to both of them.

"I'm calling from the university library in Charlottesville, Mom. I came to check it out and to get admissions materials." The silence that followed showed her just how much she needed her mother. The questions, when they came, burst out one after another, maybe faster than she could process.

"Is that where you want to go? How will you live? What will you study? And your clothes…"

As she listened, Emily knew there were a thousand other things that would need to be sorted out, and that she wouldn't be able to think of most of them without her mother's help.

"Slow down, Mom. I don't know. I just started trying to figure all this stuff out."

Of course, she did know one thing, which she didn't want to say yet, namely that she wouldn't study chemistry, as her mother had. But how to break that news to her, she hadn't quite figured out.

"Honey, we have to talk through all of this. There's so much to consider."

"Mom, we're running out of time."

"It's not fair, Chi-chan. There has to be a way…"

The two of them stretched out the call as long as they dared, and Emily promised to call again soon before removing the thumb-drive.

A few minutes later, after she'd had a chance to process the events of the morning, and to breathe a bit, she pushed through the heavy glass entrance doors and found the guys waiting for her, lounging across the front steps of the library. Although they'd enjoyed wandering around campus for the last hour, looking at dorms, the gym, the main quad outside the Rotunda, they were pretty bored by this point. More urgently, Wayne looked hungry.

"Hey, guys. How long you been here?" she asked,

relieved to be able to put the events of the last hour or so out of her mind.

"Not long," said Danny. "How about you? Did you talk to the admissions people?"

"Yes," she said truthfully, and glad not to have to lie anymore. "Plus, look at all the stuff they gave me," she crowed waving a large envelope in front of them.

"Lemme see," said Billy, reaching for the envelope.

"I'm hungry," moaned Wayne. "Anyone feel like eating?"

"Me, too," said Danny.

"The food in the student center sucks," said Emily. "But the Admissions people told me about a Greek place a couple of blocks this way."

"Let's go," roared Wayne, and off they went.

Nothing could be better, as far as Emily was concerned, than to get some distance from the part of campus where Meacham's people had been. Michael was probably right that the attack meant he didn't know she was Yuki's daughter. She wished she could believe he didn't know what her living arrangements were, or even that she was trying to finish high school. At least, she had no evidence on this point, just a good deal of fear and confusion. She had more confidence that Burzynski didn't know, though not enough to dispel all her anxieties.

They ate Greek and middle eastern food, and then bummed around the big city for a few hours. They were all quite impressed with how bright and shiny the city seemed compared to Warm Springs or Goshen. For the moment, at least, the meaning of going away to college took on a specific, concrete significance for each of them, even Danny. College meant independence, freedom, life in an exciting new place.

Later, Emily collected her bike and her new truck, and headed home. Exhausted by the time she got there, she fell soundly asleep almost immediately.

CHAPTER FOURTEEN
THE BIG GAME

Well, maybe it wasn't the "big" game. To be precise, it was really just another game, an away game, down in New Castle, against the Craig County High School Rockets. But Wayne wanted to go see it, and Emily thought it might be good to see her friends in action. She'd never attended a football game before. Of course, Wayne went to all the home games, and she could tell he really wanted to explain all the delicious details of the game to her. When Billy heard she was coming, he got her a Bath County High School Chargers football shirt. It was bright orange, and Emily wondered what she could wear with it. This was all new to her, not just the football game, but also wondering how to match clothes in an outfit. In the end, she decided just to wear it under her new UVA hoodie with some old cargo pants. In other words, back to her old style camo... except for all the orange.

Emily picked up Wayne around ten. Because of the long weekend, the game would be held a little earlier than usual, at noon. The ride to New Castle took about an hour and a half, since she chose a route that took them on winding mountain roads through the Jefferson National Forest. The trees had begun to lose their autumn colors, but it was still a glorious landscape.

She knew the roads back here pretty well, the trails less so, since she'd explored much of this area with her father the previous summer. They hiked back here for weeks, one of their more rigorous "survivalist" trips. They brought no food or water with them, just sleeping bags, some empty bottles, the usual camp tools and a slingshot. Emily had wanted to bring a bow, but her father said no, claiming it would require a special license and he didn't want to take the trouble. Of course, she knew that wasn't the real reason. He had a Sportsman's License already; he always had one no matter what. She also thought it extremely unlikely a Ranger would ever find them back in the woods. He just wanted to make her learn how to use the slings. She got to be pretty good with both kinds, though she preferred a sling to the slingshot. She didn't manage to bring down any game with either one, but she got good enough to hit a stationary target from fifty feet, even with the sling. One side effect of this training: she tended to notice little round rocks on the ground. When she checked her pockets at the end of a day, she often found one or two, even if she couldn't recall picking them up. The best, she thought, were about the size of a peach pit, though rocks about the size of a chicken egg would go further in the sling.

Wayne rambled on about the rules of football the whole way down. Apparently, each team is really composed of two separate teams that take turns wrestling their opponents for control of the ball. That part sounded dreary enough, but it seemed likely that every once in a while, one player would break out from the melee with the ball and everyone else would chase after him, trying to bring him down. This might prove to be quite exciting for everyone involved. Running away with the ball, she gathered, was Danny's role on the team. Another possibility was that someone might back away from the crowd and hurl the ball to a teammate running in the other direction. Wayne explained that it was Billy's job to see that the other team did not succeed in this effort. Emily had no deep interest in the trivialities of this arcane game, but a keen interest in seeing her friends prove themselves on a suitable field of glory.

In this case, the field was on the south end of town, a

couple of blocks from the school. There were no stands, just a big open field ringed by trees. Most people brought folding lawn chairs or blankets and watched the game from the sidelines. About four hundred people were in attendance, mostly from New Castle, but several dozen Bath County supporters had come down as well, and were mainly clustered on one side of the field, behind the benches where their team sat, almost all of them wearing orange. Emily fit right in with this group. The team arrived about an hour early in a couple of school buses, along with a small marching band and cheerleaders. The bands from each school got to perform before the game and briefly at half time. Emily found it charming that the game provided an occasion for all sorts of displays of student interests, though the cheerleading squad was perhaps a bit more mystifying. They wore bright orange outfits more or less coordinated with the uniforms the team wore, and carried orange and black pompoms as well as enormous colored cones. At various breaks in the game they would yell slogans through the cones and perform intricate gymnastic stunts. Their athleticism was impressive, though oddly derivative, and Emily couldn't fathom its purpose. She supposed that was true of the football game itself, too. But at least the game involved a struggle with opponents, however contrived it might really be, which both sides took very seriously. In it, there seemed to be an opportunity to achieve something noteworthy, perhaps even to be justly celebrated for it by the people watching.

Wayne had brought a couple of lawn chairs for them to sit in, which he placed a bit to one side of the field. While he was setting up the chairs, and chatting with other kids, Emily wandered over to the refreshment stand and got a couple of sodas and three hot dogs, two for Wayne and one for her. By the time she returned, Wayne had become the center of the contingent from Bath County, about fifteen teenagers. They all looked familiar. Emily knew some of their names, but she didn't really know them personally. She sat down next to Wayne and handed him his hot dogs. He wolfed the first one down in two bites—"Thanks, Em"—and then paused to contemplate the second one. She took a couple of little bites of hers. It wasn't exactly the taste treat she had been led to expect so she got up to go back to the stand for more condiments.

As she walked away she heard a lot of chatter and even a couple of howls. Looking over her shoulder, she saw Wayne with a blushing big smile on his face playfully push a couple of guys away. She smiled as she thought about it, since she knew Wayne was not often the center of social attention. He obviously enjoyed being seen with her, and she just liked being around such a big, kind soul. She expected some innocent gossip to result from this afternoon, and she didn't mind, since she'd never given a fig for anyone's opinion of her before, and had no intention to start caring now.

Maybe the gossip even played some important role in bringing kids together, and apart. Like a game of "telephone," idle social chatter seemed to her like a way to see yourself in the social world through the eyes of others. It could be harmful or harmless, she supposed, but not simply because it was true or false, since it was always sort of false, as all projections of one's inner life onto the social world must be. But it also provided a means of developing and unfolding yourself, of discovering new possibilities. So she didn't mind that the other kids might draw incorrect conclusions about the true dimensions of her relationship with Wayne, or that he obviously took no trouble to disabuse them of their error. Perhaps it even amused her. She liked Wayne.

Still, it did surprise her how many kids wanted to say her name, to ask her questions, to tell her what they thought about all kinds of things. She enjoyed their attention and tried to reflect it back toward them, asking about them, about their plans, their hopes and desires. She rehearsed her generic plan to go to college somewhere, but tried not to say too much.

"Aren't you the social butterfly?" a girl said to her once the game started and everyone's attention had turned to the field. "You're Emily, right?"

Emily knew exactly who Wendy Williams was, since she'd been watching the goths for a while, comparing herself to them, wondering if she ought to fit in with them.

"Yeah."

"I'm Wendy."

"I've seen you around school," she said, before catching herself staring at Wendy's nose ring. She dressed much like Emily used to, though in more somber colors and a lot of dark makeup.

"I was surprised to see you arrive with Turley, but I must say you make a cute couple."

Should she resent the presumption of this remark, or was it just the sort of banter friends engage in? Emily wasn't certain, but decided to play along.

"You and your friends go to a lot of games?" she asked, nodding to a group of goths hovering by the refreshment stand, all dressed in black. Wendy glanced over at her friends and scowled, perhaps involuntarily, or so Emily thought.

"Football is so boring. I only come for my little brother, 'cause he's on the team."

It didn't take long to see through Wendy's pretense. She made a big show of not being interested in whatever happened on the field, but it was easy to see she very much enjoyed the occasion, even if she pretended to be above it all. The paradox fascinated Emily—another girl who'd pushed herself to the margin of social life, but still longed to be included, even if she couldn't admit it to herself.

Wendy was smart and, under the goth gear, probably pretty, but trapped in a rather self-defeating form of social behavior. As far as Emily could tell from one conversation, she defined herself almost entirely by what she disapproved of, rather than by anything she actually wanted to accomplish. But Emily craved a normal social life, and to extricate herself from the web of deadly intrigue that had engulfed her family, which was her current excuse for not having been able to articulate any genuinely specific goals of her own.

"Everybody must think I'm just like her, at least before I started wearing Andie's clothes," she thought, and it occurred to her that it might be worth getting to know Wendy a little better.

The lawn chairs proved mostly superfluous during the game, since everyone stood along the sidelines in groups to cheer their team on, including Wendy, Wayne and Emily. Danny had a frustrating day on the field, tackled before he could go anywhere on almost every play, while the other team seemed to run all over their defense. On one play toward the end of the first half, Danny managed to break free from the scrum. He burst through the left side, pushed one defender aside, ran straight over another and went the length of the field for a score. Everyone in orange went wild, even Emily, and Wendy, too. He had two more long runs in the second half and scored once more.

Billy struggled in the first half against taller players who could catch balls thrown over his head. But he was quite a bit faster and didn't let anyone past him with the ball. In the second half, he stepped in front of a receiver and intercepted the ball. Later, he scooped up a fumble and ran it in for a score. Wayne cheered louder than anybody on that play, and when Billy saw Emily on the sideline, he made a mock-ceremonial bow in her direction.

Wendy noticed and teased her: "I had no idea you were so popular with the football team." Emily laughed and smiled, but said nothing.

In the end, unfortunately, her friends' heroics were in the service of a losing cause. Craig County High won by two touchdowns, and they did it with all the authority of a bigger and faster team. But at least there were a few highlights the Bath County contingent could console themselves with. Of course, Emily hardly noticed the final score at all. Sure, somebody won and somebody lost, that was inevitable, but it wasn't what really mattered in her mind. The game was just an occasion for her friends to grapple and to achieve. The fact that they were facing a bigger, stronger opponent only made their successes that much sweeter. As she saw it, everyone who played that day forged a little bit of character, developed themselves in the struggle, and were that much the better for it.

Afterwards, while Wayne congratulated the guys over by the benches, Wendy plumped down in his chair.

"Emily, how come we've never hung out before? What's it been, like three and a half years and I barely know you."

"I've been kind of a loner. I hardly know anyone," Emily replied wistfully.

"Yeah, right!" Wendy snorted. "Everyone here knows you, or wants to."

"So I noticed. I was kind of surprised by that myself."

"We should go do something one of these days. What do you think?" she asked.

"Yeah, sure. I was thinking of going for a ride up in these mountains tomorrow. You want to come along?"

"I'm not really a nature person, if you know what I mean," Wendy hedged.

"It'll be fun, you'll see," Emily persisted. "I'll pick you up at ten, okay?"

"Yeah, sure. Why not?" Wendy replied uncertainly, perhaps a little worried about what she'd gotten herself into.

On the ride back to Warm Springs, Wayne could hardly stop crowing over Danny and Billy. He was completely taken by their exploits. The only other thing he could talk about was how much smaller this new truck was. In fact, it was a little tight on him.

"I liked your old truck better, Em," he ventured. "It fit me better."

Emily laughed. "This one's better for going off road," she said, only half seriously.

One glance over at him showed her how tightly he was packed in on his side, and when she smiled, he gave her one of those looks that said he was well acquainted with all the ways an ill-fitting world might pinch. They both laughed. He had a way of communicating with facial expressions that just seemed to strike a chord with her. Hardly anyone got Wayne the way she did.

As they passed through Covington, Wayne persuaded her to swing by an ice cream stand for a snack. He got a big cone with sprinkles, and she got a fruit sorbet. They parked in the library lot by the river and sat down on a bench. From that vantage they could see past some empty fields across the river, to the mountains in the distance. Wayne was very fond of rivers and lakes. He didn't want to get wet. He just liked being near large bodies of moving water, and sometimes speculated that the evaporation cleared his sinuses. Emily figured he had a liquid soul, flexible and soft, no hard edges, but still capable of great forcefulness.

"Tell me the truth, Emily," he began in a serious tone. "Do you really know what you're gonna do next year?"

"Wayne, I'm not even sure about next week." In saying this, she spoke truthfully, even more than Wayne could possibly realize at the moment.

"Me neither," he confessed. "But you seem so together, like you've got everything under control."

"I know I'm going to college, but I don't know much more than that. I may even end up taking a year off first. The one thing I know is that I can't stand still."

This was to speak as candidly as she thought she could risk. Wayne's anxieties about college were almost a perfect mirror image of hers, she thought: she had to keep moving to create a safe future for herself, while Wayne only wanted to stay safe at home. Going away to college terrified him, and she only feared staying put too long, of letting her pursuers catch up to her. But she had to stay put, to finish high school, in order to move on. The irony of her predicament reminded her of those Chinese finger traps, if you try to pull your fingers out they only squeeze more tightly. The only way out involves pushing your fingers further into them.

"I think I want to wait a little bit, too," Wayne said with relief. "My mom keeps pushing me to do the applications, but I've got no idea how to choose. And how the hell is any school gonna want me?"

"Come on, Wayne. Don't be ridiculous," said Emily. "Lots of schools'll want you. It's not about who you are right now. Just tell 'em who you *want* to be. That's what they want to know."

"I don't know what I want, Em," he replied. It would be hard not to see how much distress he was in.

"Don't worry, big guy, it'll come to you," she said with a little laugh. "There's still plenty of time to figure it out."

She looked him in the eye as she spoke, and Wayne had never looked so directly at her before. Of course, he had long been dazzled by her, was perhaps almost afraid of her. But now, at the bottom of her black eyes, he saw a deep reservoir of human sympathy. He also saw something darker, that he recognized from the dojo. It gave him a bit of a shiver, but in the end only confirmed the sympathy he felt, and it had a remarkable calming effect on him.

"Thanks, Em," Wayne said with a deep smile.

At times, he had indulged the fancy that he had a crush on her... until now. He found her beautiful, exciting, cool. How could he not be infatuated? But what he saw in her eyes was deeper than that. He didn't quite know how to articulate it, but on some level he understood that a crush was a ridiculous misapprehension of what Emily had come to mean to him. Friend was the closest word he had for what she really was, and he thought that she may well be the most important friend he would ever have. But that meant a confession was in order.

"Those guys at the game assumed we're a couple… and I didn't set 'em straight, Em. I'm really sorry. That was just stupid… and unfair to you." His voice quaked slightly as he uttered the last few words.

"Yeah, I noticed that," she replied, and he cringed a little. "But I don't mind that stuff. That's what friends are for," she added with laugh that seemed to reassure him.

When they got to Wayne's house that afternoon, his mom was watching from the porch, waiting for them to return. Wayne turned to Emily and said "She's gonna want to meet you. I hope you don't mind."

Emily got out of the truck and walked over to the porch, with Wayne following behind. "Mom, this is my friend, Emily," he called out.

"Hi," Emily chipped in. "It's good to meet you."

Mrs. Turley said nothing for a brief moment; perhaps she seemed almost stunned. For the last few weeks, all she'd heard from her son was "Emily this" and "Emily that." She knew he was infatuated, but she had no idea the girl would turn out to be so exotic looking. Her mind went all fuzzy for a moment, until Wayne gestured to her to speak and she recovered herself.

"It is so good finally to meet you, Emily," she blurted out. "I've heard so much about you. Would you like to come in for some tea?"

~~~~~~~

Emily chatted with Mrs. Turley for about an hour, and it was almost too much for Wayne to bear. The prospect of his mother saying something to embarrass him harrowed his soul. Of course, his discomfort tickled Emily. But as it turned out, his mom was too busy gushing over Emily to remember any embarrassing stories about her son.

After Emily left, Wayne finally sat down with his mom and told her of his anxieties about college. "I don't know what I want to do, Mom. How can I even fill out an application?" She knew he was anxious, but she also knew he needed to get away from home.

"Honey, you can figure that out once you're there. You don't need to have your whole life planned out in order to go. Just think of it as an adventure."

"That's sort of what Emily told me." Mrs. Turley smiled.

"You should see more of that girl," she said with a tear in her eye.

"Mom," he replied in mock exasperation, "I already see her practically everyday in school and at the dojo. She's like my best friend."

A realization suddenly dawned on her. "You mean *she's* the girl from the dojo you guys are all afraid of? But she's so sweet... and pretty." Wayne grinned.
"Yeah, She's *that* girl."

JACQUES ANTOINE

CHAPTER FIFTEEN
BACK TO THE WOODS AGAIN

Wendy's parents ran a bed and breakfast on the north end of town. A large civil war era house with several bedrooms and a rather large dining room, they'd added a new wing on the north side of the building, which included three small studio apartments. These tended to be rented by the week all year round. A small swimming pool dominated the upper terrace in back, next to a hot tub large enough to accommodate eight or nine people. The parents lived in a small suite behind the front desk, and the children had bedrooms in the basement on either side of a large rec room that led out into the back yard.

Wendy and her brother had cleaning and front desk duties during the off-season, when there weren't many guests. During the high season, the family usually took on a couple of extra staff to handle the business. Just now, a few long-term guests occupied the studios, leaving the rest of the house empty. Even though it provided her family with a comfortable life, Wendy disliked living there intensely, and resented having to contribute to the upkeep of the house. Her family moved there from Baltimore when she was in seventh grade. She still harbored a grudge about having to leave all her childhood friends behind, and her parents watched uncomprehendingly as she gradually became more reserved and withdrawn, and began to dress more exotically with each year.

Emily pulled down the circular drive to the front porch on the dirt bike just before ten, wearing black jeans over western style boots, a deep red t-shirt and a brown leather jacket. She tossed a second helmet to Wendy, sitting on the bottom step, and her jaw dropped. It really hadn't occurred to her that this was the sort of ride Emily had in mind. "What the hell," she thought, pulled the helmet on, and climbed onto the back of the bike. They sped down the drive, spitting gravel behind them.

An hour's ride brought them as far as Potts Creek, where Emily turned east up a dirt road that connected to a network of logging trails through the forest. It was a thrilling ride up and down hills, in and out of valleys, bending around some sharp turns and over some large bumps. On a few occasions they were actually airborne. Wendy screamed most of the way. After another hour, they came out on a ridgeline overlooking a high meadow, and Emily cut the engine and leaned the bike up against a tree. They spent the next hour sitting on a fallen log in a shady spot, letting the buzz of the ride wear off, and looking out onto a lower ridge, at some tilled fields and clear pasturage on the other side, and a much higher ridge about two miles further on.

It was beautiful, Wendy told herself, the sort of pastoral scene her father always talked about visiting, but hardly ever did. She'd been driven *past* scenery like this loads of times over the last few years. Actually stopping to experience it up close felt like exploring some undiscovered country. No doubt, the thrill of the ride contributed to her giddy mood, but also the company, and before she knew it, a laugh erupted from her chest, and then she couldn't stop. Emily looked at her, puzzled and amused, and a sympathetic joy spread across her face, too. Before long the two of them were laughing together.

"Emily, I had no idea," Wendy gushed after a few moments. "Do you do this often?"

"My dad and I used to camp in the mountains all the time," she said after a moment.

"I meant the bike. Did you do *that* with your dad?"

"It used to be *his* bike," she laughed, though a shadow seemed to pass over her face for a moment. Wendy tried to look past whatever was bothering her new friend, to recapture that fleeting ecstasy.

"You are nothing like what I expected," Wendy said with a laugh.

"You were expecting something?" Emily teased.

"It's just… you seem like such a loner, you know, on the outside looking in. But you're not an outsider at all."

"What do you mean?"

"I don't think you're looking *in*," said Wendy, very pleased with herself.

Emily laughed, which Wendy took to be an admission she was right. She knew what it was to be a loner, though she'd only gone into loner-mode after her family moved out to this little town in the middle of nowhere, and maybe she just did it to get back at her parents. But Emily struck her as the real thing. She'd probably been a loner her whole life, if Wendy had to guess. Judging from what she could see in passing, in school corridors and the occasional class, Emily had completely submerged herself in private pursuits and schoolwork. Until the football game, that is.

"I've got better things to do than worry about being in or out," Emily said provocatively. "I've got more friends now than I've ever had before, and I like it. I guess I'm just Miss Popularity."

"Yeah, right," Wendy snorted. "Why do I get the feeling none of these new friends really know you at all."

"Maybe there's not all that much to know about me,"

she said, and the shadows seemed to cross her face again.

"I'm pretty sure you're hiding something behind those eyes," Wendy teased, and then immediately regretted it, when she saw how dark the shadows became.

"What about *your* friends, you know, the guys in black with the piercings? Do they know the *real* you?"

"I suppose not, but at least they're not phonies, like everyone else," she said, feeling her face grow warm.

"I don't know what you mean by phonies, Wendy. I'm pretty sure I'm a phony, you know, pretending to be what I'm not. But I don't need a uniform. All the black clothes, the death stuff, the makeup, isn't that kinda phony?"

Wendy didn't like to hear this from her new friend, even though she knew it was true… in fact, she'd been thinking the same thing for some time now. The goths were phonies like everyone else. It started as a rebellion, a way of getting back at her parents for moving out here and making her leave her friends behind. An added bonus was that because she didn't look quite presentable to the guests, she got out of doing a lot of the public duties of the bed and breakfast.

But having Emily turn the tables on her, and so quickly, telling her a cutting truth about herself… that was supposed to be her prerogative, not Emily's. She was just supposed to be her exciting new friend. But when she looked into her new friend's eyes, she saw something darker than any goth had ever imagined, though strangely, this darkness was not made of anger or frustration. Emily was a deliciously dangerous sort of friend.

On the way back home, they stopped for gas on the outskirts of Covington, and Wendy went inside to use the facilities while Emily filled the tank. Wendy prowled about the store for a moment looking for a bottle of iced tea when she noticed a dusty white SUV pulled up on the other side of the pumps from Emily. There seemed to be a heated conversation going on between a guy and his girlfriend about Emily and, of course, she was paying no attention. Finally, the girl yelled, "I'm telling you, that's the bitch from the other night!" Two more guys piled out of the back of the SUV, both quite a bit larger than the driver, one large and built like a football player, the second a bit shorter and on the husky side, but still huge. Wendy trembled as she watched the scene unfold, but she just couldn't seem to get herself to go outside.

The driver sauntered over to Emily, leaning into her face to menace her, and out of nowhere he had a knife in his hand and waved it at her. Emily hardly moved, like she was made of stone. *Was she frozen in fear, too?* Finally, Wendy unglued her feet from the floor and ran to the door just as the driver drew his arm back, as if to strike.

"Look out, Emily," she was about to yell. But before the words were even fully formed in her mouth, she saw Emily move her hands quickly towards the driver's elbow and shoulder. Once she'd taken control of the arm, his face twisted into a mask of pain, and she spun him around and stuck him in the ass with his own knife. He squealed as she threw him into the side of the SUV. He slid to the ground and Wendy gasped: "How is she strong enough to do that?" She didn't see any blood, but the knife wound must have stung like hell. The girl who'd started the whole thing ran over to him shrieking, crouched over him and removed the knife. Meanwhile, the husky guy reached for Emily.

"What the hell is wrong with you, bitch! You can't do that to my friend," he snarled trying to sound intimidating. Emily parried his hand, twisting it down and around, sending him tumbling head over heels. He ended up lying on his back a few feet away, groaning. The last guy, the athletic one, rushed toward her, no doubt thinking he would take care of her... until Emily gave him a very hard look and pointed her finger at him.

"Do you really want to risk it?" Wendy heard her say. "If I take out your knees, you'll be off the team." When he shrank back, Wendy breathed a sigh of relief, puzzled as she was that Emily had so much power in her finger, or that she'd read him so well.

By this time, the driver had recovered himself, picked up his knife and lunged towards her with an inchoate roar, and again Emily seemed so calm. Before Wendy even knew whether to cry out... Emily waved her left hand in a lazy circle in front of the driver's eyes. Such an innocent gesture, so graceful, so unthreatening, and Wendy couldn't quite understand how it happened, or how she did it. Emily had somehow controlled his arm and twisted it up and then out, sending his entire body cartwheeling into the side of the building, his shoulder weirdly misshapen.

"What's wrong with you! Are you afraid of this bitch?" the girl who started all the trouble shrieked at the last guy standing, then pulled what looked like a little gun out of her bag and tried to point it at Emily. But before she could fully extend her arm to fire, Emily knocked the gun aside, sending it skittering across the pavement, and slapped her across the face. As the girl twisted away from the second slap, Emily pressed the back of her knee down with one foot, forcing her to the ground, and crouched to whisper something in her ear. Wendy watched as the girl's face became contorted in terror. After a moment, Emily got up, swung a leg over the bike and waved Wendy over. She swallowed, and climbed on the back, and they sped off down the road, back into the mountains.

A few miles later, they pulled onto an unmarked dirt road that dead-ended by a creek. Emily cut the engine, and Wendy slid off the back. She backed away and looked at Emily, who sat by the water's edge and motioned her over. Her heart pounded in her throat as she tried to regain a little composure.

"Wh-what the hell happened back there?" she cried out, in a voice rather higher and louder than she expected to hear coming out of her own mouth. Emily looked at her calmly, though some sort of concern was clearly etched across her forehead. Wendy couldn't quite read the expression.

"Oh, that," she said, in mock nonchalance. "Just taking care of a little unfinished business."

"Emily, those guys were trying to kill you. That girl had a gun. Where did they even come from? How do you know them?"

"We met those guys the other night outside a pizza joint in Covington," she said after a quiet moment. "Wayne stumbled into the middle of a parking lot brawl and they all turned on him. Danny and Billy helped him chase them all off. I guess they were still pissed about it."

"I can't believe how calm you were. I was terrified… and how did you even *do* that? You were incredible." Wendy felt her heart shift gears as she gave in to the visceral thrill of the fight.

"Wendy, don't make a big deal out of this. In fact, I'd prefer it if we didn't mention it to anyone else."

"What do you mean? You didn't do anything wrong. They attacked you."

"I guess so," Emily said. "It's just… I could do without the attention."

"You mean from the police?"

"Yeah, sure… the police. Or anyone."

Of course, this request puzzled Wendy more than anything else she'd seen that day. She had just discovered a new side to her new friend, who was now even more mysterious than ever, and the urge to celebrate her feats was not so easily suppressed.

"But you were amazing back there," she gushed.

"Wendy, those guys were assholes, and they didn't get anything they didn't deserve. But there's nothing to brag about in what I did. In fact, I really wish they'd left well enough alone. So, please, do me a favor and keep it under your hat."

"Okay," she said reluctantly.

"Great. Now we have a secret," Emily teased. "We're

secret friends!'"

When they pulled up the drive to Wendy's house, her mom called to them from the front door. "She's gonna freak," Wendy said.

"You mean because of the dirt bike?"

"Yeah, there's that. But, I mean, you're not like the friends I usually bring home."

"Am I really so different from the goths?"

"Hi, Mom," Wendy chirped nervously. "This is my friend, Emily."

"Hello, Mrs. Williams," Emily added. "It's good to meet you."

Wendy's mom stood quietly for a moment, just taking Emily in… and when the silence began to get awkward, Wendy gestured to her and said, "Earth to Mom."

"It is really good to meet you, Emily," she said, recovering herself. "It's almost dinner time. Would you care to join us? We'd love to have you." Emily glanced at Wendy, who nodded vigorously, grinning wildly.

"I'd like that, Mrs. Williams," she replied. "That sounds nice."

"Do you need to call home?"

"No, I don't think that'll be necessary," Emily replied.

It was just turning dark, and the air had a slight chill. Mrs. Williams pulled her jacket more tightly around her shoulders.

"Your dad has the hot tub all set up. Why don't you two go join him? Wendy, you must have a suit Emily can wear. I'll be out in just a minute, as soon as I get the roast in the oven."

Wendy hesitated for a moment, not wanting to embarrass her friend. Emily smiled and said, "Sounds great to me," and followed Wendy down to her room. She only had two suits, and one was a skimpy two-piece her mom got her that she was embarrassed to wear.

"I'll wear it," Emily said with an air of indifference, and

Wendy breathed an audible sigh of relief. As they changed Wendy caught herself staring at Emily, stunned when she saw how fit and well-defined she was. Sure, she was pretty in an odd sort of way, but mainly she was long, lean and strong. Watching her change into the bathing suit took a little of the mystery out of how she had been able to handle those guys at the gas station. When they got out to the hot tub, Wendy's parents and her brother shared a similar reaction.

Of course, Emily appeared to be unaware of any of it, as if she had no insecurities about her appearance—not modesty so much as obliviousness. What Wendy wouldn't give for that sort of confidence, and it occurred to her, as she thought of the fight at the gas station, that Emily probably thought of her body more as a tool, even a weapon, than a silvered image in a mirror.

The conversation in the hot tub and later at dinner ran through the usual topics: her parents, plans for college, friends. Wendy's parents were surprised to hear Emily lived on her own, in her own apartment, that her dad was out of the country, and that she didn't know her mother. Much of this information was even news to Wendy, and she was impressed by Emily's self-possession. Could she pull off living on her own? As far as she could tell, Emily was at eighteen as independent and focused as she imagined most adults to be.

Wendy's father became especially interested when Emily mentioned the dojo. She told them about her friends there, about Sensei and her father. It turned out Wendy was really the only friend she had who didn't train at the dojo, and she was surprised to hear this, having assumed Emily had friends all over the school. That, at least, was how it seemed at the football game. "Emily really is a loner," she thought. But how can that be? She's so cool, so tough, so focused. It dawned on her how little she really understood about her new friend.

After Emily went home, Wendy had a long talk with her mother about two things: her goth friends and going shopping for new clothes.

"That Emily is really something, isn't she?" her mother said absent-mindedly. "She's not like any of your other friends."

"No, Mom, I can assure you of that," Wendy replied. "She is totally one of a kind."

"Yeah, I mean the vibe coming off her is like nothing I've ever felt before," her mother continued.

"*Vibe*, Mom?"

"She is just one cool customer. I bet nothing fazes her."

"Mom, you have no idea," said Wendy, very satisfied with herself for having a secret she shared with Emily.

Later, as she lay in bed, Wendy went back over the events of the day in her mind—the bike ride, screaming up and down the mountains, the afternoon relaxing on the ridgeline soaking up the scenery, the encounter with the toughs in the gas station, and finally the evening in the hot tub with her family. This may have been the best day of her life. Her mind kept returning to an image of Emily changing into that bathing suit. It hadn't ever occurred to her that human beings could look like that. They were roughly the same dimensions, wore the same size, but Wendy was pretty sure she didn't look like *that*. "Sure, she's beautiful," Wendy thought, "but it's more than that, like she's made of steel or something." Wendy fell asleep dreaming of cyborgs and samurai.

CHAPTER SIXTEEN
A FAMILIAR FACE

Things quieted down for awhile, and Emily heard nothing more about the incident at the gas station. She guessed those guys realized they would look ridiculous if they told the police a girl had beaten them all up. The weeks slid by with no more suspicious sightings, no one seemed to be following her. She spent Thanksgiving with Wendy's family, and they were very pleased to have her at their table. Danny and his Mom visited family in West Virginia for the weekend.

Gradually, the work of the semester wound down as the Christmas break approached. Emily sent off a few applications to colleges around the country. So far, she used the name Emily Kane, since that was the only name her teachers knew her by, and they had to write letters of recommendation about a student they knew. Fortunately, Emily had taken the SAT under that name too, and done quite well. Given her grades and scores, she was likely to be a much sought after student. She would have to figure out how to solve the problem of her name later.

She enjoyed her time in the dojo more than ever, and it was during this time that she began to see Sensei less as a teacher and more as a fellow traveler. He was "one who had gone before," but now her own experiences had brought her pretty far down a similar path. She still had lots to learn from him, but he also began to see her as a colleague as well as a student.

"*Sen*," he barked at the class one evening. "It means being decisive, taking the initiative, but it doesn't mean being reckless. You control a situation by taking the initiative away from your opponent, and this requires self-control first of all. There are three basic ways to control a fight: attack first, attack at the same time as your opponent, or attack after your opponent has attacked. In each case, you deny the initiative to your opponent. None of them is passive. Even in the last one, you don't just *wait* for your opponent to attack. You *watch* for his attack, shape the moment in which he attacks, and seize the initiative from within it. That's called *go no sen*. Those of you who have had the pleasure of sparring with Emily, I'm sure you know what *go no sen* looks like."

Emily had heard this speech in one form or another many times. But this time, it seemed to her that Sensei was needling her about something. She understood herself primarily in terms of *go no sen*. She found her initiative within the action of her opponent. It wasn't just that she was comfortable with this way of thinking. It seemed to reveal a fundamental truth about herself, about life, about the world. She certainly knew how to take the initiative in all its forms—how to attack the attack, to punch through her opponent's attack or even to meet it head on, as well as how to provoke her opponent, to attack first so as to force him into an attack prematurely. This was how her father tended to think. She saw it that night in the tunnel, and it was also a perfect description of how he would track her in the woods, moving swiftly and directly to wherever he thought she was hiding, flushing her out so that she had to fall back to a position chosen in haste. Sensei called it *sen sen no sen*, and she knew it wasn't just aggressiveness. In some ways, perhaps, it was no more aggressive than *go no sen*, and it also found the initiative within the opponent's action. Mainly, it sought to deny him the time and space to take his own initiative freely.

Still, for Emily, all forms of *sen* found their clearest articulation in *go no sen*. They were variations of it. As she saw it, initiative was fundamentally a matter of recognizing opportunity. Inopportune initiative was not truly *sen*. It was mere recklessness. To her, that meant even anticipatory initiative, attacking first, was at its heart a mode of *go no sen*.

She wondered what else Sensei wanted to tell her about *sen*—perhaps how she'd misunderstood something, maybe even allowed herself to become passive without realizing it. Of course, she took it easy on her classmates in sparring. Maybe that's what Sensei had in mind. On the other hand, she'd been involved in so many fights in earnest over the last few months that the etiquette of sparring could not help but seem to her like a narrow set of limits on *sen*. She wondered if Sensei wanted her to be more aggressive in class.

They did *bo* sparring for the second half of class, using a padded version of the *bo* staff, which was ordinarily a heavy, six foot long, tapered, hardwood staff. It was a traditional martial arts weapon, and the first one Emily had mastered. She decided to use this occasion to go in the direction Sensei seemed to be nudging her, to tilt her *sen* towards *sen sen no sen*. The beneficiary of her resolve this evening was Danny.

The instant Sensei signaled the beginning of the match, she lunged toward his groin, forcing him to block down, then used the force of his down block to rotate the other end of her *bo* into a strike to the top of his head. When he raised his *bo* to protect his head, she planted a side kick in the center of his chest, sending him sprawling backwards. The entire exchange took less than a second. Danny noticed the difference in her approach to the match and tried to seize the initiative first with a lunging strike of his own. Before he had even fully extended his arms, she had already spun outside his strike, swept his right leg out from under him and landed a strike across his face and chest. The efficiency of her move was truly stunning, and left everyone in the dojo, even

Sensei, standing with their mouths agape. One last time, Danny tried to initiate a swinging side strike, but it was much too slow. She had already struck him twice, in the head and groin, before he realized what had happened. Finally she spun her *bo* between his hands and sent his staff sailing across the room. Danny smiled at her, put his hands together and bowed. Everyone in the room laughed. There was nothing else to be said.

Emily turned to Sensei with a questioning look on her face, as if to say, "Is this what you meant?" He smiled, patted her shoulder and directed her to the back of the dojo, where she sat cross-legged and watched the rest of the matches. Most of the kids were unable to take any genuine initiative. For the most part, they tried to initiate action with a sudden reckless attack, or they waited too long for their opponent to make the first move. In neither case were they able to control the conflict. Wayne came the closest to achieving something like *sen*. Perhaps because of his size, he didn't feel threatened by any opponent, except Emily, of course. As a result, he could act calmly and decisively, but even this wasn't quite what Sensei meant by taking the initiative, since he still allowed his opponent too much freedom to control his own action. It was only the accident of his size that created the appearance of *sen*.

While Emily watched the matches from the back wall, something caught her eye on the other side of the large front window: a familiar face out in the parking lot, watching as well. Leaning against the driver side door of a large sedan, it was the woman who attacked her at the university a few weeks earlier. She had to be watching Emily—*why else would she be here?* Emily could see no point in waiting or putting off this conversation, so she got straight up and walked to the door, eyes fixed on the face in the window, pausing only to bow slightly at the edge of the main room.

An instant later, Emily pushed the outer door open and strode directly toward the woman, fully prepared to fight it out with her right there in the parking lot, alert to every detail of the woman's body, and paying special attention to her hands. The woman stepped back at Emily's approach, retreating between two cars. Emily wondered if she should just chase her off, then decided it would be better to keep her close. Instead of attacking her, much as she had with Danny a few minutes earlier, though without the *bo* staff, she adopted a slightly less aggressive posture, stepped towards her and watched the woman flinch. She didn't try to run, though it certainly looked like she wanted to.

"Is this a threat?" Emily growled, and the woman shook her head.

"No. I just came to talk."

"How did you find me?" The question made Emily self-conscious as soon as it left her lips. She glanced quickly around the parking lot, but saw nothing suspicious.

"It wasn't hard. I figured you had to train somewhere, so I just tried all the dojos in the area. Don't worry, Meacham has no idea. He isn't even looking for you anymore," she said, trying to sound reassuring. "Look, I just want to talk. Is there a private place we can go?"

Emily looked her up and down, checking for any visible sign of a weapon, and wondered if she should frisk her.

"Office," she grunted and nodded to the dojo. But before she would let the woman pass, she required her shoulder bag. They stepped into Sensei's office and Emily closed the door behind her.

"Sit over there," she said, gesturing to a spot on the floor in the corner. Of course, with no chairs in the office, there weren't a lot of other options, but it also served Emily's purpose, since she wanted to be able to control this woman if she had to. Standing over her, she looked through the bag, and found almost nothing personal in it: a key ring, a brush, a head-scarf, a chapstick and some lifesavers. A thin wallet contained a driver's license for someone named Constance Matthews, two credit cards in the same name, a card with nothing but a single email address on it, and a blank electronic access card. "This woman's definitely an agent," Emily thought. "There's nothing real in here."

"Do you have a name?" she said out loud. "I'm guessing it's not Constance Matthews."

"Can we just go with that one for now?" she asked, with a distinct note of sorrow in her voice. Emily noticed, but had no idea what to make of it.

"Fine, Constance," she said menacingly. "What was so important that you had to track me down?"

"Meacham. He's not a threat to you anymore. He suffered a setback a few weeks ago in Taipei, a major embarrassment. He's on the run for now. I don't know about Burzynski, but I don't think he was ever really a threat to you."

"That's all well and good, but you didn't find me to tell me that."

"No. There's something else. I'm not the only one looking for you. In Taipei, Meacham's group was ambushed by a Chinese hit squad. I only escaped by hiding in a sewer... and I overheard them talking about a girl they thought Meacham was pursuing, and how they want to find her, too. They didn't seem to know her name, but I think they're looking for you."

Emily listened impassively, trying not to betray any interest in front of this woman she hardly trusted.

"They also mentioned the name 'Kagami', and they think it's someone connected to Michael Cardano," the woman continued. "I know that can't be you since you're obviously Chinese and that's a Japanese name. But from the way they described who they're looking for, it's got to be you, even if they have the name wrong."

"What makes you think it's me?" Emily asked.

She was prepared to think the woman was right, and the mistake about the name offered some reassurance. But she couldn't believe it would deflect them indefinitely. On the other hand, the notion that she was of Chinese descent made her laugh under her breath. It was a common misconception at school, too... one even she labored under herself until recently. Perhaps it would prove useful at some point.

"They're looking for a warrior, some kind of super-soldier. You're the only person even remotely connected to Cardano who fits that description."

Emily mulled this assessment over for a few moments in silence. The ease with which this woman drew her conclusion alarmed her. If she could see it so easily, Emily had to wonder who else could... and if what she suspected was even true.

"Where are they looking now?"

"They were headed for the southwest. Apparently they think Cardano's hiding there."

Emily turned away, hoping to hide the distress that she feared might show on her face. From the information she'd just heard, it was difficult to tell what the Chinese really wanted or who they were looking for. Was it her or her mother... and did they even know who her mother was? She tried to collect herself and turned back.

"How long will it take them to come here?" she asked, hoping in part to create the illusion that her anxiety was for herself.

"I don't know, a month or two, maybe longer," the woman said. "But there's a security-cam video on the web of a fight in a gas station somewhere. It's pretty murky, but it shows a girl beating the tar out of three guys, and I'm guessing it was you. If the Chinese see it, they'll find their way out here sooner. On the plus side, there's no vehicle or license plate visible in the video, which ought to slow 'em down a bit."

"You found me a lot sooner."

"Yeah, but I already knew who I was looking for."

"Why did you take the trouble? What do you want from

me?" Emily demanded.

"I don't know, honey," she said, feeling perhaps a tiny bit more confident. "I guess I just got a little religion back in that bathroom stall." Emily glowered at her and the woman backtracked. "Look, I'm sorry. I owe you, I know. You kicking the crap out of me, well, it gave me a little perspective. You don't have to trust me, and I wouldn't blame you if you didn't." Emily nodded. "But if you want me to meet you somewhere, send a message to the address on the card in my wallet. Just put a time and a place, but give a date one day late. I'll be there." Emily said nothing, as she put the card in her pocket, then handed the bag back. She helped the woman up, and walked her out of the dojo, just as class was ending. The woman opened her car door, then turned back to Emily.

"You can call me Connie. That part's real," she said, and when Emily looked into her eyes, she thought she saw genuine sincerity there.

"Thanks, Connie," she said, turning back to the dojo. A few steps and she stood by the doorway to watch her drive away as the class filed out past her.

Once everyone had left, Sensei stood behind her and cleared his throat. Emily turned to look into his face.

"What was that all about?" he asked.

"I'm not sure. Have you seen her hanging around before this evening?" Sensei shook his head and grunted no.

"What did she want?" Emily paused for a moment and considered what she should tell Sensei.

"She says she's a friend. She warned me about Chinese agents who might be looking for my dad and Mr. Cardano." What she said was true, but Emily was reluctant to explain any more to him about what the Chinese might be looking for. "Have you seen any men like that?"

"No, no one like that. Chinese agents would have a hard time blending in."

"They'll probably check out the dojos around here

eventually, and if they do show up here… Sensei, we need to be very careful around these people."

"Do you trust this woman?"

"No. But I'm still gonna take her warning seriously, at least for now." Emily thought for a moment, took a deep breath and then said, "Sensei, I may have to take some time off after Christmas. I may not be back at the dojo for a while." He grumbled over what she said, and followed after as she walked to her truck, but finally had no thing to say to dissuade her.

Driving along dark country roads, Emily wanted to discuss this news with Michael. At the same time, it occurred to her that if the woman's story had been a setup, its purpose might be to lure her into making a quick call to Michael so they could somehow trace him. If she understood how the software on the thumb drive worked, and whether it would provide a secure connection if Meacham's people knew what terminal she used, she might have been willing to risk it. But driving in the dark, she wasn't confident of being able to spot a tail. Mulling it all over, she decided to wait until the next day to make that call.

When she pulled into the driveway at Mrs. Rincon's house, she found the guys installed on the front porch drinking hot cocoa and laughing. Wayne and Billy ribbed Danny about how completely Emily had dominated him in *bo* sparring, and when Danny's mother saw her arrive, she brought out one more cup of cocoa.

"Oh. My. God, Em," Danny sputtered, in mock astonishment. "I've never seen you spar like that. You were amazing. It's like you were possessed!" Emily would have laughed, but her mind was still focused on what Connie had told her.

"What happened tonight?" Danny's mother asked, in all innocence.

"Oh, nothing much, Mrs. Rincon," Wayne chortled. "Em just gave Danny a serious butt-whipping in class."

Billy started giggling and Danny blushed, while Emily remained impassive, and even a little uncomfortable joking about their match, since it seemed to her to be caught up in something Sensei wanted her to see about *sen*, and she still wasn't sure she had fully understood him.

"Well, good for you, Emily," Mrs. Rincon piped up. "I'm sure he had it coming."

Emily finally smiled, glad to see an opening to shift the conversation away from the dojo, and the boys were all happy to talk about holiday plans. Billy and Wayne would spend Christmas in town, Danny and his mom were visiting relatives. Emily said she might be going out of town, though she really had no plans. But she wanted to prepare the way in the minds of her friends, in case she had to move quickly. She halfway hoped Michael would react to her news by moving his family and Yuki, since that could well mean she would be able to meet them somewhere along the way. Maybe it would even feel like a holiday family reunion.

Later, lying in her bed above the garage, she let her mind luxuriate in the prospect of seeing her mother. Eventually, however, her thoughts turned to *sen*, and what Sensei had wanted her to see that evening. She wondered if he could see how much tougher, how much more resolute she'd become. Even without knowing the details of the encounters she'd been having over the past few months, perhaps he had sensed a change in her demeanor, in her breathing, in her *chi*. She began to think along these same lines, too, and recognized the temptation to cling to certain techniques and patterns of behavior under pressure. Over time, they could become entrenched habits rather than true initiative. Breaking out of her usual pattern in the *bo* sparring was refreshing, and she figured that had been Sensei's point, not that she should choose a different approach to *sen*, become more or less aggressive, but that she should reconnect with her *sen* in a genuine way.

CHAPTER SEVENTEEN
TORBAY

Emily spoke to Michael the next day, filling him in on what Connie had told her, and his assessment was reassuringly similar to hers: her pursuers didn't know who she was, or where, yet. He was not surprised to hear about the Chinese, and agreed that the confusion about exactly who they were looking for could prove useful later.

"How exactly did you meet this woman?" Michael asked. "Was she involved in the attack at the university?"

"Yeah, in a way, I suppose," she said, downplaying a dangerous truth. She didn't even know why she wanted to conceal this from him, or when it began to seem reasonable to try to manage what he knew about her situation. "That's not important, though. But you're sure she's telling the truth about Meacham?"

"Yes," he said. "And there's more… that ambush in Taiwan, I have a strong suspicion Burzynski tipped off the Chinese."

"If Burzynski's willing to commit treason… that's what it is, right? Then he's capable of anything."

"These are very dangerous men," he said. "They're capable of anything."

"Is it still safe for you and my mom to stay in New Mexico? You know… with the Chinese searching the southwest?"

Michael took a moment to respond, leaving Emily to twist in the silence, but finally said, "I think we're pretty well hidden, even if they come here. But I take your point. This may be the time to shift to our next position. Otherwise, we might have to move in haste, and that's never good."

To Emily's immense satisfaction, Michael also thought this might be a good moment for a family reunion, and the crush of holiday travel would make it easier to move around unnoticed. Over the next few days, he arranged for Andie and Anthony to meet them, and sent travel documents to Emily under the name Emily Chung. A week later, after several diversions through southeast Asia, Emily arrived at the airport in Auckland.

Andie went to meet her at the airport, and when she found her, she smiled to see how Emily was dressed. "Well, aren't you the stylish young commando?"

"I'm sorry about the clothes," Emily said with a blush, her face suddenly warm. "But I thought a change was necessary, given the… uh, circumstances."

"Oh, don't worry. It's a good look for you, maybe even better than on me. Anyway, I'd rather see you in them than some black-ops guy."

When they pulled into the driveway of a large beachside villa on the north end of Torbay, Yuki, who had been waiting outside nervously for over an hour, ran to the car and threw her arms around her daughter for the first time. She hung on Emily's shoulder for as long as she could… but eventually a child must pull away.

"You're so tall, Chi-chan" she cried. "Weren't you just a little girl a few months ago? And so strong, just like your father."

Emily wrapped her arms around her mother one more time, and looked down on her face. "Oh, Mom," she said, and brushed a tear aside. When she saw more tears on her mother's face, she wiped them off and said, "No crying, now. This is supposed to be a happy occasion."

The two of them spent the next few days, almost never without Anthony, who could hardly be separated from his favorite "sister," swimming in the southern ocean, snorkeling, sailing on a little boat Michael had somehow acquired—his resourcefulness always seemed endless—exploring the island wildlife preserves across the bay, hiking everywhere on the mainland, all the usual Christmas activities. Yuki seemed determined to spend as much time as possible with her newfound daughter, to share every activity, *do* everything she did. But she just didn't have the stamina for it.

"She runs for miles before breakfast," Yuki complained to Andie one morning, "and all those push ups and sit ups, and the pull ups... I had no idea."

"Oh, c'mon Mom," Emily said, standing behind her in sweats, toweling off after that morning's run. "It's just my normal routine, you know, like it's been for years."

"Then she wants to go out adventuring with Anthony for the rest of the day," Yuki continued.

"How much longer do you think you can keep it up?" Andie said with a laugh, and Emily rolled her eyes.

"I don't know, but I'm only beginning to appreciate George's energy," Yuki said, and when she looked at Emily, they both realized a limit had been reached.

~~~~~~~

In the closer quarters of the Torbay house, other eyes had taken notice of Emily's exercise regimen: Michael's security people were impressed, though perhaps none of them quite knew what to make of her. Two in particular paid special attention. Former members of Israeli special forces, Ethan and Jesse were younger than the rest of the security personnel, in their thirties. They'd heard about her martial arts training, and naturally wanted to know more. Anyone could see she was in shape, and when she practiced katas on the beach they watched closely. Ethan, the larger of the two, made a show of snorting whenever Jesse mentioned how sharp she looked.

"We're professionals," he said, "trained in the most

efficient fighting skills military science can devise. She's just an amateur, a girl. What do you really think she can know?"

In other words, he was curious, and Jesse was even more so.

"So you don't want to see what she can do, then?" Jesse asked, just to annoy him. Ethan shrugged.

The next day, Jesse approached her during one of her morning training sessions on the beach behind the house, having watched from the edge of the manicured portion of the backyard.

"Have you been training long, Miss?" he asked. "My name is Jesse," he added. "My partner and I are very impressed by your forms."

When she didn't respond right away, he fidgeted with his equipment bag and wondered if he'd crossed a line. Her position in the family was hard to figure: not a blood relative, and yet he could see everyone treated her rather differently than before the big move. Practically an afterthought in Virginia, important people deferred to her in New Zealand. Perhaps he shouldn't have presumed to address her directly.

"For as long as I can remember," she said. He rubbed his chin and squinted at her. "You asked how long I've been training."

"What exactly is your style? I didn't quite recognize the last form."

"It's a mix of things, I guess," she said. "My sensei calls it *kung fu*."

"Have you done any sparring?"

"A little."

"If you like, you can work out with us… maybe practice your sparring technique."

She mulled over the offer for a few seconds, looked him up and down and glanced over at Ethan, who had made his way down to the beach by this time.

"Israeli military, right? I guess that means your training is mainly in *Krav Maga*."

"Something like that," he said, not sure how he felt about being sized up with the sort of intensity he saw in her eyes.

"I've seen a demonstration, but never sparred with a practitioner. Sure, why not?"

"It's all about efficiency," Ethan said. "Direct strikes and hard blocks, kicks and joint locks. None of that fancy oriental stuff, with all the wasted motion."

"Okay," she said with a smirk. "How about I watch you guys first, if that's okay?"

Ethan was more than willing to oblige, and Jesse suspected it was mainly because, despite his big show of dismissing her skills, he wanted to impress her.

"We made these pads out of some old Kevlar vests," Jesse said, as he extracted their gear from his bag.

"We hit hard," Ethan snorted. "Not like the soft touches you're probably used to."

Emily tried one of the vests on, then laid it aside. "This is more like armor than padding. Too restrictive… and hard on the knuckles, I bet."

"That's why we use these old bag gloves," he said.

Jesse and Ethan's match was fierce. They punched and blocked with exceptional ferocity. Speed and strength were at the core of their skills, and Jesse hoped she would be impressed. A fight is all about aggression, he thought, which is why they constantly looked for an opening to finish the match with a single, devastating blow. But whenever he managed to steal a glance to the side of the ring they'd marked off in the sand, the expression on her face betrayed nothing, neither the awe he hoped for, nor the disapproval he dreaded. In the end, Ethan overpowered Jesse with a straight punch to the chest and a quick leg sweep. He landed on his back with Ethan's clenched fist just above his nose and had no choice but to concede.

"Pretty impressive, guys," she said, clapping her hands slowly. "I'm amazed you were able to keep up that pace for over a minute"

"Would you like to give it a try, Miss Emily," Ethan asked politely, but with a needling undertone. "We'll go easy on you."

"I'm more your size," Jesse suggested in all sincerity. "How about we give it a go?"

"Why not," she said. "But I'm pretty sure this is one of those things where size doesn't really matter."

Ethan snorted. They all knew she meant to needle him in return, but he didn't seem to know how to accept it graciously... until she flashed him a sneaky smile and brought back his good humor. He had to know she was manipulating him, Jesse thought, but he still found it irresistible, and handed her his pads and gloves. She hefted them for a moment and laid them off to the side of their imaginary ring.

"You better wear those," Jesse insisted. "I don't want to hurt you. The boss would have our heads, and who knows what Andie and Yuki would do to us."

"Okay, I'll wear the gloves, but not the shell. It's way too heavy for me," she said smiling at Ethan again. "But don't worry about hitting me. I won't tell if you don't."

"Fine! Then I'll take my pads off too. I guess I'll have to just do those little taps, like they do in karate sparring." Emily laughed, and Ethan joined in.

"Don't worry," she replied. "I won't hit you any harder than you try to hit me."

Ethan was overjoyed by Jesse's embarrassment.

Jesse stood ready and looked her in the eyes, trying to read her, to develop a series of feints so he could tap her a couple of times, sweep her legs and force her to concede without risking any hard punches. He knew he had an advantage in quickness and strength, which meant he could risk more, since even if she snuck something past his guard, it wouldn't have enough force to put him down.

He bluffed a low kick followed by a left hook, and she

leaned in to block each one just as he expected. The next series of punches to her head and chest, quick as he could make them, ought to finish her before she'd be able to back out of range. *Why didn't any of them connect?* Somehow, she blocked them all one after another, soft blocks at first, barely nudges, just enough to send them off target, leaning out of the way; then her blocks became more forceful, and even began to smart as she struck his forearm and then his biceps. Even more frustrating, she'd managed to force him to retreat just when he expected to be moving forward. He didn't want Ethan to accuse him later of being fooled by this girl's wiles, and tried to turn the tide by stepping forward into a more aggressive attack. But before he could put his left foot down, Emily kicked it out from under him. He fell forward and to his left, and she hit him lightly with several quick strikes to his chest and throat. Just before he hit the ground, she grabbed his right wrist and twisted him over so he landed face down in the sand.

Jesse let out a sorrowful moan. Emily hadn't hurt him, but he knew he had been decisively beaten. And so did Ethan, who roared his approval. At least she'd done him the favor of letting him hide his face so Ethan couldn't see the expression of utter perplexity written so unmistakably across it. *But how had she done it?* Everything had been going so well, and she hadn't overpowered him, and she certainly wasn't any faster than he was. It felt like the punch and block duels he and Ethan had everyday… but Ethan had never managed to do anything like that to him. Finally, he let the truth slip into his consciousness: the point hadn't even been close.

He picked himself up, dusted off the sand and faced her, ready to try again. This time she controlled the terms of the fight much more thoroughly. He made the first move again, lunging in with a left jab, followed by a right uppercut, but instead of blocking, she stepped back and swirled her arms around both of his. Her movements made no visual sense to him and he found it difficult to focus on her hands, and before he realized what was happening, she'd grabbed hold of his wrists and twisted them over and then under. It proved impossible to keep his footing as the pain in his elbows and shoulders forced him to bend his entire body to one side. He expected to end up kneeling, and hoped to find a way out from there, but the twisting movement accelerated and he found himself flipping head over heels, ending up on his back in the sand. Before he could gather his wits, Emily was on top of him and he was defenseless.

In the third point, she made the first move, perhaps reacting to his growing sense that she'd tricked him into acting first before. *Krav Maga* is, after all, a deeply conservative fighting style. So he watched and waited, until she looked directly into his face and caught his attention, distracting him for an instant, just long enough to kick him lightly in the chest before he could react. The force of the kick, and the sheer surprise of it, rocked him back slightly on his heels, and when he leaned forward and tried to anticipate another kick, she stepped directly through his block. In a sudden epiphany, he thought to grab her—*What else could he do?*—but she slapped his hands aside and planted a side kick into his chest that sent him sprawling backwards onto the sand. He lay on his back for a moment shaking his head in disbelief, with absolutely no idea how she had managed to dominate him so thoroughly.

Ethan laughed after the first two falls, but now even he was agape. Watching attentively from the side, he still had not been able to comprehend her technique. Emily turned toward Ethan and smiled demurely at him.

"You want to have a go? Don't worry, I'll go easy on you."

Ordinarily Ethan would have reacted to a challenge like that with an easy laugh or some bravado. But Jesse could tell he was shaken by what he had just seen… and he thought she knew it, too. Of course, Ethan couldn't decline, not in front of the friend he'd mocked a moment ago. He stood in front of Emily with visible trepidation, no longer so confident in the huge size advantage he had over her. In the event, he fared no better than Jesse had. She sent him sprawling face down into the sand each time, playing on his desperate aggressiveness.

After the third fall, she walked over, extended her hand and helped Ethan up, leaning back for leverage. She smiled at the two of them graciously and, strangely, Jesse felt better about the whole thing. When he turned to look at Ethan, he was surprised to see him blushing.

Both of them fully expected to hear all about their defeat at the hands of this girl from the rest of the security team for weeks to come. Of course, they heard nothing at all about it from anyone.

"Thank goodness," Ethan said to him that evening.

"I think our secret's safe with her," Jesse said, with a nervous smile.

The next day, they asked her to be their teacher.

~~~~~~~

The only witnesses to the events of that morning were Andie and Yuki, who watched from behind a hedge fronting the back patio. Yuki wasn't surprised Jesse and Ethan had noticed her daughter's workout regimen. But it hadn't occurred to her that she would end up sparring with them. When she saw her toss the pads aside, Yuki had to suppress a little shriek, having seen how ferociously those guys tended to fight when they sparred.

"I'm sure they'll have the good sense to take it easy on her," Andie said.

But when the sparring began in earnest, two jaws dropped—Jesse attacked her so fiercely. Moments later, they watched, thunderstruck, as Emily turned the tables on him and he ended up face down in the sand. They looked at each other and giggled. For the first time, Yuki began to realize just how much the martial arts must mean to her daughter.

"I always thought it was just a hobby," she said.

"Yuki, she just manhandled a couple of professional soldiers, as if they were schoolboys. I hope they aren't mortified by what just happened."

In the end, Yuki found an activity she could share with Emily, one that had no limits for her: clothes shopping. It was every mother's dream, and finally she got to indulge in it, too. They drove into Auckland, just the two of them, and hit all the fancy shops. Yuki could have done this for the rest of the holiday if she'd had her way… but finally even Emily had had enough. Yuki picked out all sorts of stylish clothes and accessories, so much, in fact, that she had to buy her new luggage to haul it home in.

"I don't see why my duffle bag won't do," Emily said.

"You are just like your father," Yuki said. "He had no sense of the proprieties either."

They had lunch in a little Japanese restaurant near the university, which didn't surprise her. She figured Emily had just steered the car toward wherever the young people were, as if by some sort of powerful sympathy. Yuki had a bowl of *udon* with fish cakes, and Emily had a sashimi plate with pickled vegetables. While they ate, Yuki wanted to tell her about her father, but Emily seemed uncomfortable with that topic and diverted the conversation into a question about college plans… and Yuki felt her face grow warm with the fire in her eyes. She had so much to tell her daughter, and so much to find out about what she wanted to do.

"Mom, I already applied to five schools. I think it's probably too late to do any more applications."

"With your grades, you could get into a good Japanese school," she said, hearing the tremor in her own voice, knowing all too well that the problem wasn't in getting accepted somewhere, but in surviving until the fall. That little worry, catastrophic in its dimensions, lingered in the back of all of Yuki's joy and satisfaction. Her daughter never ceased to amaze, but she was also in danger; they all were, but none more than her.

"What do you want to study, do you know yet?"

"I don't really know, Mom. Maybe history. I'm sorry."

"Sorry about what, Chi-chan?"

"I know you wanted me to do science, and I like that stuff. But right now history looks more interesting."

"It's okay, Sweet Pea," she said, unconsciously reverting to another one of George's pet names for their daughter. "You have to follow your heart, and you can always change your mind later. I just want you to go to college and find your own way."

Yuki's pleasure in this conversation was almost indescribable, even greater than what she experienced on the shopping spree. She couldn't remember ever being this happy. And it was easy to see the pleasure it gave to Emily, as she listened to her recount every detail of her domestic arrangements, the apartment, how much she liked wearing Andie's clothes, her new style, the truck and the dirt bike.

And her friends… Yuki wanted to hear all about them. Why hadn't she ever met any of them before? What were their families like? Emily's description of Wayne was especially captivating; he sounded like a kindly walrus, or maybe a sea lion.

After lunch, they strolled over to Albert Park and found a bench with a view of the clock tower. The park was usually crowded during the lunch hour, but by now most people had gone back to work, leaving them the place pretty much to themselves. She told her daughter all about her father, and Emily seemed ready to hear it now… how they met, how much she came to love him, about her early childhood in Hawaii and later in Virginia. They both wept and held each other. Reliving their loss together, working out their feelings with each other, this was how they would become the family they had never truly been before. When they looked up, the rusty sun brushed against the horizon and sent its fading beams through the treetops. The drive back to the villa gave them time to recompose themselves for the rest of their new "family."

~~~~~~~

Naturally, Yuki and Andie had to crow over all of Emily's new clothes, and made her try everything on, oohing and aahing over each outfit. Michael watched from a distance with a little smile, but Anthony was a still too young at twelve to appreciate this scene. Later, at the dinner table, they talked over all the events of the day, and afterwards Emily sought a quiet moment with Michael to talk over the trickier points of her going to college, the problem of changing the name on her school records, and related matters. Michael had a couple of suggestions.

"Emily, you know I can change all the records for you, seamlessly, craft an entire identity for you. You don't have to stay in Virginia any longer."

"Don't worry, I know you can," she said. "But I want to have a genuine identity. I want to come from the place where I really grew up. I can't do that if I leave now."

She was absolutely determined on this point, and Michael saw this right away. He knew well enough the nature of her determination. But he really wanted to find some way to be of service to her, no matter what shape it eventually took.

"If you stay, you'll have to stay as Emily Kane, at least until graduation. You can change all your records after that. There's nothing shady or illegal about it. The only records that matter are the school transcripts."

"So far, I've been changing over some things to Hsiao or Chung. Car registrations, driver's license, that sort of thing. Of course, I came here as Chung. But in person, everyone who knows me calls me Kane."

"That's probably the best you can do, for now," he said.

"But any of those names you use now, you'll have to leave behind completely at graduation. Are you ready for that?"

"Yeah, I guess," she replied after a moment. "I can just tell everyone I was using an informal family name, and that my legal name is Michiko Tenno."

The subtle simplicity of her plan struck Michael right away. Her friends and acquaintances, and the school officials too, would recognize her by whatever name she offered them. After all, she had the legal documentation for that name, and he'd always been impressed by the contrivance of this identity. George and Yuki had crafted it on their own, through their own connections, without his assistance. He had only heard about it for the first time a few months ago. He also knew for it to be of any real value, it was important he not have any discoverable connection to it, no matter how closely anyone looked.

"The problem of the recommendations is a little stickier," he sighed. "If you go to one of those schools, you'll have to change the records there after you're admitted. That means you'll probably need someone from your high school to affirm that you are both people. There's a risk in that. It increases the number of people who know you under both names."

"I know," Emily conceded. "I don't see any way around that. But once I'm living elsewhere, the high school won't have any record of where I've gone. And I can destroy whatever they have in their files about Emily Kane once I'm enrolled someplace. A search for her would come up empty." Michael thought about this for a moment.

"There is another option," he began. "The service academies don't base admissions decisions on recommendations from teachers. They rely on congressional recommendations."

He watched as she mulled this suggestion over. It could resolve the difficulty about the letters, as well as allow her to change over the records at her school sooner, insulate herself from her dangerous identity more completely. He suspected the discipline of the service academies would appeal to her, even if it entailed some narrowing of academic possibilities.

"But won't the congressman who recommends me want some documentation of who I am?" she asked.

"Yes, but as it happens, I have an acquaintance on the House Armed Services Committee. I'm sure I can persuade him to recommend you."

"Won't that link me to your influence forever? I mean, even if the congressman keeps the secret, his staff might reveal the connection."

"That's true," he said "Michiko Tenno is only completely safe if it grows naturally out of your childhood connections."

"Michael, I'm going to need your help in a thousand ways, I know," she said. "But I think I have to solve this problem on my own. It's not just about a name. I have to decide *who* I'm going to be"

"I see your point, Emily," he replied. "Here's one thing you can do, right now to shore up Michiko's history. When you fly home you'll have a stopover in Tokyo, and then fly home through Hawaii. You should clear customs as Michiko, not Emily."

Over the next few days, Michael watched Yuki and Emily together, and wondered how Yuki could have been so near Emily for all those years without revealing anything. He supposed the pain she felt then must have been roughly the reciprocal of the joy written across her face now.

"I can barely imagine it," Andie said one morning. "How many years have we known her... and Emily, she grew up under our noses."

"They are an enigmatic family," he said. "George was more reserved than either one of them."

"Yeah, but now that I know her secret, Yuki's like an open book... it's so strange. And who knew how pretty Emily would turn out to be, as soon as she got some decent clothes."

Michael was less impressed by how she looked in her new clothes than in how, in a few short months, she had gone from a petulant adolescent to a mature young woman, so resolute, yet so sympathetic. He saw how open she could be with her mother, with all of them really, an impossible combination of grit and grace.

When Andie took her back to the airport a couple of days later, she handed her a new thumb drive and some new travel documents Michael had sent along. She sat with her in the airport cafe for a few minutes before her flight.

"I really hope you don't mind about the clothes," Emily ventured, half-apologetically.

"How could I," she teased. "You look so great in them. I wish I looked that good." Emily blushed and Andie wiped away a little tear from her left eye.

"Well I'm glad you feel that way. Your clothes really helped me find my way when I needed to. I hope that makes sense."

"It does, don't worry. I think I know what you mean."

"Well, I'm grateful."

Andie looked at her face and was struck by how simple and open she was. At the bottom of those deep black eyes she saw a perfectly innocent soul. She had always thought of Emily as a tough, resourceful kid, but now she saw a mature young woman with the heart of a small child. As they got up to go to the gate, Andie put her arms around her and held her tight, like she was her own daughter, and whispered in her ear.

"We are all very proud of you, sweetheart. Let us help you if you ever need us."

Emily smiled and turned to walk to the gate. Andie watched her make her way through the terminal, smiled wistfully and headed back to the villa.

CHAPTER EIGHTEEN
KYOTO

Emily landed at Kansai Airport, which, having been built on an artificial island in Osaka Bay, is one of the most expensive public works projects in human history. The trick had been to keep the island from sinking into the silt of the bay under the weight of the terminal structures and the runways. It was a monument to civic resolve, or perhaps just stubbornness. Emily passed through border control as Michiko Tenno, native, citizen of Japan. She had spoken Japanese from childhood—Yuki had made a point of speaking to her in her native tongue whenever possible. Although her vocabulary was limited, her feel for the character of the language was practically that of a native speaker. She felt at home in it. A couple of summer classes at the community college showed her how the grammatical presentation of a language could be cold and unhelpful, and she concluded that she already knew more from her mother than a class could teach her. It felt especially good to speak her mother's tongue now.

Michael had arranged for her to have a layover here for a few days. She would fly out of Narita airport in Tokyo and on to Honolulu, finally from there to the mainland. Each leg of her journey was booked independently of the others, which made for a long trip, but Michael wanted her to have an opportunity to size up her situation along the way, not leave a trail directly back to her home. Perhaps he also wanted her to have a chance to spend some time in one of her homelands.

Whatever Michael intended, Emily took a train to Kyoto and checked into a little *ryokan* near the Yoshida shrine on the west end of the city. The city felt wonderfully familiar to her, though this may have been merely the effect of seeing herself surrounded by crowds of people with long, straight black hair, people who looked like her. She loved the sound of their voices, the smell of the food, the bustle of their busy lives… and the fact that she could walk around the city in almost perfect invisibility, except for being so tall. She wasn't absurdly tall, but she still towered over most of the women she saw by a good five or six inches. She also walked differently, with a calm self-assurance that must have seemed masculine to the people who noticed her. Nothing deferential in her manner, she strode through the streets of Kyoto for the next couple of days like a tomboy, the gait so familiar to her friends in Virginia.

At first, she visited the important shrines and temples, the Shogun's castle, played the tourist, but the university eventually captured her attention. Perhaps she would find a clue to her own future in the young people she saw buzzing about the campus, especially since they didn't seem all that different from the students she had watched at the university in Charlottesville. They carried books in backpacks, walked to and fro with friends, listened to music, idled in the plazas and walked along the avenues. The campus of Kyoto University didn't feel quite as pastoral as the one in Charlottesville, probably an effect of the many tall buildings, and the scarcity of trees and lawns. It felt more industrial, as if learning here were a product, and there a leisure activity.

Eventually she attracted a little more attention than she

wanted. Sitting in one of the campus cafés, she noticed a couple of girls arguing with two young men who looked to be a bit older than they were. One of the girls noticed her sitting alone and pulled the other girl over to her table. She asked very politely for permission to join her, and then promptly sat down without waiting for a response.

"Is there a problem?" Emily asked.

Before the girls could answer, the men came over and barked at the second girl that she should come away with them immediately. She shuddered and buried her face in her hands. The first girl told them to leave, and stood up in their faces. They pushed her down rudely. As the girl fell backwards, Emily stepped out of her chair and propped her up, then glared at the men, staring directly into their faces, in a posture they seemed to take as a challenge, and perhaps they found her glower a little unnerving, not to mention the fact that she was as tall as they were.

"Can I help you?" she asked, in perfectly polite Japanese.

"You are not wanted here," the larger man spat back at her as he turned toward the crying girl. When he reached as if to grab her arm, Emily quickly inserted herself between them.

"You're the one not welcome," she hissed. As she said this, she grabbed his hand, twisted it back and pushed him to the floor. Everything in the room seemed to stop for a brief moment, and it felt to Emily as if every eye had turned her way, though perhaps no one was paying any attention.

The young man on the floor writhed in agony from the insult he felt he had just received, and sprang back up, ready to fight, though perhaps uncertain as to whether he could actually strike her in public. When Emily appeared unmoved, which only infuriated him the more, he reached for her, as if he meant to grab her arm and shake her, and his friend moved to seize the girl at the same time. Emily grabbed across the first man's wrist and twisted it up and out, spinning him into his friend and sending them both crashing to the floor. Now people in the room began to take notice.

She stood over them and growled, "Stay down, unless you want to risk even greater humiliation."

The two men looked up into her eyes and apparently thought better of challenging her again. Whatever calculation they'd run through, it seemed to give them no confidence they would be able to save face in this sort of confrontation. Slowly edging away from her looming figure, they picked themselves up and tried to walk away with some dignity, and just as they left the room, the first man hurled a curse over his shoulder at Emily. She shrugged and turned back to the table where she had been sitting.

The girls looked dumbstruck. It must never have occurred to them that they could stand up to men in such a way. Still, they'd been drawn to seek shelter at Emily's table. On some level they must have sensed something reassuring there, but now they looked at her with a mixture of amazement and horror in their eyes. She had protected them, but at what cost?

"What did they want?" Emily asked. The girls stared back at her, speechless. "Why do you tolerate such behavior?"

Again, they were silent. She figured they understood her perfectly. Still, they seemed to have no idea how to respond. Seeing that this inquiry was going nowhere, she leaned over to look directly into their faces and said, "You are on your own now. Stand up for yourselves." She flashed them a little smile and walked away.

The next day, she boarded a train to Tokyo. The route took her through the lake district near Kosai, where her mother's family came from, though it seemed unlikely she had any relatives living there anymore. The thought occurred to her to get off and catch a later train, but in the end she decided to stay in her seat and content herself with watching the scenery pass by through the window.

Her mind returned to the scene at the university, and she still found it hard to fathom why those girls allowed themselves to be treated in such a way. *How could they act as though they were helpless, at the mercy of a bully? Why did no one else object?* It all seemed incomprehensible.

Even more puzzling to her was how isolated they seemed from their own inner strength. They could resist, if they would only choose to do so. But, somehow, they had completely lost sight of that dimension of their own personalities, making themselves into victims and waiting for the next bully to take them up on their offer. They had doomed themselves to spend their lives in a cringing existence, hiding from boyfriends, and later, husbands. Certainly such behavior did not seem to her particularly Japanese. Her own mother would never tolerate such treatment, nor would she ever allow Emily to do so. It made her angry just to think about it, and frustrated to realize there was nothing she could do to help those girls in any lasting way.

She spent that night in a hotel in Tokyo, and boarded a plane for Honolulu out of Narita airport the next day. After a long, uneventful flight, on which she slept most of the way, she cleared border control in Honolulu, as an American citizen of Japanese descent. The border security agent asked a couple of perfunctory questions, and she grunted a couple of bland replies, and passed on through. Almost no notice was taken of her first official act as Michiko Tenno, but she still found the experience not a little bewildering. It was, after all, exactly how she wanted to live, as an ordinary citizen, the sort of person government agencies take no special notice of. But as the pieces of her identity fell into place around her, she couldn't help feeling almost numb. As she walked away, she slapped her face lightly and snapped into an alert mode. She needed the rest of her stay to be as uneventful as her entry had been.

After a quite circuitous journey through the terminal,

with her eyes peeled for any suspicious looking people, really anyone who betrayed an unhealthy interest in her—no one stood out—she brought her luggage to a ticket counter on the upper level of the terminal and checked it through to Los Angeles, except for a small overnight bag. Her flight departed the next evening, giving her a bit more than a day to spend in Honolulu.

She took a room in a motel near Kapiolani State Park, and found a seafood stand around the corner where she had lunch. Later, she rented a scooter to explore the area around Diamond Head. Her parents had come to Oahu when she was just an infant, though they probably lived further around the point, up towards the Marine base at Kaneohe Bay. The scenery was spectacular, but it didn't feel familiar.

"It isn't home," she thought. "That's in Virginia, for better or worse."

Emily spent the next morning wandering around the capital city, enjoying blending into the melting pot of American, Asian and Polynesian cultures she found there. She didn't stand out at all among the Chinese, the Vietnamese, the Koreans and the Japanese. They were all Americans, like her; they shared her manners, her culture… even her gait didn't stand out, not like it had in Kyoto. No one would think she looked out of place here. And yet, she felt someone was watching her. She couldn't quite put her finger on it, couldn't quite see who it was, but she felt it all the same. The problem with blending in was that danger could blend in, too.

She made her way back to the airport, looking over her shoulder the whole way, and noticed nothing out of the ordinary. Airport security might make it easier to spot a tail, she figured, and after she passed through the checkpoint, she went to a nearby restaurant and took a seat where she could watch whoever came through after her. A raisin bagel with cream cheese and a glass of orange juice gave her an excuse to spend some time on this little vigil, but she saw nothing suspicious, and wondered whether she even could spot a trained operative. After about twenty minutes, she walked to the gate and boarded her flight.

Several hours later, she arrived in Los Angeles, and congratulated herself that her instincts seemed to have been correct—if there were any Chinese operatives in Honolulu, they hadn't tracked her onto the plane. At least, she didn't see any suspicious types, nothing to set off any alarms, even though she found excuses to walk down the aisle a few times during the flight. She left Los Angeles without any further incident, and flew on to Charlottesville, arriving that evening.

CHAPTER NINETEEN
BACK HOME AT LAST

Emily's flight landed at Charlottesville-Albemarle airport late, around 11:00. A regional carrier handled the last leg, riding on a commuter jet, three seats across. Choppy weather bounced the plane around quite a bit—a real roller coaster ride—a few passengers turned green, and at least one threw up, all of which kept the flight crew busy tending to the queasy. Emily peered out her window and wondered at the amount of light visible even at night. The country looked like a Christmas tree, though near the end of the flight, she noticed a jagged, dark gash to the south that must have stretched for miles, like a chasm amidst all the surrounding lights. She guessed it must be the forests around her home, and got lost in one of those perspective paradoxes: seen from above, the mountains looked like a dark hole in the bright valleys. The idea offered her some little reassurance: a dark haven from the lights... and she felt safest when she was in the woods, and exposed when she went into the towns. That's the lesson she learned from all those camping trips with her father. But now it struck her that she might also be hiding in a hole, living a buried life. Unless, perhaps, by something like an optical illusion, she was really living on a mountaintop, free in the bright, thin air.

She made her way to the baggage claim, and while she waited for her luggage she thought of those two girls at the university in Kyoto. They thought of themselves as helpless, and that had become their reality, as if someone were hiring victims, and they couldn't help but apply for the job. The one girl had tried to stand up to those guys, but crumpled at the first sign of aggression. The other one merely cried the whole time. Had they ended up like that by chance, or was this an expression of who they really were? Or were they merely living out some eternal human type? The obvious comparison to her own situation was impossible to ignore: she lived in hiding, trying to craft an identity she could use to live out in the open. Was it really only temporary, or was she merely seeking another hole to hide in?

Her luggage tumbled off the conveyor belt on to the carousel and slowly circled toward her. She grabbed the biggest piece and hoisted it up.

"Damn, this is heavy," she groaned.

Before the obvious next thought could come to full expression, she noticed the nametag hanging from the handle, and couldn't remember if she had written her information in it. Out of curiosity, she lifted the flap and noticed the curious double characters, kanji over English letters. She knew she hadn't written *that*. And then it struck her like a thunderbolt: it was her mother's handwriting; *she* had written her daughter's name: *Michiko Tenno*.

A sign doesn't arrive with more fanfare than this one had, and she could hardly fail to recognize a message from her mother about who she should be. She scrambled to pull the rest of her luggage off the carousel and sat down next to the stack, the name her mother and father wanted for her dangling right there before her eyes. They'd devised it on their own, without any input from Michael, or any other outside source.

As she pondered the meaning of a message from the other side of the world… and beyond, the next thought presented itself.

"How am I gonna get home?"

An electronic sign hanging from the ceiling warned her that the last shuttle left in fifteen minutes. It would drop her in Goshen, where she could get a taxi to Warm Springs, if one could be found at this hour. Her predicament seemed even less pleasant the more she contemplated the task of hauling the luggage all the way to the other end of the arrivals terminal to catch the shuttle. Just then, she saw some familiar faces: Wayne rushing towards her, long legs thundering through the terminal, bellowing her name the whole way, with Danny and Billy trailing behind him.

"Hey, Em! Over here."

"We're just in the nick of time, by the looks of it," Billy piped up.

Before she could even find the words to express her pleasure at seeing them, they'd grabbed all her bags—"Gee, Em, did you have all this with you when you left?"—and began hauling them to Billy's parents' SUV.

"How did you guys know when I was coming in?" she asked incredulously.

"It's just one of those 'friend' things, ya know," Wayne asserted in his best mock-heroic tone, while Billy snorted behind him. "We just sensed your need, and leapt into action."

"We figured you had to be coming in today or tomorrow, because school starts on Monday," Danny said. "Wayne wanted to stake out the terminal for the last few days."

"Yeah, he just wouldn't listen to reason," Billy said with a laugh. "Thank God his mom's car's in the shop, or we would have been practically living here."

Emily had to laugh along with him, and at herself for only just realizing the pleasure their company gave her. She loved her friends, and felt the truth of it tickle its way down her spine in the warm reflection on the fact that they loved her.

"I'm starving, guys. Can we stop and get something to eat on the way?"

"Now that's what I'm talkin' about," Wayne roared. "The telepathy between friends. I'm ravenous!" Everybody laughed, and Danny hedged a little.

"I'm tapped out, guys," he said.

"This one's on me, everyone," Emily trumpeted.

"See what I mean," Wayne roared again—he was in a mood. "It's that ol' psychic connection." In other words, he was broke, too.

"I know a diner on the way that's probably open late," Billy piped up.

"Step on it, my man," Wayne commanded imperiously. "My stomach growls hideously." They all laughed, and Billy stomped on the gas pedal.

They sat in a large semi-circular booth in the back of the diner, one of those places with seats covered in lime green vinyl and hammered nickel upholstery nails. Ribbed art-deco chrome edged all the tables and counters, and there was a drain in the center of the checkerboard tile floor— Emily wondered if they hosed the place out in the middle of the night. Each of them ordered some form of breakfast from the menu, with Wayne getting more than anyone, while Emily got a fruit plate and a bagel with cream cheese.

They all clamored to know every detail of her trip, which hardly came as a surprise to her, since she'd kept a pretty tight lid on her plans beforehand, for fear of committing herself to a story that might have to change later. But maybe this was the moment to open up to her friends... *since there no longer seemed to be anything to gain from concealment, at least not from them.*

"I went to Japan," she said, figuring she should keep New Zealand to herself, in case Michael planned on staying on there a bit longer. "I spent the break with relatives." That last part was true, though not exactly consonant with the way in which the first remark was.

"Japan?" Danny said. "I thought your family was from China."

She could see that Wayne and Billy shared his perplexity, judging from their faces, and Emily couldn't help laughing. She didn't know exactly how it happened each time, but for some reason people always seemed to assume that about her. She was tall for a Japanese, she supposed, and maybe she didn't give people much to go on to avoid the error.

"I'm sorry guys... there's a lot I have to tell you, stuff I've been keeping from you, and I'm sick of it." She paused to take a breath, and the guys were all expectation. "Here goes. My dad is dead."

She had to stop right there. Her friends gasped, as if there were no more air in the room, and she struggle to hold back the tears. It still hurt to say it, even in front of friends, since it just made the event real again with all the same vivid pain. One more long breath helped her sigh it out, and she went on.

"He was killed in a crossfire at the estate," she said, speaking quickly so as to get through it more quickly, though the fixed horror etched on the boys' faces threatened to stall her effort. "His boss was targeted by covert operatives in the intelligence community. They invaded the estate one night in October and he died trying to keep me safe."

This last was too much even for her. The image of the scene broke over her once again, and she wept openly.

"Oh my God, Emily," Wayne cried out, finally able to give voice to what they all felt. "I'm so sorry." He wanted to say so much more, but the words just didn't come, and the three of them sat in silence for a long moment, as if to observe a moment of silence for Emily's father... though of course they all thought only of her.

"There's more, guys," she said in a tremulous voice. "My name is not really Emily. That's just an informal family name, Emily Kane. My legal name has always been Michiko." Now utterly perplexed, the boys were reduced to silence again. "Don't worry, you can still call me Em."

She found herself smiling again, almost involuntarily, and the boys laughed nervously, no doubt relieved to find that she was open to humor.

"Michiko," each one said, almost simultaneously, trying out the feel of it in their mouths. "That's kind of cool sounding," Danny said.

"It means 'the way' or maybe wisdom, or a whole lot of other stuff. I think I like 'the way' best," she added, trying to normalize the name for them.

"So, do you, like, speak Japanese?" Billy asked, with an odd look on his face.

"Yeah, I do," she admitted, feeling a little guilty that so much of her personality had been concealed from them. "But don't worry guys. It's just the same old me. I'm still the Emily you know from the dojo and school, you know, the one who kicks your butts on a regular basis."

They all laughed, and she began to feel better. Sharing a deep, dark secret with them, trusting them, it felt like shedding a great burden, especially when she saw their embarrassment, which she figured was because none of them had any secrets on this scale.

"There's one more thing," she said. "It's kinda bad, and I'm most sorry about keeping this part from you all. Those men who invaded the estate, the one's who killed my dad… he was afraid they were looking for *me*, and I've been hiding from them, sort of, ever since. But I'm sick of it, and I'm not hiding anymore," she said with a ferocity that scared them all a little bit.

"What do they want from you?" Danny asked, though he looked like he didn't really want to hear the answer.

Emily paused for a moment, pondering what it would

be safe to tell them, what would be safe *for them*. There was no easy answer, so she just decided to push on with it.

"There's no good reason," she spat out, contemptuously. "My dad said they think I carry some special gene, something engineered in a lab, like, a secret code." She paused, took another breath, and continued. "There is no special gene, but they've fooled themselves into thinking there is, and they'll stop at nothing to find it."

"Holy crap, Em," said Wayne. "This is all pretty wild, cloak and dagger stuff. You're not just goofing on us, are you?"

"I wish I was, believe me. These assholes have destroyed my family, and I'm not letting them take anything else from me. I'm especially not gonna let them cheat me out of my friends. I love you guys."

This last statement stunned the boys, though she could see they were thrilled to hear how she felt about them. Of the few things she knew about boys, the most obvious one was that no matter the danger—and this one might well prove to be illimitable, despite its obscurity—it's in the nature of a boy's soul to minimize it, especially when it looms over a friend or, even worse, the girl he loves. A warning only sharpens his determination to stick by her, since he can't bring his mind to focus on the danger. Only the girl is real for him. Her sense of this truth, imperfect though it was, gave her no small anxiety for their safety.

"Here's the important part," she continued. "These are dangerous people. If you *ever* see a suspicious person around the dojo, or around school, or anywhere near me, you *have* to keep clear. You know me, I can handle myself. But I can't risk your safety."

"You mean someone like that woman at the dojo before Christmas," Danny asked.

"Yes, exactly like her. Steer clear of her and anyone like her. Also, suspicious Chinese guys… don't approach anyone like that. You have to promise me you'll keep away from anyone who looks wrong." Emily spoke in deadly earnest now, and they all sensed it. "Guys, I mean it. You have to promise me!"

They all reluctantly grunted and nodded their heads in some sort of vague assent. That would have to do, she supposed, especially since she didn't expect to get anything more explicit out of them. But she desperately hoped they would take her warning to heart.

Emily spread her glances over all of them, looking each one in the eye, this time not with a demanding glare, but with affection. Finally, she wiped the last tears from her eyes, tears of joy for the love of her friends.

"Let's go, guys," she said. "It's getting late."

They all nodded and went out to the SUV as Emily settled the bill with the waitress. On the way home, she told them about her second encounter with the guys from the pizza place.

"There's a video of it on the web. You can probably find it if you search for 'ass kicking gas station' or something like that."

Wayne had already found it on his phone before Emily had a chance to ask them not to tell anyone it was her.

"Whoa, Em, it's those same guys," Wayne chortled. "You really kicked that guy's ass!" Danny grabbed the phone and replayed it, hooting through the whole thing, and Billy had to pull over so he could see it, too.

"Did that girl pull a gun on you, Em," Billy asked, beginning to appreciate how awful that moment must have been. "What did you say to her?"

"I asked her if she wanted me to mess up her pretty face. You can see it had a powerful effect on her."

"That guy you threw into the building, he's not moving. Is he dead?" Billy asked nervously.

"No, though his arm's probably still in a sling. But that's my point. The whole thing was gross. There's nothing to brag about in it. I really wish they hadn't insisted on a fight.

And Wendy was there… she saw it all… so be careful what you say around her. I think she's still a little freaked about it."

"What's the deal with her anyway, Em," Danny asked. "Isn't she one of the Goths?"

"Yeah, I guess so, but she's pretty cool, you know. You guys should give her a chance."

"Yeah, like I saw her wearing non-black clothes before the break," Billy observed.

"Next it'll be non-black nails, eyes. Who knows what else," Wayne said with a snort, and Billy and Danny laughed along, until Emily brought them up short.

"Like I said, she's just a poser like the rest of us. So, let's cut her some slack, okay guys?"

They murmured another vague assent, and even she was surprised by how vehemently she'd spoken to them about Wendy.

When she finally got back home, Emily was exhausted. She dropped the luggage by the door and tumbled into the bed, where she fell asleep almost instantly. The next morning, she unpacked everything and put it all away. It was a good thing the apartment had a large closet, since the clothes her mother had bought her completely filled it. Six months earlier she couldn't have imagined it, though her mother would get immense satisfaction if she knew, but Emily found it quite comforting to see all her new clothes hanging in her closet. It was a bit of ancient maternal magic her mother was working on her from afar.

She spent the rest of the day getting ready for school, buying groceries, household sundries, cooking for the week, laying out clothes, all the domestic tasks she had foreseen a few months earlier. She also sorted through the changes that would have to be made in her various papers in keeping with her new resolve. This would include changing the name on her truck and dirt bike, of course, maybe even selling them and getting new ones. Most important of all, she would speak to the secretary in the front office at school and get her to change the name on her school records. She would also need to reintroduce herself to all her teachers as Michiko. That by itself would probably suffice for the rest of the school to hear of it. Undoubtedly some wit would be broken over her as a result, but that didn't really concern her. It was important to bring her real name out in public, to live openly as who she really is, as the person her parents wanted her to be.

CHAPTER TWENTY
MISS M COMES OUT

A white haired, older woman, the school secretary was probably in her sixties, though to Emily's eye she might as well have been a hundred. Mrs. Telford had been working in the front office for the last three decades, and the records for thousands of students had passed through her hands. She remembered some from many years ago, but her memory was not what it once was, and she couldn't exactly recall who this pretty girl in front of her now was.

"Emily Kane, ma'am."

"That's right, honey, I remember," she said, trying to hide what didn't need to be hidden. "And you want what now?"

"It's my name, ma'am. We need to change it in my records, to put my legal name on the records."

"Has your name changed?" she asked.

"No, not really," Emily began, hoping her story would put an end to the need to tell any more lies about herself. "Emily Kane is just a family nickname. It's what my cousins used to call me. But my legal name has always been Michiko Tenno."

"But what does it say on the birth certificate we have on file?"

Her records had been carried over by the school district from when her father had first enrolled her in elementary school, and Emily didn't really know what might be in the file. This was a sticky point she hadn't anticipated last night—had her parents devised some sort of birth certificate for her under the name Emily Kane? If so, it would be hard to explain how she had another one now, with a different name. Her mind raced through the possibilities as Mrs. Telford shuffled over to the filing cabinets against the back wall. A moment later, she returned with a thick folder in her hand.

"Well I'll be," she exclaimed. "There's no copy of a birth certificate in here. How on earth did that slip by unnoticed?"

Emily breathed a heavy sigh of relief.

"I don't really know, but I guess that's why the name on my records has been incorrect for all these years. Kane is my father's family name, so it's always seemed natural to hear it. But when I started doing college applications, I realized there was a problem."

That story seemed plausible to Emily, though she wasn't sure Mrs. Telford would buy it. But the old lady looked at the photo attached to the file, and this was obviously the same girl sitting in front of her today. She had no reason to doubt what Emily told her, even if it was a bit unusual. She'd seen stranger things in her time.

"Do you have your birth certificate with you, dear?"

"Yes, and my passport, too."

Emily showed her the documents, and Mrs. Telford was impressed. This was more documentation than she was used to seeing. She made a photocopy of the birth certificate and handed everything back.

"I'll change the name on your records in the computer and put a note in the paper files with your new information."

"Can't we change the name on the paper records, too?" Emily asked.

"Well, I don't know. I'll print out your high school records with your new name and put them in the file, of course. But the older records, the ones from elementary school, aren't in my computer. We'll have to leave those as they are."

Emily thought that might be good enough. She toyed with the idea of switching out the files herself at some later date. Mrs. Telford would be unlikely to remember this conversation, especially since she barely remembered who Emily Kane was in the first place. If the files for Emily Kane simply disappeared sometime after graduation, no one would be the wiser. It was a tempting notion, though she wasn't absolutely convinced it would be necessary.

"Thank you very much, ma'am," Emily said politely, and smiled as she got up to go.

"You're very welcome, dear. I'm glad we got that straightened out, Miss… Tenno."

"Oh, you can still call me Kane, if you like. It's my dad's name after all," Emily said, as she stepped out the door into the main corridor of the school.

She had a few minutes before lunch, so she headed to her locker to retrieve the bento box she'd prepared that morning, and to change out books. She walked by Mr. Jameson's room, her US History teacher, on the off-chance he was available, and seeing him through the window working at his desk, she stuck her head around the door.

"Ah, Miss Kane, what can I do for you?"

"Well, that's just it," Emily began. "My name, it isn't really Kane."

That was blunt enough, she thought. Jameson looked puzzled.

"If that's not your name, what is it?"

"You'll probably get a note from the office about it soon. Kane *is* my name, sort of. It's my dad's name. It's what people in my family usually call me. But it's not my formal, legal name. That's Tenno, Michiko Tenno."

"You know, it's the strangest thing," he said, looking a little embarrassed, "but all this time I've been assuming you were Chinese. Judging from your name, though, I suppose you must be of Japanese descent."

Emily smiled. "I get that a lot. My mom's from Japan."

"I see. Well, should I call you Miss Tenno now?"

"That's up to you. Either name is fine with me."

Emily walked through the halls to the cafeteria feeling very pleased with herself. She knew Jameson would pass the word around the faculty, and from there it would make its way around to the students. But she especially enjoyed showing indifference to her names. Of course, the difference between the names meant the world to her, but it would still please her to answer to either one.

~~~~~~~

At lunch, Wendy sat with her, and looked enviously at Emily's lunch. Her mom had made her some sort of sandwich and a bit of cole slaw, but Emily had an exotic meal: pickled vegetables with tofu on rice and what looked like teriyaki sauce. It hardly seemed fair to Wendy.

"Where did you get *that*, Em?"

"I brought my lunch from home, just like you."

"I know, but yours looks so much better. Did you make that?"

"Yeah, it's like one of my mom's recipes. You want some?

"You bet," growled Wendy hungrily. Emily slid it across the table and ate some of the cole slaw. Wendy gobbled Emily's lunch down. She'd eaten more than half of it before it occurred to her that she should give it back.

"I'm sorry about that, Em," she said sheepishly.

"It's okay, Wendy. If you like it that much you can have

it. I'll just eat yours." Wendy giggled with delight and finished it off. Billy and Wayne sat down a moment later. Emily ate half of the sandwich and toyed with the cole slaw.

"Hey, Wendy," said Wayne, with a sidelong glance at Emily. "How you doing?"

"I'm okay. Thanks, Wayne."

"You going to the dojo tonight, Em," Billy asked.

"I wouldn't miss it. How about you guys?" Just then Danny joined them.

"Hey, Wendy," he said, in a suspiciously ordinary tone of voice, as if there were nothing unusual about her sitting with them at lunch. She nodded and grunted, utterly bemused at how easy it was to join these guys, especially since she'd spent so much time disdaining them from a distance, imagining they were phonies. She felt a little guilty to be the recipient of their openhearted welcome.

"You gonna eat that, Em?" asked Wayne, gesturing toward the other half of Wendy's sandwich. Emily looked at Wendy and they both laughed.

"You can have it," she said with a smile and slid it over to him.

"You guys go to the dojo every night?" Wendy asked.

"Nah," said Danny. "Just most nights. You should come check it out. Sensei won't mind. He likes it when people watch class."

"But what if it's meditation tonight? She'd be bored silly watching that," Billy said.

"You should come, you know," Emily offered. "But bring a book in case it's meditation. You can ride over with me."

To be the subject of this much attention caught Wendy off guard, and she really was curious about the goings on at the dojo. Her old habits would have her turn them down with a sneer, and she struggled with this for a moment, but finally relented.

"Yeah, sure, what the hell," she said, with all the grace

she could muster.

Emily and Wendy drove over to the dojo after school, and arrived about twenty minutes before class. Emily showed her a bench on the side of the room where she could watch and sip some tea, and then went to change into some athletic gear. Tonight she brought a form fitting, black running outfit, and Wendy almost snorted tea out of her nose when she saw her come out of the changing room wearing what looked to her like some sort of cat suit. She was reminded once again how fit Emily was.

~~~~~~~~

Before the class began, Emily ducked into the office to talk to Sensei, to tell him about her name change. He seemed pleasantly surprised to hear it. She also wanted him to understand fully her new resolution about living a secret life.

"I'm just tired of hiding. That's not how I want to live, Sensei."

"Are you sure that's wise, Mi-chan?" he asked, shortening her new name in the way that made most sense to him.

"It's probably not, but I refuse to let these people dictate the terms of my life to me anymore," she said in a decisive tone.

"What do you need me to do?"

"I don't know yet. Maybe nothing. Maybe everything."

"Well, if you're no longer in hiding, maybe you want to go to the tournament next month. It would certainly inspire everyone in the dojo to see you there."

Emily smiled at this suggestion, but not for the reason Sensei had in mind. She thought it might be a way to bring her pursuers out into the open. In fact, it might be the best way to come out of hiding.

"Maybe I will," she said slowly and deliberately. "Let

me think about it. By the way, a friend is here to watch class today. Let's not do a long meditation this time, for her sake." Sensei smiled and nodded.

As the rest of the class filed in, Emily introduced Wendy to Sensei, and he was gruff, but kind, as usual. They worked on leg sweeps and grappling for most of the night. To see how much control a little joint leverage could give, even over much larger opponents—like Wayne, who was Sensei's demonstration partner for much of the class—kept Wendy on the edge of her seat. His huge bulk flew all over the dojo, much to his consternation, though strangely enough, Sensei managed to arrange it so that he remained uninjured.

For the last twenty minutes, they practiced with *nunchaku*, a pair of wooden clubs connected by a short cord. These are too dangerous for sparring, but they allow for intense speed and reflex training. Sensei walked the class through a few easy techniques that had the students swinging their *nunchaku* around their shoulders, arms and waists. There were a few slight mishaps, but nothing serious: Billy clunked himself in the head a couple of times.

At the end, Sensei asked Emily to give a full speed demonstration of a particularly complex pattern. She started slowly, letting the class get a good look at the sequence of moves, and then gradually accelerated. By the end, her hands were moving so fast the *nunchaku* were nothing but a blur. Finally, Sensei brought a couple of target pads over, and Emily struck them several times in quick succession without disrupting the pattern. When she finally stopped, the entire room burst into applause. Danny let out a loud whoop, and everyone started laughing, even Wendy and Sensei. After a truly impressive performance, Emily smiled and bowed—what else was there to do under the circumstances?

On the ride home, all Wendy could talk about was that last demonstration. Emily tried to draw her attention to the other things she had seen, especially the grappling techniques that had so captivated her earlier.

"Don't get distracted by the flashy stuff. It's the simple stuff that really matters, like learning how to stand your ground, even against someone bigger or stronger."

"Yeah, yeah, I know. But what's wrong with enjoying the flashy stuff, too?"

Emily laughed. Of course, she was right, there was nothing wrong with it.

"What's the deal with your name? I heard you changed it. What's the story with that?" Emily laughed to hear how the news had spread, just as she'd hoped.

"I didn't change it, but Emily is really just a family nickname. My real name is Michiko. *You* can still call me Emily if you like," she teased, "or just Em."

"Well, aren't you full of surprises?" Wendy sat silent for a moment as Emily pulled up to the bed and breakfast. "It's good you're back, you know," she said. "I really missed you."

"Yeah, without me, who'd make your lunches?" Emily said.

"Oh, yeah, I'm sorry about that." Wendy paused for a moment, then said "Oh, and I like your friends. They're alright."

"I think you mean *our* friends."

CHAPTER TWENTY ONE
THE TOURNAMENT

Martial arts tournaments are surprisingly common events around the country. In most states, one tournament or another is held just about every month, somewhere. These are often small, local affairs, attracting mainly little kids, who make up the bulk of any dojo's students. A few times a year, larger tournaments are held that attract more adults and higher-ranking practitioners. Mostly the tournaments are sponsored by karate organizations, some local or regional, a few even national in scope. But typically, they aren't limited to karate-style practitioners. Competitions are held in katas, both empty-hand and with weapons, and in sparring. For the kids and the adults in the lower ranks, the sparring is narrowly controlled and heavily padded—no full-force contact, no take-downs and no contact to the face. For the black belts, some tournaments allow more open bouts, with little or no padding and fewer restrictions on contact, grappling, and take-downs.

Sensei suggested the East Coast Regional Martial Arts Competition to Emily, an annual tournament held this year in Norfolk. Most competitors would come from eastern

Virginia, Maryland and North Carolina, though some people would come from further away, and a few even from abroad. Because of its proximity to several military installations, it would also attract a lot of military personnel, which would guarantee a large field of competitors in the black belt division. Emily registered for the advanced *kumite* as a black belt. When the boys heard about it, they all clamored to register for the tournament, too, and she had some misgivings about this, since she expected to encounter the Chinese there and didn't want the boys to be caught in the middle. Of course, she also knew there would be no way to keep them away.

The next few weeks in the dojo, classes focused on tournament preparation, especially polishing katas and fine-tuning sparring mechanics. Emily spent almost every extra moment there working with her friends, showing them in much more detail than she usually had time for how they made themselves vulnerable inadvertently, going over every technique in slow motion. She seemed infinitely patient with them and, of course, they couldn't get enough of her attention. Fighting Emily was always a very intimate affair, even if it always ended with a humbling defeat, but her care for them came to the fore, and the boys couldn't get enough of her wisdom… though how much of it actually sank in was perhaps a different question.

Naturally, Wendy became increasingly envious of the boys for monopolizing her friend's time. The only solution was to come to the dojo, cheer them all on, and poke fun at them, too. Eventually, Wendy became a fixture there, even though she never expressed any interest in becoming a student, and Sensei did everything he could to make her feel welcome, since it was apparent that's what Emily wanted.

"I don't see how I'm making any progress," Billy moaned, finding himself once again on his back after a bout with Emily. Wendy giggled from the bench at the side of the room.

"You've improved a lot from just a week ago," Emily insisted.

"Not compared to you!"

"Billy, that's not about strength and speed. I'm not better at this because I'm faster," Emily said for the umpteenth time. "It really is all about *sen*, just like Sensei always says."

"Why can't I get it?" he whimpered.

"That's what the meditation is for, dummy. Sensei wants you to learn to listen to yourself, even just your breathing, so you can hear what your opponent is doing. That's how I do it. I listen to you, I 'hear' your decisions as you make them." She could see he was hardly persuaded by what she said, and she could hear Wendy snort in disbelief from the side of the room. "Don't worry about it. No one in the brown belt division will be able to do that either. You'll do just fine against those guys," she said, to reassure him. Perhaps it was unrealistic for him to think he could train against someone like Emily, but she thought a little humility would probably serve him well in the tournament.

As the big day approached, decisions had to be made. Since it would be about a five-hour drive, Emily wanted to catch a flight out of Shenandoah Valley, but Danny couldn't possibly afford that, and she didn't want him to feel excluded. The next best thing was to drive in a big group, and they were going to need a couple of hotel rooms, but Emily figured she could take care of that without embarrassing anyone in particular. Since the tournament would take place in the ballrooms of one of the big downtown hotels, she quietly booked a three-room suite for the weekend. Wendy's parents let her have the minivan they used for guests for the weekend, and Friday morning they all set out for Norfolk: Wendy, Emily, Wayne, Danny, Billy and Sensei. Emily sent a message to the email address Connie had given her.

The hotel turned out to be a huge complex a few blocks

from the water, with large parking lots on all sides of a crescent shaped central structure, as well as two smaller outbuildings across the parking lot from the convex back of the main building. One of the outbuildings was a wedding center with a small garden reception area, the other a taller, not yet completed business suites wing, the top floor of which was only partially enclosed.

"Whoa, Em, how on earth did you pull this off," gushed Billy when they got up to their suite in the main building.

"Convention discount, doncha know," she said, with a sour look on her face. Habits of deception are not so easy to break. "Wendy and I have this room, you three take that one. Sensei, you've got the couch out here. Sorry about that."

He grunted his assent and tried to look put out, though it was apparent that he couldn't care less. Later, when they were alone, Emily talked over the dangers with him.

"We need to be careful here, Sensei," she said. "If there's trouble, keep those guys away from it."

"What about you, Mi-chan?" he asked.

"I have to find my own way through this, Sensei. But I can't bear to have my friends in danger. Promise me you'll watch out for them." He grunted and nodded gravely, though with obvious reservations about her safety.

After an early dinner at a nearby restaurant, they went down to the tournament to watch the sparring finals for the younger competitors. The competitions were held in the largest ballroom in the hotel complex, which accommodated six separate rings, marked out by red tape stretched along the carpeted floor. A wider ring marked a safe zone around each one for the audience, and rows of banquet-style chairs positioned around each ring reinforced the buffer. By the time they arrived, eight or nine hundred people had already found their way into the main ballroom. Most of these were competitors and their family and friends, but plenty of spectators who appeared to be unconnected with any particular participant had come as well. By the time of the final sparring events for the black belt division the following evening, the audience would have swelled to a couple of thousand people, and even at that size, the large ballroom still seemed roomy.

The first competitions involved the youngest kids, some as young as six or seven years old, and as the day progressed, the organizers included more and more of the older kids, until by the end of the day, the final matches for the pre-adult division would be held. Emily liked to see the courageous way in which the finalists faced their fears, overcame them and won, or lost. If only her friends could attend to the same things she did. She nudged Wayne to notice this very thing when Sensei caught her eye and, with a tilt of his head, indicated a woman standing by the door. Emily glanced over and caught sight of Connie, scanning the room from the door. Her own observations of the room had revealed nothing more suspicious than she might be, all by herself, so she walked to the refreshment stand across the room, and Connie went to meet her, while Sensei kept the attention of the boys on the sparring.

~~~~~~~~

"The Chinese are here," Connie said, matter-of-factly.

"How many?"

"I'm not sure, maybe seven or eight. I think they're still uncertain about who they're looking for."

"They won't be for long," Emily muttered.

"What are you planning?"

"To compete."

Connie knew exactly what that meant. "What do you need from me?"

Emily hesitated before replying, looking directly into her face. For the first time Connie was able to look into those eyes without flinching, either out of fear or shame. It felt as if she had undergone the beginning of some sort of catharsis, an almost spiritual purification, and could now just begin to imagine measuring herself against this strange girl. Emily gestured to the ring across the room where her friends watched the sparring.

"Do what you can to keep them out of danger."

Connie nodded and walked off, quickly disappearing into the crowd.

The next morning after breakfast, with Connie keeping a discreet distance, Emily and her friends went down to watch Wayne take part in the adult *kata* competition. Of the fifteen or so other brown belts in the adult division, most performed very elaborate *katas*, some of their own devising. At Sensei's suggestion, Wayne chose to do a traditional *Shotokan kata* called *ninja shiho*. His performance was very precise and quite forceful, but the judges preferred a flashier *kata* done with a good deal of verve by another competitor, and Wayne took second place. Still, he was thrilled and accepted the result as an affirmation of all his hard work.

Later, Billy and Danny competed in the brown belt *kumite* and, as Emily had predicted, they did quite well even though they did not possess a profound sense of *sen*. They were stronger and faster, because of their athletic training, than most of their opponents. Billy did particularly well by attacking first and unsettling his opponents, forcing them into ill-judged counters. He won several matches in a row with this tactic. But in the final match, his opponent was as aggressive as he was and attacked his attack. Billy lost the advantage his aggressiveness had given him in the earlier matches, and was unable to regain his initiative through counters. He also ended up with a second place trophy, and Danny came in fourth. Wendy cheered them on from the side, along with Wayne and Emily, and she was crestfallen when Billy lost his last match.

"That was so unfair," she protested. "The judges missed at least two points Billy should have gotten."

"You are really into this, aren't you," observed Wayne. "I had no idea."

Wendy blushed a little. "I guess I'm just a fan-girl," she said.

Emily couldn't resist using the occasion to teach something to Danny, who was standing next to her watching the match. He'd been cheering Billy on and was especially impressed by his aggressive control of his earlier matches.

"You saw why he lost, didn't you? It was the same reason he won the earlier fights."

"Something about *sen*, I suppose."

"Not something, *everything*," Emily replied. "He didn't really control any of those matches. When he met someone as aggressive as he had been, he had nothing else to respond with."

Danny knew what she would say next, that initiative was not the same thing as aggression. He'd heard it many times before from Sensei, and maybe he even saw the way in which Billy had failed to control the *sen* of the last match. It was harder to see how that could be so in the matches he had won, but Danny knew he had not felt in control of the matches he himself had won. He had taken chances in them, and they had paid off, until finally they didn't. He had a pretty clear idea of what *sen* was not. It was just a lot harder to see what it was.

"Em, I feel like I am so far from really knowing what you and Sensei mean."

"Good," she said with a smile. "That might mean you're on the way."

The black belt *kumite* wouldn't start until after dinner, and Wayne was hungry, so they went out to a Lebanese falafel place around the corner. The conversation focused on the boys' triumphs, and Sensei and Emily heaped praise and congratulations upon them. Wendy was particularly effusive in her praise for Billy's sparring, and still a little miffed at what she perceived as an injustice in the scoring of his last match. Wayne was curious about what sort of clothes Emily was planning to wear in her competition, since she didn't appear to own a *gi*.

"Yeah, Em. What *are* you gonna wear?" Danny asked.

"I guess one of my running outfits," she replied. "I haven't really given it much thought. Why? Does it matter?"

"Well, you know, the tournament has a rule that all participants have to wear some sort of uniform," Sensei said, trying to conceal a sneaky smile. "The judges might make a fuss if they think you're dressed too informally."

"Oh," she said. "That hadn't even occurred to me." She began to look a little flustered, something none of her friends had ever seen before.

"Well, the thought had occurred to us," Wendy announced with unconcealed glee. "That's why we all pitched in and got you this!"

With a grandiose flourish, Wayne produced a package wrapped in shiny foil, which took Emily completely by surprise. She didn't really care about uniforms, but she cared deeply about her friends, and she was practically moved to tears by their thoughtfulness.

"I tried it on to make sure it would fit you," Wendy piped up, "since we're about the same size. It feels fantastic, all soft and smooth. Open it."

"Yeah, open it," they all cheered.

Emily tore it open, and discovered a jet-black kung fu style outfit with dark red clips on the jacket. It was made of some sort of performance synthetic, like rayon, only much tougher. And it did feel really cool, just as Wendy had said. "Oh my God! Thank you so much, guys. This is wonderful," Emily gushed. She had to wipe away a little tear. "I can't wait to try it on. Let's go back. Are we all done here?" Wayne stuffed what was left of Wendy's gyro into his mouth and mumbled, "all done."

When they got back to the hotel, Emily rushed up to the room to change into her new outfit. It fit her perfectly. By the time the rest of the guys got up to the room, she was already leaping off the couch doing flying kicks over the coffee table, tumbling around on the floor and out into the hall, springing up into what looked like a spinning double side kick. She was like a kid on Christmas morning. Wendy and Wayne were astonished by her form on a leaping, spinning kick.

"Whoa! I've never seen you do *that* before," Wayne burbled, and Wendy was speechless.

"How do I look, guys?"

"You look fantastic, Em," said Danny, and they all chimed in: "Fabulous," "Amazing!"

"Smokin'," shouted Billy.

"Absolutely marvelous," Wayne intoned, with all the authority of a fashion designer.

"We better head downstairs," suggested Sensei, herding them all toward the elevators.

CHAPTER TWENTY TWO
A FOOT IN THE DOOR

As it happened, there were no other women in the black belt division who had signed up for the *kumite*. The tournament organizers were in favor of simply giving Emily the first place trophy for the women's division and proceeding to the men's division. She protested and insisted on being allowed to compete in the men's *kumite*. Sensei and her friends made a big fuss about it, much to the consternation of the officials. They finally relented after devising a special liability waiver for her to sign, which she did without hesitation.

Some twenty or so other competitors lined the center ring, most of them from karate dojos, and about half of these came from the Norfolk naval station. These men were exceptionally fit, and looked very focused. They had an impressive intensity about them. The judges decided it might be simplest just to put Emily up in the first match against one of the tougher looking sailors. No doubt they hoped she would be eliminated in the first couple of rounds and be out of their hair. Her opponent was unimpressed by his first pairing, and may even have felt the judges had slighted him, and Emily had a notion that he would attack her with special ferocity. They met at the middle of the ring where the referee reminded them of the rules: five points, no full-force contact to the head, no strikes to the back of the head, spine or kidneys, and any strike that draws blood results in a penalty point. They bowed and looked each other in the eye.

"I hope you're ready, young lady," he said with a sneer.

"This isn't play fighting anymore." Emily smiled, and he stepped back, shaking his head.

Emily's friends couldn't hear that last remark, but they could guess from his facial expression what its import had been. Danny was especially concerned, since even though he knew first hand how formidable her skills were, he couldn't help but be alarmed by how much bigger and stronger her opponent was. His heart seemed to be thumping against his ribs and pounding in his ears. He wasn't sure he could bear to watch, and yet he couldn't bring himself to look away. Connie also watched discreetly from the door, as she scanned the room. She was concerned for Emily as well, but less from the threat posed by her current opponent than from another danger that might be lurking in the room, quietly observing the match.

The referee began the fight with a vertical hand gesture. Emily seemed unprepared as she stood and watched her opponent launch a front kick, three quick straight punches and a round house kick. He meant to force her back with the first few strikes to place her in the proper range for the roundhouse kick. Danny was aghast at what he saw, and thought she was dazed, like a deer with its eyes caught in the headlights of an oncoming car—Emily didn't step away from the onslaught. Instead, she twisted away from the first kick, then leaned back under the three strikes. When he tried his final kick, her opponent was stunned to find that she was too close, right up against his chest. By the time he realized his error, she had already hit him three times in the head and shoulders. As he tried to stagger out of her reach, she planted a side-kick firmly in the center of his chest.

He lay on his back on the mat, fuming. Emily knew he would think he hadn't been aggressive enough, so she disabused him of that error in the next two points, beating him to the punch in each case. In the fourth point, she blocked a series of strikes back across his body, completely locking his arms up until his upper body was immobilized.

By the time he realized what had happened, they were nose to nose and she was staring into his eyes. He saw for the first time what he was really up against, and recoiled. She released his arms just in time to deliver a double palm heel strike to his chest, sending him stumbling backwards. One last side-kick laid him out on his back. The final point was almost an anti-climax. Emily simply punched through a feint he had hoped would lead to an opening for a quick front kick. Match over. He stood across from her, looking utterly bewildered, and bowed grudgingly as the referee announced his defeat. She nodded her head slightly. He slouched over to the side of the ring and sulked in the row on the floor reserved for competitors. He knew he had been eliminated from any possibility of a first place finish.

Emily walked over and sat next to him. She knew he felt humiliated by this unexpected turn of events. He grumbled and muttered as she sat down, and watched the next couple of bouts in cold silence. Eventually, he came out of his funk and turned towards her.

"How did you do that?" he asked incredulously, as if the meaning of the result was still somehow a mystery. Emily just smiled at him. Finally, he gave in to the truth that was trying to work its way into his consciousness and said: "It wasn't even close, was it?"

"No," Emily replied with a kindly expression on her face. "You were pretty damn good, maybe as good as any of these guys," she said, tipping her head to the rest of the competitors in the row next to them.

"What am I not doing right?" he asked with genuine and uncomprehending sincerity.

"*Sen*," she said. "We can talk about it some time, if you like." He was stunned by her generous, open spirit. She was willing to talk to him, to teach him. Just then, it dawned on him that she was beautiful.

Danny had been half hiding behind Wayne throughout the match, peeking around his shoulder, at one point digging his fingers into Wayne's arm. No one in the whole room seemed to be expecting her to win, and when she did the crowd sat in puzzled silence. Danny punctuated the moment with a loud yell of exultation. Wayne and Billy roared next to him, and Wendy let out a little shriek. Sensei just smiled at his girl, and thought wistfully of her father.

Connie walked out into the parking lot behind the hotel to make her plans. A white van with tinted windows was parked off to the left, about fifty yards from the back entrance. Suspicious Asian men came and went, and she concluded that the Chinese strike team was using it as a base of operations. She looked for lines of sight, fire lines, and generally scoped out the positions she might take later. They were unaware of her presence, she had been very careful. Satisfied, she went back into the hotel.

The first round of matches ended, and twelve people had lost once. The level of skill of this field was very high, and her first opponent was indeed about as good as most of the others. Emily studied them as they fought, and saw that most relied primarily on speed, strength and aggressiveness in their fighting. Two of them had something more, something that might even turn out to be *sen*. One was a young man, not much older than her, or much taller, and he had long black hair pulled back into a pony-tail. He may have been an Asian mix like her, though it was not entirely clear. Whatever he was, he had a quiet way about him, and didn't win his first match through mere aggression. He had countered his opponent's attacks effectively, and worked through a long sequence of blocks and parries until he found an opening to deliver his strike, approaching his bout more like a chess match than a fight. It was clearly an intellectual process for him, and this left him vulnerable to a couple of quick takedowns, as he appeared to be too hesitant on a couple of occasions.

A second man, who looked to be in his late thirties or early forties, also seemed to have a rather more sophisticated style of fighting. Not a *very* large man, perhaps not quite six feet tall, but very solidly built with a good deal of upper body muscle development, he looked very much as you would expect a Marine Corps drill sergeant to look. It didn't surprise Emily to see that he fought in an extremely disciplined style, quite conservative, like the *Krav Maga* she had seen Ethan and Jesse practice. He studied his opponent, blocked effectively and waited for an opening. Every once in a while, he would attack first, but this seemed to Emily to be merely a calculation on his part to conceal the essentially conservative nature of his overall style. He scored most of his points when his opponent tried fancy spinning kicks, and he lost two points to simple reverse punches.

The next few rounds played out much as she expected. Her opponents were very aggressive, but were unable to control the match. She won the first one with a series of takedowns, relying almost entirely on leg sweeps and throws. The second one, against a hyper-aggressive man, she won through *sen sen no sen*. She attacked first each time, either scoring immediately or directly after his first block. She finished him off with a flourish that brought the crowd to its feet, blocking his punch with a quick reverse crescent to the back of his arm that led seamlessly into a leaping roundhouse kick to the side of his head. The force of her kick sent him spinning across the floor, and as the crowd roared its approval, she crouched over him tentatively, hoping she hadn't hit him too hard. When he finally opened his eyes, he looked into her face and just lay there for a moment smiling at her, as she sighed in relief. That match was over in less than a minute.

Throughout the tournament, she was intent on not giving the rest of the field a coherent sense of how she fought. She created the illusion that she was given to one sort of technique or another. Each competitor thought they had her figured out, and each one came to a different conclusion about what her strengths and weaknesses were.

After four rounds only four competitors were undefeated, Emily, the guy with the pony tail, the drill sergeant, and another rather larger man with long legs and arms. In the next round, she was paired with him. He was very fond of his left round house kick, and liked to keep his leg in the air, balancing on one foot, threatening his opponent with a sudden long range blow. It was obvious to Emily that he was nervous about close-quarter combat and used this technique to keep opponents at a distance. She took the first point by leaning out of the way of the first kick and then stepping to her right behind his raised leg, forcing him to bring his foot down. Just as he was about to touch the floor and put his weight on his left foot, she kicked it out from under him, sending him twisting to the floor, helpless. She hit him with three quick, light strikes to the jaw, armpit and chest as he fell. He lost the second point in a similar fashion, this time trying to follow his initial roundhouse kick with a wheel kick from his other leg, and hoping to catch her as she came up out of the lean she used to dodge the first kick. But before he could bring the wheel kick around, she struck the back of his left knee, and he went down again as she took the point with another series of quick strikes to his head and shoulders. In the subsequent points, he tried to initiate the action with front kicks followed by hand strikes, but Emily either kicked his foot before he could begin his kick, or hooked it on the way down and pulled him off balance. Again, he became immediately vulnerable to close quarter strikes to his head and chest.

Up to this point, she had yet to lose a single point. No one had even come close to making any contact with her, and the fellow who lost to her in the first round was in much better spirits. He was now openly cheering her on, and Danny and Wayne went over and stood by him to offer moral support to Emily's newest fan.

The judges decided that in the final round Emily should face both remaining competitors, even though the drill sergeant had lost to the guy with the ponytail. Of course, it was more or less a matter of indifference to her. Perhaps she even preferred it this way, not wishing to give anyone the occasion to think she had somehow evaded a potential opponent.

The first match was against the drill sergeant, who was determined to make up for his one loss by defeating her, and thought she had gotten off easy in her previous matches. He decided he needed to intimidate her early in the match and was willing to *bend* the rules, as he saw it, to do it. As they met in the middle to bow, and before the referee had signaled the beginning of the fight, he suddenly swung his fist into her head. She reacted in time to avoid the full force of his punch—it was a glancing blow that struck the edge of her jaw. But it still hurt. The crowd roared its displeasure, and the referee signaled the side judge to award her a penalty point. Emily looked at the referee and shook her head.

"No, give him the point," she said loudly enough for everyone to hear. Then she turned to her opponent and in quieter tones said "Shall I hit you as hard as you tried to hit me?"

"Give it your best shot, sweetheart," he said, with obvious contempt.

Emily looked at the referee and he nodded. She took that as tacit approval for what she was about to do. Connie, watching from the door, caught a glimpse of Emily's expression and winced slightly. She knew what it meant to be on the receiving end of that look. She also thought she understood the mentality of Emily's opponent, having received much of her training from men like him, men who took an obvious pleasure in dominating trainees, especially women. She awaited the event with a smirk on her face. A hand gesture restarted the match.

The drill sergeant evidently thought he had gained a mental edge over Emily, and tried to capitalize on it by attacking with a series of fast and powerful strikes to her midsection and head. Emily blocked them all, first pushing them across his body and then allowing him to swing wide. She stepped into the opening he left and landed a blistering array of strikes to his head and chest, finishing him with a full force reverse punch to his solar plexus. He staggered back, struggling to breathe for a moment, and stood at the edge of the ring, bent at the waist with his hands on his knees. The referee asked him if was able to continue, and he brushed the question aside angrily, and tried to stare her down. When she looked him in the eye and smiled, he shuddered visibly, as if a chill had just run up his spine.

Another hand gesture restarted the fight. He led with a left jab and tried to follow with a left kick to her knee that he hoped would leave her open for a head strike, but Emily slapped his jab back across his chest, swept his left foot out from under him and punched him hard on the left ear as he spun down to the floor in front of her. He tried to roll over onto his back as soon as he hit the floor, hoping somehow to counter attack from the floor. But before he knew what had happened, Emily landed on him jabbing her elbow directly into his solar plexus. He grimaced in pain and was again unable to breathe for a long moment. The referee asked him if he could continue and he brushed him aside again. He stepped to the center of the ring to face her.

He was convinced he needed to be even more aggressive in his attack and began this time with a ferocious series of strikes of every kind in rapid succession. That he meant to hit her as hard as he could was apparent to everyone watching, but Emily blocked them all one after another without giving any ground. To his great consternation, he found himself backing up even as he was attacking, much as Jesse had on that beach in New Zealand. And, like Jesse, he tried to force her back with a quick forward step and punch. But Emily anticipated his step and swept his foot before he could set it down, then grabbed his wrist as he fell backwards and twisted it hard, forcing him to flip over as he fell. He ended up on his back with Emily's elbow once again planted in the center of his chest. More or less completely disoriented, he lay on his back with a look of perplexity etched deeply across his face. His anger and frustration were palpable, so much so that it seemed to cloud his mind, keeping him from understanding just how profoundly he was out of his depth with this girl. He stood up, ignoring the referee and stood opposite Emily. She smiled at him and asked if he was okay.

"You better believe it, sister," he snarled.

"Well then, bring it on, tough guy," she said, meaning to provoke him.

When the referee dropped his hand to restart the match, he charged forward as if he meant to tackle her. Like a matador, Emily side-stepped him and swept his foot as he went by, sending him sprawling face first onto the floor. He picked himself up off the floor and lunged toward her again, this time trying to punch her hard in the face. Emily parried and twisted his wrist, first one way, forcing him into a deep, awkward crouch, and then the other way, forcing him up and over. He tried to resist the movement she was forcing him into, but to do so was unbearably painful. Finally, he felt himself leave the ground as he flipped over and out of control, ultimately landing several feet away, on his back at the edge of the ring. He lay there for a long moment, staring up at the ceiling, and Emily walked over, crouched down next to his head, and looked him in the eyes.

"Maybe you've had enough," she offered.

He looked up into her face and saw her, maybe for the first time. He seemed finally to understand the generosity in her words and nodded his head. The depth of compassion he saw in her eyes triggered a wave of nausea that washed over him, and he finally recognized it for what it was: shame.

"I'm sorry," he said in a small voice. "I behaved badly. Forgive me, Sensei," he said, casting about for the right word to express the respect he now felt he owed her.

"It's okay," she replied with a smile. "I hope you're not hurt."

He shook his head, and Emily helped him to his feet. With one fist held inside an open palm in front of him, he bowed deeply to her. The audience cheered thunderously. Then he bowed to the referee and the judges, and stepped out of the ring. The match was over. He had conceded the last point. There was nothing else for him to do.

Watching from the door, Connie found herself measuring her own behavior against that of the drill sergeant. She had behaved much worse than he had when she attacked Emily in the bathroom at the student center. She had been the recipient of Emily's mercy that day, but perhaps not her compassion, and she found herself longing to gaze once more into Emily's eyes, to search in those depths for the redemption she hoped to deserve. The thought that those eyes might be closed to her forever this very evening terrified her, and she staggered for an instant, and reached out to steady herself against a nearby wall. She took a deep breath and looked inside herself for the resolve to make sure that didn't happen. By the time she had regained her full composure, her face was locked in steely determination and her own eyes seemed like black mirrors, as if fashioned from obsidian.

The final match was anti-climactic by contrast to the one Emily had just won. The guy with the ponytail was careful and precise, and wanted to approach the match like another chess game, a problem of thoughtful calculation, but Emily refused to allow him the time or the space to think through his strategy in that fashion. She took the first two points with quick, ferocious attacks designed to force him into desperate defensive maneuvers that left him vulnerable. She fought as she imagined her father would, in each case, finishing him within three quick moves. He tried to adjust in the next two points by being more aggressive, but his initial attacks were just too slow to catch her off guard, and she was able to use each of his attacks to develop the vulnerability she needed to finish him. In the final point, he tried to use a left front kick followed by a left jab to create an opening, but Emily kicked his foot before he could fully extend it and slapped his jab back across his chest, leaving him completely vulnerable. She hooked his foot with hers and pulled him down with it, finishing him with a series of light taps to the side of his head. He knew he had lost decisively, and when he bowed to her, he said, "Sensei."

In a brief ceremony a few minutes later, the referee presented her the first place trophy, and the crowd roared its approval. The rest of the black belts in the *kumite* competition looked on from the front row. After the announcement, they stood up together and bowed to her, and she smiled, and returned their bow. Her friends rushed onto the stage and huddled around her, hugging her and shouting congratulations. When Wayne finally found his way to her side, she gave him a knowing look, and he put his hands on her waist, and lifted her high above his head so the whole crowd could see her, and she them. She leaned forward and spread her arms as if she were flying, and Wayne did a complete turn. Cheering filled the room and even seemed to shake the stage. The judges and the tournament organizers pushed through the crowd to meet this impressive young woman again, and to congratulate her once more. In the end, she thanked everyone, shook what seemed like a thousand hands, smiled graciously and waved to the crowd. Eventually, the swell receded and the crowd thinned out. Emily and her friends came down off the stage and made their way to the main door, when she spied Connie at the far side of the room, near another exit.

Here, guys," she said, handing the trophy to Wayne. "I'll meet you upstairs in a few minutes. I've gotta talk to someone."

She gave Sensei a meaningful glance and then headed across the room, while he herded the rest of them out the door and toward the elevators.

"The Chinese are using a van in the parking lot. They saw your matches. I imagine they're hoping to grab you in the middle of the night."

"Show me," Emily replied.

They walked out a side entrance and peered carefully around a corner, where Connie pointed to the white van. "That's where they'll gather to plan their attack," she said. "There's been some activity on the roof over there. I think it's one of their men. I don't think they mean to shoot you. He's probably there to cover their departure."

"Can he see us now?"

"Not from this side of the hotel." Connie guessed the rest of the strike team would gather at the van around midnight and try to grab Emily once the hotel quieted down, an hour or two later.

"We're gonna have to take care of the guy on the roof before I deal with the rest of them. I'll meet you there," Emily said, motioning to the building where the sniper was positioned, "just after twelve."

"Did you bring dark clothes?" For an instant it sounded like the sort of thing a mother would say to her daughter. Emily smiled at Connie and nodded, and then went back in to the hotel.

When she got up to their rooms, the guys were still in full celebration mode. Billy had managed to video Emily's matches and was playing them back through the TV. They had already watched them all a couple of times. She picked up the phone and called room service, seeing that Wayne was obviously gonna be hungry again soon, and they all needed something to go with the festive mood.

"I couldn't believe it when you kicked that guy upside the head," Wendy gushed. "I mean, he literally flew across the ring."

"Whoa, yes, that was amazing," Billy agreed. "It was like you launched yourself at him. I've never seen you do anything like that before."

"Yeah, I got a little carried away with that one," Emily said, putting the phone down. "I hit him too hard. I was really kinda worried he was hurt in a serious way."

"What did he say to you when you went over to him," Wayne asked.

"You know, he didn't really say anything. He just smiled up at me. I think he was a little groggy."

"What about that jerk who hit you? What did he have to say?

"Oh,… him. Yeah, that was unfortunate." Emily paused, rubbing her cheek, and Billy played the video of the first point.

"That was so cool when you stepped inside his last punch," Danny said. "I mean, you just unleashed all these strikes, and there was nothing he could do. He was like totally helpless."

"I bet that was the last thing he was expecting," Wayne snorted.

"Yeah, and he deserved everything he got," Wendy clamored. "I was glad you really unloaded on that guy."

"You know, he acted like a jerk," Emily said over her shoulder as she went into the other room to change. "But in the end, I think he wasn't so bad. I mean, you gotta give everyone a chance."

She put away her new kung fu uniform and put on black jeans, a black t-shirt and shoes, and went back out just as the room service arrived. Of course, Wayne was thrilled. Emily had read his stomach precisely. A large tray of scrambled eggs, French toast, bacon, sausage, fruit, bagels, juices, beckoned from the center of the room. Everyone crowded around and piled up plates, without asking any questions, even Wendy, who seemed to be as hungry as anyone. While her friends were occupied, she drew Sensei aside and told him her plans. He was, naturally, dismayed.

"There has to be a better way, Mi-chan!"

"There isn't."

"We can notify the authorities. Let them handle it."

"We don't know which authorities to trust here, Sensei. But even if we did, that would just delay the inevitable. *This* is the moment to confront them," she said decisively.

Sensei's shoulders visibly slumped as he let out a long sigh. He knew he was not going to be able to change her mind.

"What do you want me to do?"

"Keep these guys here. Don't let them go out. Don't let anyone in."

She motioned to Wendy, and led her into the other room.

"I've got to go take care of something in a few minutes, and I don't want the others to follow me. You've gotta help Sensei keep them up here. Can you do that for me?" Wendy's face turned pale and her upper lip quivered.

"Emily, what's going on? What are you going to do," she asked tremulously, tears forming in her eyes. She looked a little unsteady on her feet, and Emily helped her sit down in an armchair. "Can't you just stay up here with us?" She couldn't possibly know what the danger was, but she seemed to feel it as vividly as if it were looming over them both right then, or as if a cold, dark hand were closing around her throat.

"Wendy, you've have to help me with this. Sensei can't do it by himself. He's gonna need your help." Wendy sobbed as she stared at Emily. "You know me. I can take care of myself. But I can't keep them safe at the same time. You've gotta do this for me."

Wendy nodded and tried to collect herself before going back out to the other room. She went into the bathroom and splashed some water on her face. Emily put on a close fitting synthetic vest and a black hoodie. She was now dressed entirely in black from head to toe. She pulled her hair back into a short ponytail and glanced over at Wendy, who gave her a shaky smile. Emily slipped out into the hall and walked quietly to the elevators.

~~~~~~~

Connie crept up to the roof of the hotel's unfinished business suites building, expecting to have to subdue the Chinese sniper. But Emily was already there, and the sniper lay in a confused heap off to one side. Connie could surmise that she had hit him on the side of the head with a fierce roundhouse kick, since she had personal experience of the efficacy of Emily's foot. She took out some cord she had prepared for the purpose and bound his hands and feet while he was still unconscious. Then she hefted his rifle, examined the clip, peered through the scope, and said, "This'll do nicely." Finally, she settled in by the railing and rested the barrel on the pad he had prepared.

"Whatever you do, don't shoot any of them to protect me. Just keep 'em from going in the hotel. And absolutely don't kill any of them, even this guy here." Connie nodded reluctantly. It would be so much easier just to take them out one by one from here. She had been trained to do just that.

She looked through the scope at the van for a moment, then panned around the parking lot. It was a good position, commanding the entire area between the van and the hotel. She looked up to say something to Emily, something about how she shouldn't underestimate how dangerous these guys were, but she was already gone. She quickly looked through the scope again, sweeping the area on the near side of the van until she spotted her—dressed all in black, she was hard to notice in that landscape, practically a shadow.

Connie watched as Emily walked slowly but deliberately to the van, and she noticed her gait perhaps for the first time, like a tomboy's, with a slight saunter, even a little swagger. She paused to admire the strength that seemed to emanate from Emily's body. Then the van came into the field of view of the riflescope and Connie felt a wave of panic wash over her. What was she going to do? Had they seen her already? Was it too late for Emily to run away? She was tempted to rake the side of the van with bullets, kill them all. Her finger throbbed on the trigger, but she remembered Emily's words and held off. Then she was next to the van, and suddenly thumped her fist on the side panel. Connie could hear the hollow sound all the way up there.

The side door slid open and two men tumbled out, and then two more! Before she knew it, six guys men had surrounded Emily. Some of them were big, much bigger than her. Two wore gray suits, obviously government issue, and the rest were dressed like a grunge band, apparently in an effort to blend in with the locals. Their age spoiled the effect, and they just appeared even more dangerous. Connie watched as they looked Emily up and down. She seemed strangely calm, glancing at each one, but not making any move.

The largest one, one of the suits, stepped forward and wrapped her up in both arms from behind, lifting her feet off the ground... and she didn't even resist! She just seemed to let him do it. Connie placed his head in the crosshairs, her finger dancing on the trigger. Every fiber of her being wanted to make his head explode with the bullet, but Emily's voice still echoed in her ears: "Don't shoot any of them to protect me." The words seemed to make no sense to her at that moment, but she struggled to honor them, to honor Emily.

She watched helplessly as the others closed in, one of them holding what seemed to be a syringe. Why wasn't she resisting? *She should fight back.* Connie knew what Emily was capable of. Why wasn't she doing anything? Was she sacrificing herself just to protect her friends? Was she just gonna let them take her away? She desperately wanted to squeeze the trigger.

But then something did happen, though she wasn't

quite sure what it was or how exactly it started. She noticed Emily wriggle ever so slightly in the arms of the man holding her from behind. It seemed so harmless, so insignificant a movement. He leaned forward to adjust his grip on her, and as soon as her feet touched the ground... she must have gotten control of his arm, somehow... there was no other way to account for it. He seemed to tense up as if in extreme pain, and then suddenly swung around, crashing into the man with the syringe. Connie had no clear notion how it had happened, but the two men lay dazed in a heap as Emily grabbed the syringe and stuck it in one of them. An instant later, she seemed almost to fly through the air at two others, kicking one on the side of the head from an impossible angle, as she evaded the kick of the other. She landed behind him, and before he could turn to face her she had kicked out his right knee and then spun into a wheel kick to his head. What Connie saw was a black whirl, a little too fast to track from that distance.

Four men lay in a heap in the twinkling of an eye. The two others looked anxiously at each other, as if to work up their courage. One of them produced a knife. *That was it... she'd seen enough.* Connie placed the crosshairs on his head, and was ready to fire when she saw Emily looking directly at her in the scope. She relaxed her finger. Did Emily know what she was about to do? Had she really been looking *at* her?

Just then, the door on the far side of the van slid open and someone got out. The last two men froze, apparently waiting for this last man to appear. A moment later, he was in sight, waving them off. He snapped his fingers and uttered a sharp command, and his men picked themselves up and limped away to a safe distance. He seemed somewhat older than the others, perhaps in his mid-forties. For a long moment, he said nothing to Emily as he looked her up and down, and she sized him up, too. Connie recognized him from the incident in Taiwan as the man who had orchestrated the ambush of Meacham's teams, and she couldn't help but think of him as a cold, implacable enemy. She situated his head squarely in the crosshairs of the riflescope.

Then suddenly, he surged forward with a left front kick followed by a lightning fast series of kicks and punches, moving much too fast for Connie to keep him in her sights. She couldn't shoot him if she wanted to, at least not without endangering Emily. All she could do was watch as Emily blocked and parried all of his attacks, finally controlling his right wrist long enough to land a palm heel strike to his jaw just below his ear. He stepped back, clearly surprised that she had been able to hit him at all. He spun into a high wheel kick followed by a right back fist and a sneaky left hand reverse punch. But Emily leaned away from the kick and the back fist, and stepped inside his left hand to land her own reverse punch to the center of his chest, striking him hard, harder than she had hit anyone in the entire tournament. The force of the blow drove him a few steps back, and he gasped for breath as he stared at her.

He attacked one last time with even greater ferocity than before, a seemingly endless rain of strikes and kicks. Emily was able to defend it all, though it seemed to Connie that she was pushed nearly to the limit of her abilities. He must have been the most formidable opponent she had ever faced, but with each block, she forced him to commit his hands and feet more and more completely, until finally the two of them were locked together, face to face—he stared into her eyes and she into his. From the rooftop, Connie found herself straining to see whatever it was they saw, but she couldn't quite manage it. It was infuriating and tantalizing for her. But through it all, Emily seemed completely serene. She didn't appear angry or even offended by this man who was attacking her in a parking lot in the middle of the night. If Connie could have inspected her face more closely, she would have said she seemed to have no mood at all as she stared at him. He recognized this too. Finally, he smiled and gently pushed her away.

Connie saw she was of no further use to Emily on the roof. She cut the cords binding the Chinese sniper who was beginning to come to, then brought the butt of the rifle down across his nose, effectively stunning him again. Then she packed up his rifle and went down to the parking lot. As she walked over to the hotel entrance, the rifle case slung over one shoulder, she watched Emily talking to her assailant, though at first she couldn't make out what they were saying. As she got closer, she could see that Emily no longer seemed serene, and she caught bits and pieces of their conversation.

~~~~~~~~

"*Sifu*, you are not the girl we are looking for," the man said, in heavily accented English. Emily looked puzzled. He continued in Japanese: "You are not the one, Sensei. My men do not understand *Nihon-go*."

"I don't believe you," she replied testily, also in Japanese. "I *am* Yuki Kagami's daughter. Who else *can* you be looking for?"

"I know who you are, but when I look into your eyes, I see only a gentle breeze in the pine trees. You are not a genetically enhanced warrior."

"How can you be so sure?"

"I saw you hold back against your opponents in the tournament, and just now against me and my men. You could have killed us all, but you didn't. The person we are looking for would not be able to show such restraint, such compassion."

"But those were only choices. I have often felt the urge to kill the people who killed my father. How can you know that isn't who I really am?"

He smiled at her. "You are no genetic freak. You are just supremely well trained. I would gladly have you as my teacher."

"Surely you didn't come all this way just to discover that," she muttered, deadpan.

"I had to be sure. My masters think there is a genetic super-soldier. They will stop at nothing to find it. They are fools. You and I both know, deep down, there *is* only training."

"That's *not* all there is," she cut him off. "They destroyed my family… my grandfather, my father and my mother. I am alone."

He couldn't help hearing the depth of pain in her voice, seeing it swirling at the bottom of her dark eyes, and it seemed to cut right through him like a jagged blade. Here was someone capable of feeling the magnitude of the wrong that had been done to her, and the dishonor it reflected on him.

"I am truly sorry, *Sensei*," he said in a soft, deep voice. "The chain of events that has led us here began two decades ago, but if I could undo any of it, I would. Please forgive me."

He must have glimpsed in her eyes just then the immense wellspring of compassion and forgiveness that made its home there, and sighed as his shoulders visibly sagged, perhaps under the weight of the knowledge that she could indeed forgive him.

"What is your name," she asked.

"Tang."

He bowed to her and then snapped his fingers. His men limped into the van.

"What will happen to you if you return empty handed?"

He looked back at her and said: "Nothing you can do anything about."

He got in the van and they drove off. She followed with her eyes as they turned out of the parking lot and down the street, then took a deep breath and let it out slowly as she walked back to the hotel.

Connie waited for her by the entrance, searching her face, trying to read her expression for the meaning of the events in the parking lot. Emily smiled wanly at her, put her hand on Connie's shoulder and said "Thank you."

Connie drew her into a hug and whispered "Anytime." But she knew Emily had not really needed her help. Her debt was not repaid, not by a long shot, and she knew it. But she felt that her personal redemption was underway, and all thanks to this puzzling, enigmatic girl.

CHAPTER TWENTY THREE
HOME AT LAST

On the ride back to Warm Springs the next day, the boys sat in the front of the minivan with Sensei, and Wendy sat in the back with Emily. Billy and Wayne crooned teasing songs about heroes returning home, and Danny searched the videos of all their matches for dazzling moves to hoot and crow over. This was more attention than she generally cared for, but she didn't want to spoil everyone's enjoyment of the moment. Her own pleasure came from the relief she felt at the result of the weekend, and had almost no connection to the tournament. For the first time in months, she could finally relax, even if Wendy couldn't exactly.

"What happened last night?" Wendy whispered. "You know, out in the parking lot."

"Nothing, really."

"C'mon, Em. It didn't seem like nothing when you left the room. And don't try to tell me that scary-looking woman was just a casual acquaintance."

"You saw her?"

"I'm not stupid," Wendy said. "You can trust me, you know." At these words, Sensei glanced over the seat back in front of them and shook his head.

"Okay, Wendy, but you have to keep it to yourself. I mean, not even the guys need to hear about it. Are we clear on that?" Emily said in a low voice, with both eyes fixed on her friend. When Wendy nodded, she continued. "I confronted the people who've been following me for the past few months out there in the hotel parking lot."

"Who were they?" Wendy asked, eyes wide as saucers.

"Chinese intelligence operatives."

"Holy crap," Wendy gasped, until Emily touched a finger to her mouth. "Did you have to fight them? I mean, was anyone hurt?"

"I had to give a few of them an attitude adjustment," she said, with a quiet laugh. "But, no, nobody was hurt in a serious way." Sensei shook his head, as if to signal that she shouldn't divulge anything else.

"I still can't believe you did that, I mean, all by yourself."

"Oh, I had help. That scary woman had my back."

"Who is she?" Wendy asked. "And what did the Chinese guys want from you?"

"There may be some things you don't want to know." Emily said, in a tone of voice that signaled to Wendy to let it drop. "It's over now. That's all I care about."

After lunch at a diner outside of Richmond—pork barbecue for the guys and salads for the girls—Emily climbed into the back of the mini-van, laid her head on Wendy's shoulder, and fell fast asleep for the rest of the journey.

That evening, she called Michael and her mother to tell them the news. Naturally, she tried to spare her mother the bit about fighting foreign agents in a dark parking lot, to the extent possible.

"You did what?" Yuki exclaimed, and Michael whistled in the background.

"Don't worry, Mom. Everything worked out."

"But how did you even get to speak to them?" Michael asked, having grabbed the phone.

"Did you have to fight them?" Yuki called over his shoulder.

"Let's just say we came to an understanding." When Yuki left to fetch Andie a moment later, Emily could afford to be more explicit. "I took out their sniper, and then confronted them in the hotel parking lot."

"Holy crap," Michael said.

"Their leader, a man named Tang… we came to an understanding."

When Yuki returned with Andie, Emily regaled them with descriptions of the tournament, and her friends. Andie wanted to know all about Wendy, and how her new wardrobe went over at school.

One evening a few days later, she pulled the truck into the driveway at Danny's house, and climbed the stairs that led to the apartment above the garage. Taped to the door, she noticed an envelope addressed to Miss Kane. Inside, she found an old photograph and a short note. It said:

"Don't get too comfortable, because it's not over yet. Sorry, kiddo. You can count on me." It was signed, "C."

Emily scanned the yard and the street. If Connie could find her, maybe Meacham also knew where she lived… and she didn't even like the idea that Connie knew. The thought occurred to her that it might be prudent to dig out the sleeping bag and camp out under the rhododendron again. She glanced absentmindedly at the photograph held casually between two fingers as she pushed the door open, and *then she noticed him*—the recognition froze her for an instant—her father, in fatigues and standing on a wooden dock, next to a single-engine seaplane. The image must have been from his days on Okinawa, or maybe Manila; he looked so young and carefree. Two other men stood around him, one with his face obscured by a wing strut, and a tall woman leaned casually against a piling, all four of them in military gear.

When she examined the photo more closely, holding the photo under the kitchen light, she recognized the woman: Connie.

Later, lying in bed, she held the picture close to her chest, or held it up to check again, just to make sure... Eventually, she dozed off, and dreamed the familiar dream: walking through a cool forest glade, leopard shade decorating her face, dirt and leaves crinkling underfoot, and the sound of rushing water in the distance. She recognized the spirit of the place, her father's spirit—this was his place, where she could always find him.

The End

BONUS PREVIEW OF *GIRL PUNCHES OUT*

CHAPTER ONE
SPARRING

Billy Codrow peered over his gloves at Marty Gibson. He waited for the feint. He thought it would come from his right hand. Marty's left foot moved. Billy was all nervous energy. A front kick! He stepped back and blocked the kick across Marty's body, then moved to follow through with a sweep of the right leg. But the kick *was* the feint. Marty used the energy of the block to start a spin. As he came around, he swung the back of his fist into Billy's right ear, and the force of the blow crumpled him.

"What the hell was that," Danny Rincon yelled in protest.

"What's your problem, Marty," Billy moaned from the floor.

"I want the next match," Danny said, in a vengeful tone.

Danny was a bit bigger than Billy, stronger too, but Marty was much larger than either of them. They were all on the football team, but he was on the defensive line and they were only backs.

Sensei stepped in and growled. "Sit down."

Emily watched from the side through the whole match. Marty and his buddy, Jeff Schenk, joined the dojo last week. It was a special promotion: first two weeks free. They seemed wrong, somehow insincere. They already had some skills, especially Marty, but they'd roughed up everyone they were paired with, apologizing each time for their seeming lack of control. It was getting to be quite annoying. The monthly sparring party was supposed to be rather more convivial. For Danny this was the last straw.

"C'mon, Sensei. They've been punching through the target all week," he said.

"And you think you can do something about it." Marty sneered at him across the mat, and Jeff snickered in the background.

Danny leapt to his feet again, and Sensei stepped over, placed a hand on his chest and guided him back down. Danny still fumed, even though he couldn't resist Sensei's hand. Emily pushed herself up off the mat and nodded to Sensei.

"I think it's my turn." She turned to pick up her pads.

"Yeah, right," Marty snorted. "Am I supposed to hit a girl?"

"Don't worry about me, big fella. I'll take my chances."

Everyone in the room went silent. A moment later Sensei dropped his hand between them in a sharp gesture starting the match. Marty looked perplexed. Clocking Billy was one thing, but he didn't seem prepared to hit her. They circled around each other for a few seconds while he looked for an opening, and she pushed out a long breath and let it seep back in.

Her breath moved in and out, back and forth: an endless cycle… soothing. Just beneath the sound of her breathing, the beating and sloshing of blood in her veins was audible. The hum of the day drifted into silence. Time crawled along. Underneath it all was a cavernous emptiness, cool and dark at first, then gradually filled with a warm glow.

It grew more intense until becoming a white-hot intensity, then faded into a crystalline clarity.

The muscles in Marty's neck and shoulders tensed, and his eyes moved restlessly over her body. Behind them a chaotic energy peeked out, visible to anyone who knew how to look for it – anxious and fearful, yet filled with sneering arrogance, the usual contradictions of adolescence. His jaw clenched, then unclenched, and his breath shuddered unevenly.

It was plain, he wouldn't move until she did. He wanted to block an attack, to figure out how to touch her by blocking her. Then he might feel more comfortable hitting her.

"Don't be shy." She flashed him a mocking smile.

"Ladies first."

The last word had barely left his mouth when Emily kicked him lightly just below the left knee. Before he even had time to complete a block of the first kick, she flicked her foot up to the side of his head. The ball of her foot gently nudged his headgear, and it was obvious to *almost* everyone there that if she'd wanted to, she could have knocked him off his feet with that combination. His eyes were wide as saucers.

Sensei dropped his hand a second time. Marty jabbed urgently with his left hand and followed with a right hook. Emily leaned out of the way of the jab and slapped the hook across his chest, but didn't give any ground. His right foot came up off the floor, perhaps in preparation for a roundhouse kick that was no longer possible. Before he could put it back down she kicked it out from under him. Off balance, falling backwards, his best option was to roll out of it. When he spun back up, he found the heel of a sidekick just in front of his nose. She pulled her foot back and stepped away.

Sensei dropped his hand once more, and Marty surged forward with a frantic series of strikes. He seemed to think a flurry of punches might succeed where a more careful approach had failed. Oddly, Emily didn't seem to react. She didn't block his strikes or step back. She merely leaned out of the way of each one. In the end, he was surprised to find her right up against his chest, too close for his long arms and legs to kick or punch. By the time he thought to grab her, it was too late. She had already hit him with a short, hard reverse punch to the center of his chest, and he staggered back, gasping for breath. A crossover side-kick planted firmly in the same spot sent him sprawling across the floor. Match over.

No one had hit him with any real force before this moment. Fortunately for him, the pads and gloves protected him from serious injury. He lay on the floor for a moment looking at the ceiling. Emily stood over him with a menacing sneer playing across her face.

"How'd I do, Marty?"

"This is bogus," Jeff shouted. "She punched through... and he didn't want to hit a girl."

"Shut up, Jeff," Billy snarled. Marty picked himself up and tried to shake it off as Emily walked back across the room.

"Tell 'em, Marty. That wasn't fair."

"You wanna try your luck against me, Jeff?" Emily asked over her shoulder.

He didn't respond right away, his eyes fixed on Marty, who stood off to one side, still shaking his head.

"I, I... I, uh," he stammered out.

"Shut up, Jeff," Marty whispered.

"How about this: I'll take you both on. Two on one," Emily said. "You two think you can handle a girl?"

There was more stammering and agitated whispering between them. Emily stood in the middle of the ring and waited for an answer, though anyone could see they had no choice but to face her.

Finally Sensei dropped his hand again. She listened for the sound of her breath, still reassuringly there... always there. The somber blackness, the light, was such a contrast to the cacophonous energy of the boys, and their breathing so hasty, nervous, uncertain. It left room for only the most blinkered of thoughts: it ought to be easy enough to kick her in the legs or the back, maybe knock her to the mat, and once she was down they would have won the point as far as anyone could tell.

The boys flanked her on two sides in a surreal scene – she was so much smaller than either of them. She circled back to her right, putting Jeff between her and Marty. They tried to flank her again, but she circled around the other way to bring them back into line. It gradually became clear that she could outmaneuver them indefinitely. Jeff lost his patience and lunged at her. She controlled his right wrist and twisted him down to his knees. Marty tried to take advantage with a roundhouse kick to the back of her head, but before he could bring his foot around, she slipped a sharp side-kick under his raised leg, striking his thigh from below and lifting him off his feet. He fell backwards and hit the floor hard.

"Nice one, Em," Billy yelled. "Not so tough now, huh Marty."

Emily turned to shoot him a dark look, and he sat back down quietly. Jeff saw an opening and swung a hard right hook into the side of her head as she was turned away. She spun down to the floor and rolled away from the blow. He had made solid contact, and everyone gasped… except Billy, who stared fixedly at the floor.

Emily stood up and rubbed her jaw. She took off her head-gear and the rest of her pads except for the gloves.

"I guess you've had enough," Jeff gloated.

Emily ignored him as she pulled her hair back into a ponytail. She nodded to Sensei and walked back to the center of the ring. Her breath came in and went out, and she turned her attention to it once again. It filtered its way through the hectic breathing of Marty and Jeff, past the stillness in Sensei's chest, to the rush of anticipation around the ring. Breath enveloped all.

Just as Sensei was about to drop his hand she turned to Jeff and said, "Do you want me to hit you guys as hard as you hit me?" He seemed at a loss for an answer.

This time she let them flank her, and her friends looked worried: what was she up to? Marty looked like the same question had occurred to him, and he was frozen by it. She turned to face him with her back to Jeff, who couldn't resist the apparent opening. He stepped right in, meaning to kick her in the small of the back, but she pivoted away just before he made contact, and kicked his other leg out from under him in the process. He landed flat on his back and lay groaning on the floor.

She sprang back up to face Marty, who was now ready to fight. She glowered at him in the eye, and he flinched, and before he could react, she used the same combination she had tapped him with earlier—a front kick to the knee and a quick roundhouse to the side of his head—but this time she hit him *much harder*. The force of the second kick laid him out on the floor sideways.

Jeff picked himself up in time to see his friend go down. He roared something incoherent and charged at her... and once again, she parried his right hand and controlled his wrist. A sharp twist forced him down, and then brought him back up again, yelping in pain the whole way and unable to resist complying with the direction she forced him in. He must have hoped he would merely end up in a hard crouch, but the movement only accelerated until he left his feet altogether, flipping head over heels. He landed on his back a few feet away. Emily loomed over him gigantically, her black eyes aglow with a dark fury, and he shuddered at the sight of her. He was done.

Some of the boys stood up, as if to cheer, and she glared around the room with an intensity that made them all sit down again. Her gaze lingered an extra moment on Billy.

She walked over to Marty and crouched beside him. He was staring at the ceiling again, and the ferocity in her eyes had subsided a bit. When he finally met her eyes, his own wide-eyed and queasy, she spoke in a soft, firm voice.

"You only came here to make trouble." He blinked and tried to look away. "Don't come back until you're ready to learn something."

She stood up and offered him a hand, leaning back to balance his weight, then looked around the room sternly. Everyone sat in silence as she showed him to the door, and Jeff picked himself up and limped out after him like a lost dog.

When Emily returned she glanced around the room again. "That wasn't sparring," she said, in a forbidding tone. "That was a fight. It was ugly and I hate it. I don't want to hear a word about it in school tomorrow. No taunting. No bragging. Nothing."

Everyone was dumbstruck. Was she angry at them? Some indistinct grunting and nodding made its way around the room. She took a deep breath and let it out slowly, then disappeared into the office. A prolonged awkward silence hung over the dojo. No one seemed to know what to say, or to have the breath to push the words out if they did know.

"Let's take a few minutes, everyone," Sensei said, breaking the spell. "We'll start the *chambara* competition in twenty minutes, and then it's pizza and cupcakes."

The group broke up, wandering out to the courtyard or milling about in the parking lot. Sensei turned into the office, where he found her sitting on the window sill rubbing her jaw.

"Well, it's clear you can take a punch," he said.

"Did we really need more data on that point?"

"I guess not."

"You knew those guys weren't on the level all along, didn't you?"

"Yes. And so did you, right?"

"Yeah, but you could have kicked 'em out a lot sooner, you know, like before I got sucker punched," she said, in an increasingly annoyed tone of voice.

"I suppose so, and I'm sorry if it hurt too much." He paused to gauge her reaction. "But your control was impressive even after their shameful behavior." She stewed over this last remark. "Chi-chan, the people hunting you will fight much dirtier than those idiots. Your self-control will be your most important weapon against them." Emily let out a long breath, and her shoulders slumped.

"I suppose it would be unrealistic to think the Chinese were my only enemies."

"It would be wise to assume there are others."

The mood was lighter after the chambara competition. This is a form of dueling, with lots of padding and foam covered PVC "swords." Initially it looked like frenetic flailing. Soon enough the kids developed a subtler economy of attack and defense. The best among them even approached a taut serenity, moving the sword only to block or to exploit an opening.

Billy was glad to be able to celebrate several victories. Danny, too. They all teased each other over pizza. Even Emily joined the mood. Afterwards, she drove Danny home.

"Why did those guys even come?" he asked from the passenger seat.

"I have no idea."

"Well, I think you got 'em to see the light."

"You know, I hate fighting. It's about inflicting pain, and it sucks… and it hurts, damnit." She glanced at him with a rueful smile and rubbed her chin.

"Well you're certainly good at it. Don't you get any satisfaction from that?" His tone probably sounded more importunate than he intended.

She shot him a withering glare, but there was also an air of uneasiness about her. He blanched a bit, and she forced a shaky smile.

In the driveway, his face looked like an unasked question. Was he still thinking about the sparring? He said goodnight and closed the passenger door. Later, lying in her bed, she could hardly help musing on the irony of the day. Boys like Marty playing teenage intimidation games in her dojo, while she needed to guard against truly terrifying dangers. Still, she desperately wanted to fit herself into high school social life. At moments like this, it could seem like an open question which was more important to her, survival or friendship.

ABOUT THE AUTHOR

By day, Jacques Antoine is a professor at a small college in the southwest, by night he writes action-adventure stories. At first, he wrote "kung fu" tales just for his daughter, when she was a little ninja studying karate. As she grew up, the tales evolved into full-length novels focusing on the dilemmas of young adults, but always set against the background of martial arts adventures. When he's not writing or teaching, he enjoys walking his dogs in the Sangre de Cristo Mountains outside Santa Fe.

21231934R00171

Printed in Poland
by Amazon Fulfillment
Poland Sp. z o.o., Wrocław